PRAISE FOR BIANCA SLOANE

WHAT YOU DON'T KNOW

"Riveting and terrifying! The very definition of a thriller! This is what I call, "an all-nighter." Once you start, you won't be able to stop! Chilling all the way down to your bones! *What You Don't Know* is what nightmares are made of."
–**@Elizabeth.Ness.56**

"[*What You Don't Know*] was a 5/5 for me ... Brilliant."
–**@Momfluenster**

"It was pure joy to read and edit *What You Don't Know* by Bianca Sloane. Alternating between the violence unfolding at the Gilbert's and investigative interviews with their friends and family, Sloane transports us into a terrifying, brutal home invasion while constructing a brilliant plot that reads like an episode of Dateline. I was mesmerized and petrified through every page. Masterful and gripping, this is a suspense novel that any thriller lover will devour."
–**Samantha M. Bailey, #1 bestselling author of WOMAN ON THE EDGE**

"Sloane creates complex characters within multi-layered plots that will have you flipping pages to the very end."
–**Cindy Reads & Writes**

"I read [*What You Don't Know*] in roughly 24 hours, and when I was near the end I was carrying my Kindle around the house so I could sneak in a page or two because I had to get to the end, I had to know

what happened. I actually turned the shower on and stood in the bathroom so I could read the last few pages. This book is that good."
–@The_Towering_TBR

"[What You Don't Know] . . . [was] such a thrill to read . . . We have been looking for a thriller that captures our attention from the first page and holds it until the last. Bianca Sloane's ability to plot and pace such a universally scary event was masterful. We were absolutely petrified reading this book. . ."
–@audioshelfme

"My favorite thing about being a book reviewer is discovering new authors and Bianca Sloane was a new to me author who has me ready to read more of her books after devouring this one in just two nights. I was quickly hooked on this story [and] Sloane's writing style is fast-paced and totally gripping."
–GripLitGrl

THE LIVE TO TELL SERIES

"Bianca Sloane sure knows how to make a page turn."
–Whatisthatbookabout.com about TELL ME A LIE

"...Once again, [Bianca Sloane's] fast-paced, nail-biting, on-the-edge-of-your-seat style of suspense had me gripped from the first page to the last."
–Goodreads Reviewer about LIVE TO TELL

"...You will sail through these fast-paced thrillers."
–Ashley Gillan, eBookNerdReviews.wordpress.com about LIVE TO TELL and TELL ME A LIE

EVERY BREATH YOU TAKE

"Once you start reading this book, you won't want to stop."
–Ionia Martin, ReadfulThingsBlog.com

"...Will have you chewing your fingernails down to the quick. The author has a deftness for building suspense and tension, leaving you wondering what's coming next."
–The Haphazardoushippo.Blogspot.com

"The character buildup ... is beyond perfection. Highly recommended."
–San Francisco Book Review, 5 Stars

SWEET LITTLE LIES

"It is impossible for a reader to relax their grip on *Sweet Little Lies*. The story elements are crisp and exciting with multiple twists and turns."
–Night Owl Reviews

"The mystery [of *Sweet Little Lies*] deepens from the very beginning and comes to a satisfying but shocking ending. I feel that anyone looking for a good thriller would be hard pressed to find a better one."
–Green Embers Recommends

"From the first few pages, you get instantly hooked. When you first read about the premise ... you think you know exactly how the story might unfold. There is no amount of predictability that would have foreseen all the twists and turns that came from reading [*Sweet Little Lies*]."
–Whatisthatbookabout.com

"Once again, Bianca Sloane has written a fast-paced mystery that is the perfect choice for some exciting reading escapism."
–SheTreadsSoftly.Blogspot.com

"I could not put this down until ... I found out what would happen. The ending was a big shock. I loved this and would recommend it to any thriller fan."
–WiLoveBooks.Blogspot.com

KILLING ME SOFTLY

Thriller of the Month by www.e-thriller.com (May 2013)
"2013 Top Read" by OOSA Online Book Club

"[A] cross between 'Sleeping with the Enemy' and a superb murder mystery."
–a CrimeReadersBlog.Wordpress.com

"[*Killing Me Softly*] is a book that will leave the reader scratching their head trying to figure out the villain. And, just when the reader thinks they have it all figured out - think again - AND AGAIN!"
–Examiner.com (New Orleans)

TELL ME A LIE

A NOVEL

BIANCA SLOANE

Cover design by Nick Castle Design: www.nickcastledesign.com/

ISBN-13: 9781096581031

To sign up for the author's newsletter, visit www.biancasloane.com

First Paperback Edition

V4

❀ Created with Vellum

BOOKS BY BIANCA SLOANE

STANDALONE NOVELS

Killing Me Softly (Previously published as Live and Let Die)

Sweet Little Lies

What you don't know

THE EVERY BREATH YOU TAKE SERIES

Every Breath You Take

Missing You: A Companion Novella to Every Breath You Take

The Every Breath You Take Collection (Box Set of Every Breath You Take and Missing You)

THE LIVE TO TELL SERIES

Live To Tell

Tell Me A Lie

White Christmas (A Live To Tell short story)

TELL ME A LIE

1

WHAT MAKES A MURDERER?

I suppose the experts would point to childhood trauma, mental defects, DNA, environment, and the like.

In my case, it's not really any of the above.

I became a murderer out of necessity.

No, my life wasn't in imminent danger, or anything so dramatic. I mean, yes, my life was at stake, but my husband wasn't out to kill me.

However, he *was* out to ruin me.

We didn't start out that way. It never starts out that way. At first, you're brimming with misty-eyed dreams of white picket fences, 2.5 children, dozens of dewy roses every week, love letters dripping in mush and sentimentality. You vow to be *that* couple, the couple everyone alternately loves and hates because they wish they were you, because they know they can never be you. When you're *that* couple, the world swings on a string. He's handsome and successful. You're beautiful and charming. You have adorable, do-no-wrong moppets who grow into handsome/beautiful do-no-wrong adults. You're slavishly devoted to one another. The perfect little couple with the perfect little family.

Of course, that's not at all how it unspooled between Charles and me. When it all goes south in a marriage, one of you always pulls the trigger and the other always takes the bullet.

I took all the bullets. Every last one. I bore the brunt of our marital woes. For all intents and purposes, I was a single mother to our two sons, what with Charles devoting every spare second to his medical career, the leftover crumbs sprinkled across the golf course. I often thought if he had it to do over again, he wouldn't have married me. He would have remained unencumbered by the banality of a wife and children in favor of some ridiculous Swinging Single, Rat Pack lifestyle with a bachelor pad in the city, a bearskin rug on the floor, Dean Martin on the hi-fi, and a disco ball twirling above the rotating circular bed.

As I said, it wasn't always bad. In fact, if I may trot out a tired chestnut, it was magical. For so many years. It would not be a lie to say he swept me away. He was my prince. I'd seen him around town several times—Cambridge being the quintessential little college town and all—so it wasn't hard to notice the same tan, blond God, even among a cadre of tan, blond Gods. Charles with his comfortable swagger, cerulean eyes full of wit, and a constant wry, easy smile, was different. He hadn't noticed me, which was yet something else that set him apart from the pack. Men always noticed me. Being a slinky, blue-eyed blonde with porcelain skin and an aloof manner tended to have that effect. But not Charles. I had to be the one brazen enough to approach him that warm fall day. It was a happy accident I'd even seen him that afternoon. Indian summer was blowing over us and I'd decided to abandon Russian Lit for a few hours of meandering through the tiny boutiques of Cambridge, topped off with a demitasse of espresso and nibble of pastry at my favorite little café. I was cutting through Harvard Yard, when there he was, head dipped into the creases of *Gray's Anatomy*, oblivious to anyone around him. I decided this was the day I'd make my presence known. I pulled the most predictable of ploys—asked him for a light. He didn't smoke, of course, but it didn't matter. I knew once he saw me, *really* saw me, I would have his full attention.

And indeed, I did. For a long time. I knew on our first date we would marry. It took Charles longer to come to that inevitable conclusion, but it was okay. I could wait.

I mustn't leave out the passion we had for each other. A relentless, exhilarating tidal wave of passion. It was like that for years, the two of us lapping each other up like the little hunks of saltwater taffy I'd loved as a child. It was all rather tawdry, so very un-debutante like. Yet oh-so-delicious. My mother would have died if she knew how many times a day Charles and I used to have sex, not to mention the places we had it. Furtive groping in public places wasn't exactly a chapter in the Main Line debutante's handbook. I used to wake up in the middle of the night yearning for him, would dream about it during the day, impatient for night to fall so I could just *be* with him. There was no one I would rather have defile me a hundred different ways than the love of my life.

I can't really pinpoint the moment he began to despise me. Perhaps it was little by little, like a dripping faucet that merely annoys you in the beginning. The next thing you know, a flood of hatred washes over you and all that's left is to lay awake at night to ponder where it all went wrong.

I guess none of that really matters now, since, as the saying goes, what's done is done. I suppose I could have divorced Charles instead of murdering him. That would have been too easy.

And after years of being the one to take the bullet, I decided it was his turn.

2

My husband was dying.

As he lay on the floor in front of me, gasping and sputtering for air, clutching the bloody crater in his stomach, courtesy of the bullet I'd just fired into him, a ripple of sadness shuddered through me and, dare I say, a flash of regret. Thirty plus years of marriage, two sons. Love. Laughter.

Still, I couldn't let Charles live.

Not when his life would mean my death.

He gasped. "Jillian. Please. Help me."

I continued staring down at him, unmoved by his wheezing plea. The saltiness of his blood comingling with the acrid stench of gun powder floated through the air. He reached for his pants pocket and I knew he was going for his phone. I bent down, dropping the gun softly onto the rug next to me, and clamped my hand against his until it was immobile. I couldn't risk moving the phone or having my fingerprints on it. Our eyes locked. The life was draining out of him and I knew it would be over soon. I cupped his cheek.

"Just let go, Charles. Let go. There's nothing—"

"You fucking bitch." He grunted. "You'd just let me die here, like this?"

"Yes, Charles. I would."

He opened his mouth to say something else, but coughed instead, expelling clumps of blood. Sweat bubbled down his face.

I stood up, intending to call 911, when I looked down. Not a drop of blood anywhere on me. I sighed and glanced at Charles. It should at least *look* as though I made some sort of effort to revive him. I dropped to the floor and let my hands roam against the warm, blood-soaked terrain of his body until they were as slick as he was. I wiped my hands on my white button-down shirt, the outside of my coat, my skinny black pants and even ran a little across my cheek and chin for good measure. Satisfied, I grabbed my own phone from my purse, managing a few robust smears of red across the case and buttons in the process.

Charles continued to writhe and moan, his eyes suddenly lighting up as he extended a shaky hand toward the gun just out of his reach. I ran over, kicking it away before turning my attention back to my phone. My finger hovered over the keypad. Our bedroom light caught my eye from the top of the stairs. The bedroom window faced the front of the house, visible from the driveway. I couldn't very well say I didn't know Charles was home if the light was on. I scoffed. One more detail. I ran upstairs to flip off the light, chuckling at the sight of his packed suitcase waiting patiently for its owner to whisk it away to parts unknown.

Don't hold your breath, suitcase.

Mission accomplished, I descended the stairs, my eyes locked onto Charles as I resumed standing over him, watching as he heaved and sweated and bled.

It was time.

I tensed a muscle in my neck to trigger tears. My cousin, Lee, taught me that trick. It was how she drove five husbands to divorce her and got her father to placate her never-ending whims until his grave. She had nothing if not ingenuity. The tears spouted from my eyes at once. I paced across the living room to elevate my heart rate, bring some color to my cheeks, force a few dribbles of sweat to burst from my pores, a squirming, groaning Charles under my watchful eye the entire time.

When I felt I was sufficiently *in a state*, I dialed 911. I glanced at my husband, fading faster, disappearing before my eyes.

"911, what's your emergen—"

"I just shot my husband."

"Did you say you shot your husband?"

"Yes, yes, yes—I—Charles, oh my God—"

"What's your address ma'am?"

I spit out our address in a frenzy. "Please, please hurry, please—"

"Okay, ma'am, is your husband conscious?"

I looked down at him, clinging to a thread of nothing.

"Yes, barely."

"Does he have a pulse?"

I bent down and put a delicate finger against his neck, the faint tingle of pulse descending rapidly. I was about to pull my hand back when Charles grabbed my wrist, managing to yank me toward him. His mouth groped for words, but he couldn't quite make any sound come out. I gasped and yelped as I struggled to break his grip.

"Ma'am, are you still there?" the dispatcher asked. "Does he have a pulse?"

With some effort, I managed to snatch my hand free and Charles attempted to crawl toward me. I ground my heel against his palm and he collapsed, wailing, the momentary gush of adrenaline fading back to black.

"What should I do?" I asked.

"Ma'am, did you apply pressure to the wound?"

I folded one arm across my torso and leaned against the arm of the sofa. "No. I ... What do I ...?"

"Ma'am, what I need you to do ..."

I tuned her out and resumed pacing as I looked at Charles, his face a contortion of reds, blues, and purples. I let a smile slip across my lips. God, he looked terrible.

The scream of sirens hurtling down the street outside caused me to whip my head in the direction of the front door.

"I think the paramedics are here," I said. "Did you hear that, Charles, sweetheart? Help, it's here—"

"Okay, ma'am, I need you to stay on the line with me just to be sure. Did you put any pressure—?"

The front door exploded in a burst of pounding and announcements that the paramedics had arrived. I dropped the phone and wiped my phony tears with the back of my hand as I hurried to answer it, flipping on the living room light along the way. A blast of cold December air smacked against me when I opened the door to the paramedics.

"He's in the living room. Please—"

A band of men and women shrouded in puffy, navy jackets and matching cargo pants trampled over me as they rushed toward Charles. I hurried into the living room, wringing my hands and crying, throwing in some whispered prayers for effect as they strapped an oxygen mask on him. Someone started CPR and as voices shouted directives, blue and red flashed across the swarm of faces from the door, still standing open, the temperature seeming to have dropped even in those few minutes. I bolted in Charles's direction—all for show, of course—when a hand clamped itself against my shoulder, stopping me. Within seconds, the face of a burly police officer was inches from my own.

"Ma'am, we're gonna need you to stand back and let them work—"

"But please, I—"

"Ma'am, tell us what happened here tonight."

I looked over at Charles again. The room started to spin as heat crawled up my cheeks. Despite the questioning face in front of me going blurry, like tissue dissolving in water, I opened my mouth to answer him.

And then I fainted.

3

I JERKED OUT OF SLEEP, heart racing, blood thrumming, legs and arms flailing.

The hard clank of metal jerked my hand back. Handcuffed. I was handcuffed to the rail of a hospital bed. I rattled the metal, panic swelling in my veins as I used my free hand to try to wrench my bound hand through the hard metal loop in a wild attempt to extricate myself.

What had happened? What the hell had happened?

Charles. A bullet exploding.

His face rushed toward me. His moans pounded in my ears. I looked down, expecting to see blood across the front of my white shirt. Instead, the pristine blue and white diamonds of a papery hospital gown stared back at me. My head swiveled around in a panic as I took in the sky blue walls, oversized framed photo of birds, and small white dry-erase board filled with indecipherable scribbles in green marker. I had honest-to-God fainted. It was a mystery as to why. I wasn't usually prone to those types of hysterics. In fact, I'd never fainted once in my fifty years. Perhaps I took my role a little more seriously than I had intended.

"Help," I screamed, rattling the handcuff, still doing my damndest to extract my hand from the metal clamp. "Someone help me. Please!"

A uniformed police officer poked her head into the doorway one second before a young nurse came running into the room, long dark curls flying behind her, concern crinkling her face.

"Mrs. Morgan? Mrs. Morgan, you need to calm down," the nurse said.

I rattled my newfound jewelry, the metal upon metal screeching hysterically. "What the hell is this?" I hissed. "Why the hell have I been chained to this bed like an animal?"

"Mrs. Morgan, the police—"

"I don't give a damn about the police. I want you to take these off me, right—"

"Mrs. Morgan."

My head snapped toward the door at the unfamiliar voice. Two men sauntered in without invitation. One suave, one slovenly. One middle-aged, one far past. Both with brown hair and brown eyes, though one had more hair than the other. Straight out of a bad cop show. I squinted as I realized I actually knew them. The same detectives who'd cornered me as I'd come out of Pilates some months ago to harangue me about the state of my marriage. The same two detectives who'd paid a visit to the house to needle Charles about his slut and her murder.

Why are they here? They told me they were with the Chicago Police Department, not Winnetka. Isn't this out of their jurisdiction? Wait. Of course. You just gunned down the prime suspect in the murder they were investigating.

"Detectives." I flipped through my mental Rolodex to recall their names, though I couldn't immediately remember which was which. "Potts. Travis."

The fat, old, balding one in the dirty, too-small overcoat laughed. "Oh, good. She remembers us."

Ah, yes. That would be Potts. For his grotesque pot belly. Sweaty, jowly, pasty white, red-faced Potts, in a perpetual state of huffing and puffing.

"I guess that means you didn't hit your head or anything when you wiped out. No amnesia or anything," he continued.

"What is going on here?" I asked, rattling the handcuffs.

"We need to talk to you about what happened tonight," the suave one—Travis—said. The opposite of his partner in every way. Tailored suits, high sheen loafers, his smooth olive skin affirming no immediately discernable ethnicity.

"Maybe first you can tell me why the hell I'm handcuffed to a bed, being treated like a common criminal—"

"For all we know, that's exactly what you are," Potts said, sneering at me.

"Excuse me?"

"Your husband was pronounced dead about an hour ago," Travis said.

"I—what?" My head pivoted between the two, my voice quaking. "He died? Charles is dead?"

"We're sorry for your loss," Travis said, cocking his head.

To my surprise, tears slid down my face and I wiped them away with my free hand, too stunned to say anything. I'd actually done it. I'd murdered my husband.

"She cleared medically?" Potts asked the nurse.

"Well, I need to check her vitals—"

"We need you to answer some questions for us, Mrs. Morgan," Potts said, ignoring the nurse.

I squared my shoulders, lifting my gaze to meet his. "Am I under arrest?"

"We're just gathering information about what happened at your house tonight," Travis interjected. "You can do it here or we can take you down to the station."

"Mrs. Morgan just woke up. Can't this wait?" the nurse asked.

"No," Potts said. "It can't."

"I believe I asked you a question," I said.

"No, Mrs. Morgan, you're not under arrest." Travis paused. "However, we'd like to talk to you while the details of what happened tonight are still fresh. You understand. Like I said, we can do it here, or take you down to the station."

I slammed back against my pillows, thoughts careening across my brain like a rogue ping-pong ball. I needed to focus. Stay calm. I rubbed my forehead and took a few deep breaths.

"I'd prefer to do it here," I finally said.

"Please, I need to check her vitals first," the nurse said, hovering over me, protecting me.

Potts held up his hands in surrender and the nurse quickly busied herself with shining lights in my eyes, checking my pulse, and taking my temperature. This gave me time to collect my thoughts, form my story. Travis shoved his hands in the pockets of his coat, his eyes trained to the shiny floor tiles, while Potts went into the breast pocket of his jacket for a roll of red cough drops, depositing one glossy lozenge into his mouth, never taking his eyes off me.

"We through here?" Potts asked as the nurse scribbled notes on a chart.

"Yes." She clapped the metal chart shut and looked at the two men. "Don't take long."

The cop squad didn't say anything as the nurse left the room, closing the door quietly behind her. Travis walked over to the other side of the bed, heels clicking against those shiny tiles, and narrowed his eyes at me.

"Mrs. Morgan, we need to take some pictures of you," he said as Potts went out and called for the female officer to come into the room.

"Pictures? For what?"

"Document any markings, injuries, that kind of thing. For the investigation."

"I don't—"

"It's all standard procedure," Travis said as the officer who'd been drafted into duty unlocked the handcuffs and instructed me to hold out my hands.

I didn't get a chance to revel in my liberation from the handcuffs, as I was commanded yet again to submit my hands for review. I shook my head, my jaw agape at the bloodstains seeped into my skin. But, I complied, my fingers splayed as the officer snapped endless photos, instructing me to turn my palms up, down, to the side. There was at least the dignity of a partition as I was told to get out of bed so the female officer could photograph my arms, legs, feet, thighs, face, neck, and shoulders. I flinched with each click of the camera, humiliation and anger heating my cheeks. I avoided eye contact with her, and to her credit, she was the model of efficiency, snapping her photos with as much emotion as if she'd just picked up a book of stamps at the post office. After the photos, she swabbed my hands, explaining that she was testing me for gunshot residue. All of this allowed me to calm down enough to imprint my story into my brain.

"Let's try this again, Mrs. Morgan," Travis said as I climbed back into bed, wincing as I was once again chained to the railing. "We need to ask you some questions about what happened at your house tonight."

I inhaled a few more times, my pulse subsiding a bit.

Stay calm. Stay cool. Stick to the facts.

"You'll have to forgive my earlier behavior," I murmured. "I'm not accustomed to waking up shackled to a bed."

Potts rolled a stool over to my bedside as he pulled a tiny digital recorder out of the breast pocket of his jacket. He clicked it on. "We'll be recording our conversation, make sure we don't miss anything."

I bit my lower lip. I could do this. I was back in control of the situation. I would not be undone by hysterics. Far too many people were sitting in jail today due to panic and unfocused thinking, which led to slips. I would not be one of them. I would compose myself. I would talk low, a bit rushed at times. There would be the occasional wavering and well-timed tears. Tempered frenzy when needed.

I would walk away from this. Clean. Unscathed.

Potts coughed and Travis pulled out a tiny spiral-bound notebook and pencil from his own jacket, licking the lead point. Potts squirmed around on the seat a few times, tugging at the ends of his jacket and sniffing a few times before he settled in.

"This is Detective Ernest Potts, here with my partner Detective Dorian Travis and we're in room five-one-seven at Evanston Hospital, the time is 00:15 hours. The date is December twenty-ninth, 2017. We're here with Jillian Morgan. Mrs. Morgan, what is your full name?"

"Jillian Elizabeth Vaughn Morgan."

"And your date of birth?"

"June nineteenth, 1966."

Potts rocked back on the squealing stool and cleared his throat, reaching for another lozenge. Travis was stone, a statue, any eagerness he might have felt at questioning me seeming to hide beneath an impassive face.

"All right, Mrs. Morgan, we're investigating the death of your husband, Dr. Charles Morgan," Potts said. "How long have you and your husband been married?"

"Thirty-two years in July."

"Any children?"

"Two. Our son, Chase, is twenty-four and Gabe is eighteen."

"And does either son live in the home with you?"

"No, Chase will be starting his final semester of law school at Harvard and Gabe is in his freshman year at Columbia University in New York."

"When were you made aware of your husband's extramarital affair with Tamra Washington?"

Well, let's just get right to it.

"When he was arrested for her murder."

"And that was your first indication?"

"Yes."

The furious scratching of Travis's pencil against his own small notepad unnerved me.

What on earth is he scribbling? I've barely said anything.

"Did Dr. Morgan have any other extramarital affairs?"

"Not to my knowledge."

"How would you characterize your marriage—aside from the infidelity?"

Other than that, how was the play, Mrs. Lincoln?

"I suppose like most marriages, we had our ups and downs. Charles had a very demanding career, I ran the household, raised the children. It could be stressful."

"You indicated on your 911 call that you shot your husband. What happened?"

I took a shaky inhale. Time for the show to begin.

"I came home this evening and heard a noise upstairs. My in-laws took my boys to Telluride for New Year's and they're not due back for three more days and as far as I knew, my husband—" I let a tear run down my face, which I wiped away with my free hand. I took another gulp of air before continuing. "As far as I knew, my husband was in jail so he shouldn't have been in the house and I just—I panicked."

"Where were you coming home from?"

"Dinner with my girlfriend, Suzette."

"And what time did you get home?"

"Seven forty-five."

"Do you have an alarm system, Mrs. Morgan?"

"No, I—well, I never really saw the need for one. I mean Winnetka..."

"Right. Winnetka." Potts paused. "So, you come home, you hear a noise. Where did you say the noise was coming from?"

"Upstairs."

"And you were downstairs?"

"Yes."

"Did you come in through the front door?"

"Yes," I repeated.

Potts went into his pocket again for his cough drops, popping another one before continuing. "Okay, so you came through the front door. And you always come through the front door?"

"Yes."

"No side door, no garage door, nothing like that?"

"No."

"Did you slam the door?"

"No."

"How long was it after you came into the house that you heard the noise?" Travis asked.

"I don't—not long. Seconds, really. I'd barely walked through the front door when I heard the noise."

"What did it sound like?" Potts asked.

"I'm not sure what you mean," I said, shaking my head.

He was trying to trip me up.

Potts shrugged. "I mean, what kind of noise was it? What did it sound like? Describe it for us."

"It was—" What would sound plausible? What would be something I could recall later?

Of course. So simple. "It was our landing. There's this spot on our landing that squeals, or squeaks when you walk across it and that's what I heard."

"Huh. Okay, so you heard this squeal or squeak and that led you to believe you had an intruder in the house," Potts said.

"Yes." I nodded. "That's what I thought."

"So, what did you do?"

I went to swipe my shackled hand through my hair, grimacing at the clatter it made, annoyed with myself both for the impulse and for forgetting. "Well, I just froze. I wasn't really sure what to do."

"How close were you to the front door?" Potts asked.

"A few feet. I was standing next to the table in our foyer. I was going to put my purse down on the table when I heard the noise."

"Okay, so you're a few feet from the front door, you hear a noise from upstairs—a squeaking or a squealing, a noise that's ordinarily familiar to you, but tonight was unfamiliar and put you on alert." Travis looked up from his notepad. "If you were standing so close to the front door, why didn't you just slip out of the door, get in your car and drive away? Call the police once you were in your car?"

Nervous laughter fell from my lips. "Hearing you say it now, it sounds so simple. I wish to God I had."

"Where was the gun, Mrs. Morgan?" Travis shuffled through his notebook. "A Glock 19?"

"In my purse."

"You got a permit for it?" Potts asked.

"Yes, I—" I patted down my hospital gown with my free hand, my head swiveling in search of my purse, not even sure of where it was. Had it made the trip with me? Doubtful. "My purse—"

"We'll do a search on it," Potts said as he sniffed. "So, what happened then?"

"Well, the lights were off, and I heard the noise and I froze. Then I heard footsteps, as though they—whoever it was—was coming down the stairs. All I could see was this person across the room, in the dark, heading toward me, not saying anything and I panicked, grabbed the gun and fired." I fell back against the pillows, allowing sobs to wrack me once more. "I just fired."

The two snuck a glance at each other. Due to my somewhat frazzled state, I couldn't quite discern what code they were passing between them. I was usually fairly good at reading people. Or as I used to tell my boys, I had eyes in the back of my head. All seeing, all knowing.

"Was it pitch black in the house?" Travis asked.

"I—well the lights were off."

"Right, but was it pitch black? No moonlight, no light from other houses ...?"

I shrugged and shook my head. "I mean, I don't know that I can say it was *pitch black*, but it was definitely dark enough that you couldn't make out anything from a distance."

"All right, so you grabbed the gun out of your purse?" Potts asked.

"Yes." I nodded, sniffing. "That's right."

"When did you realize you'd shot your husband?" he continued.

"Right away. I—as soon as he fell to the ground, I realized it was Charles."

"And that's when you called 911?" Travis asked.

"Yes, I—as soon as I realized it, I called 911."

"Was the gun still in your hand?"

"What?"

"Where was the gun?" Travis asked. "What did you do with the gun after you fired it, while you were calling 911?"

I scoured my brain trying to remember. What *had* I done with the gun?

Charles reached for it. I kicked it away. It didn't go far.

"I—I don't know. I must have dropped it on the ground."

Travis shuffled through his notes. "So, unaware your husband had been released from jail, you thought someone had broken into your house, you panicked then fired."

"Yes," I said. "That's right."

"Huh." Travis looked up and down at the scribbles of his notebook for a few seconds, rustling the pages and reading silently to himself.

Around and around we went like this for hours, as the two men turned my story every which way—dropping it, kicking it, shaking it, smelling it—hunting for any inconsistencies. To my credit, I didn't waver, sticking firm to my story at every poke and prod.

Finally, Travis and Potts nodded at each other, a seeming indication the inquisition was coming to an end.

"Are we through here?" I asked.

"For now." Potts shut off his recorder and dropped it into his jacket pocket.

Travis called for the officer standing outside my room to come in and uncuff me. "Don't leave town, Mrs. Morgan," he said.

"Thank you," I said to the officer as I was unlatched, rubbing the grooves of my wrist. "I assure you, I won't be going anywhere. And I'll answer any questions you have."

"Good." Travis reached into the breast pocket of his suit jacket and extracted a small white card, holding it out to me. Potts did the same. "We'll be in touch."

"Thank you." I palmed both cards, wondering where the trashcan was. I'd wait until I got home to toss them.

"Do you have someone you can stay with, Mrs. Morgan?" Travis asked.

I blinked. "Why?"

"It's going to take some time to process the crime scene, so we won't be able to turn the house back over to you for a while," he said.

"How am I ..." I groped for the words, exasperated. Exhausted. "How long will that be?"

"A couple of days at least." Potts paused. "You've got a big house."

I let his snark slide. Antagonism was usually my stock in trade. However, it had been an excruciating day and I just wasn't up to any verbal jockeying. Besides, there was no point in playing any role other than the shocked and grieving widow and accidental murderess. I couldn't call any unnecessary attention to myself.

"I can stay with my neighbors for a few days. Or my in-laws."

"Which neighbors would those be?" Potts asked.

"The Ladds. Francine and Raymond Ladd. They live a few blocks away."

Potts nodded as he made a fresh notation in his notebook. "And your in-laws? Where do they live?"

"Lake Forest. Celia and Clayton Morgan."

"Ceeeelia and Claaay." Potts slammed his book shut and looked at his partner who nodded.

"Oh, Mrs. Morgan, where are your clothes? We'll need them," Potts said.

I grimaced. "My clothes? For what?"

"Evidence," Travis answered.

"I have no idea."

Potts smacked Travis's arm with the back of his hand. "Probably under the bed."

"What—if you're taking my clothes, what am I supposed to wear when I leave here?" I asked as Travis dropped to his knees and peered under my hospital bed. The scrunch of thick plastic accompanied his heavy grunt as he stood up.

"I'm sure the hospital can get you something to wear," Travis said, tucking the pouch under his arm. "Or your neighbor can bring you something."

"But you just said I can't get back into my house."

"You're a smart lady," Potts said. "You'll figure something out."

"All right, well, when will I get them back?"

"We'll let you know," Potts said.

"Like we said, Mrs. Morgan, we'll be in touch," Travis said.

My head wobbled on my spine in disbelief as they took their leave, my clothes in tow. I put up no resistance as I floated back into the flat, floppy pillows. I rolled to my side, my eyes slamming shut. My head pounded. The heavy sounds of my breath ballooned across the tiny room. Chase and Gabe's faces flashed in front of me briefly. What would I say to them? Somehow, some way, I'd have to figure it out.

"*Jillian.*"

I jumped up, looking around.

Charles. His voice. That unmistakable cultured tenor. He was in the room with me.

"*You won't get away with it, Jillian.*"

I leapt out of bed, my eyes darting around the room. I dropped to the floor, the tiles hard and cold against my palms and knees, as I searched beneath the bed.

I stood up shakily and looked around one more time.

"Charles." I swiped my hands through my hair. "Stop it. Stop it right now."

Silence.

Trembling, I climbed back into bed. Charles's dying face, purple, and twisted, floated in front of me. Blood hammered against my ears. The crack of the gunshot exploded in my head.

I slapped my hands over my ears and squeezed my eyes shut.

"I'll win, Charles," I whispered. "I'll win. I always do."

4

"I wish I would have gotten to you before you spoke to those detectives."

"I don't have anything to hide. I want to cooperate fully with the investigation."

Joss Hamilton sniffed, her face still buried in her phone. "Lot of folks sitting in jail who said the same thing, Mrs. Morgan."

I looked up from sliding my foot into one of the pink-toed tennis socks Francine Ladd had brought me that morning. She'd also come bearing a lawyer, one Joss Hamilton, much to my surprise, and if I were being honest, slight chagrin.

And truthfully, looking at this woman, I couldn't say I would have chosen her. She was younger than me, late thirties, early forties perhaps and craters of acne were visible beneath a thick wedge of orange foundation. I mustn't leave out her hot pink lipstick, primal streaks of matching blush, French manicured acrylics, and ... well, the less said about those excruciatingly appalling embellishments, the better. Neither her obviously expensive royal blue jacket and matching skirt, nor the Hermes scarf wrapped around her wide neck could contain the gargantuan, mannish figure, so like my mother's.

There'd been scant pleasantries, as the minute her foot had hit the door of my hospital room, she'd launched into an interrogation about what had transpired the night before and what I'd said to the police. My story seemed to hold up against her assault. She might have looked a tad gauche, a tad *too much*, but she was sharp, I had to give her that. Perhaps I would keep her around.

Francine stood in front of the window, her face pale and pinched, similarly focused on her phone. Her wiry chestnut hair was pulled back from her pale, makeup-free face into a severe bun, a burgundy tracksuit hiding beneath her coat. "Ray just texted me, said he drove past your house and there's a horde of media camped out."

"All the more reason for you to have counsel present," Joss said. "You're not to say a word to them, not even 'no comment.'"

"I won't," I said.

"Same for the police. You don't say a word until I tell you to. Understood?"

"Yes, of course," I said, my voice calm, giving no hint of my agitation.

Play nice.

Joss held up her phone. "There's already a trough of stories about this. Whether you realize it or not, you're in the crosshairs, Mrs. Morgan."

"Well, I suppose this type of story is right up their alley," I said as I put on the other sock before shoving my feet into Francine's borrowed running shoes and lacing them up, my toes snug against the mesh tops.

"Of course, I'm less worried about the media than I am the police," Joss muttered. "I just hope that little impromptu interview you gave them last night doesn't get you in trouble."

"I told you everything I told them," I said.

"I'll have to get a copy of the statement, make sure it tracks with what you told me," she said more to herself than to me, before grabbing her phone and tapping out something, an e-mail, a text, I wasn't sure. "Scour it for any discrepancies."

"I just didn't think they'd be out so early," Francine murmured as she looked out the window, also in her own little world. "Although, I guess I shouldn't be surprised. Considering."

It had been a tumultuous night. Truthfully, I didn't have to stay at the hospital overnight. I didn't have a concussion and nothing was technically wrong with me physically. However, after the long cross-examination from the police, I was exhausted and had fallen into a fitful sleep. Charles's voice echoed in my ears and visions of him running into my room, followed by the explosion of the gunshot, continually jolted me out of what little sleep I'd been able to obtain. When I wasn't cowering from Charles, I worried about my boys and what I would say to them. By six a.m., I gave up and miraculously, was able to pluck Francine's cell phone number from the tatters of my brain and called to ask if I could stay with her for a few days and if she would bring me something to wear, too. She flew to my side, bearing a bag of toiletries and one of her trademark velour tracksuits to shrug into.

I stood up. "I guess I should get this over with."

"When we get to Mrs. Ladd's house, I want to go over your story one more time," Joss said. "I've e-mailed my paralegal and asked her to get a copy of your statement from the police."

"I parked in the back, so hopefully, if there are any reporters out there, we might be able to duck past them," Francine said, opening the door, colliding with Detective Potts.

"Mrs. Morgan," he said as he glanced at me, before sizing up my attorney, a smile tugging at the corners of his lips. He knew the drill. "Excuse me."

"I'm Joss Hamilton, Mrs. Morgan's attorney," she said stepping in front of me, effectively blocking Potts. "Please direct all questions to me."

"We'd like your client to walk us through the crime scene," Detective Travis said over Potts's shoulder.

I looked at Joss, confused. "What do they mean?"

"They want to make sure that what you told them last night

matches the crime scene," she said. "Detectives, my client has just been released from the hospital. She's suffered a terrible trauma and is in no shape for a field trip."

Potts scanned me up and down. "Looks all right to me. And it's to her house, not the moon."

"Detectives, we'll be in touch about when—"

You don't have anything to hide. Be the model of cooperation.

"No, it's okay," I interrupted Joss, who turned to look at me, visibly fuming. "I'd rather go ahead and do this now. While it's fresh."

Joss opened her mouth to protest, but I gave her a wan smile and slight nod. She folded her arms across her surprisingly flat chest.

"Fine. But I'll be accompanying my client every step of the way."

Potts opened the door. "After you."

They hustled me silently down the hospital corridor. Joss glued herself to my side as we marched down the hall, the squat heels of her sensible black pumps pounding authoritatively against the floor, the nude pantyhose wrapped around her tree trunk thighs swishing mightily. Doctors, nurses, and assorted other personnel gawked momentarily at this motley little crew of ours before returning to their charts, carts, and I was sure gossip about me. I ignored them, my own gaze pinned to the exit signs, the borrowed running shoes pinching my feet as they gripped the glossy tiles beneath me.

We reached the sliding glass doors and I peered through them, relieved to see a parking lot filled only with cars, not teeming with media vans. The blast of cold, gray air walloped me as we stepped outside and I realized I didn't have a coat. I clamped my arms across my chest.

"Oh, honey, I didn't even think to bring you a coat. I'm sorry." Francine grimaced as she shoved her hands into the quilted shell of her Burberry. "Do you want mine?"

"Don't worry about it, Francine. You've already done so much. Besides, it's only for a little while."

"I'll follow in my car," she said. "Meet you at the house."

I nodded and she turned on her heel toward her own car.

Stay calm. They don't have anything on you.

"My client will ride with me," Joss said, pointing out her SUV.

No sooner had the words left her mouth than a flock of cameras, microphones, and shouted questions came zooming toward me from some far, unseen corner of the parking lot. The car was a good fifty feet away. Running seemed undignified. Of course, with a lawyer and two police detectives at my elbow, that wasn't going to happen anyway. I would just have to slog through the throng as best as I could.

"Mrs. Morgan, why did you kill your husband?"

"Did he confess to murdering Tamra Washington?"

"Are you turning yourself in to the police?"

"Mrs. Morgan, are you under arrest?"

Travis and Potts each took an arm as I put my head down against the barrage of questions. I felt a hand press against my back and I hoped it was my attorney. I swiveled my head to avoid the glare of the lights, finally putting my hand in front of my face to shield my eyes.

"Jillian!" someone screamed.

I froze. I knew that voice. I looked up, searching the crowd for its owner. I locked onto the pinched, distressed face of my sister-in-law, Charlotte. She plowed toward me, her Prada wool coat flying open to reveal a black turtleneck, jeans, and black riding boots, her normally smooth and meticulous long blond hair a greasy, tangled mess. Her breath swelled out in front of her as she mowed through the chattering, ravenous crowd.

"Charlotte—"

I never saw the slap. Cold, stinging, and raw. The already raucous roar of noise exploded around us in a torrent of clicking cameras and flashbulbs as the media flock clamored for more discord between sisters.

Travis stepped in front of me, one hand in front of him as if he were holding Charlotte at bay.

"Ma'am, I'm gonna have to ask you to step back—"

She snaked around him, her finger inches from my face. "Did you really murder my brother?" she demanded. "Did you really gun down my brother in cold blood?"

"Ma'am, you need to step back—"

"My client—"

"What the hell happened, Jillian?" Charlotte screamed over Travis's warning, Joss's posturing, and the cacophony crashing against us. I twirled from one side to the other, searching for an escape. The noise, the lights, the questions, the arms, the legs, the voices, swallowed me like quicksand. Charlotte managed to worm her way around Travis until she was standing in front of me. On an impulse, I pulled her to me, my mouth searching for her ear.

"It was an accident," I whispered. "A terrible accident."

She pulled back, rage, confusion, and agony warping her year-round, sun-kissed beauty. She shook her head slightly and yanked me toward her.

Potts attempted to get between us. "Ma'am, this is the last time we're going to warn you—"

"You better hope that's what it was," she hissed, inches from my face. "If I find out otherwise, I will slit your fucking throat."

"Ma'am—" Potts tried again, succeeding this time in planting himself in front of Charlotte.

"I'm done, I'm done," she screamed, tears streaking her cheeks. She looked at me again. "I'm done."

She stalked to her still-running black Escalade, the driver's side door hanging open to welcome her back. Confusion flooded the jackals' faces, unsure if they should pursue the distraught sister or continue grilling the dazed wife. Half ran after Charlotte, half continued swarming across me. Joss locked her arm around the crook of my elbow and shepherded me toward her cream-colored SUV, finally managing to deposit me inside. She slid behind the steering wheel and laid on the horn as she inched forward in a controlled attempt to encourage the throng to scatter peacefully. A few suctioned themselves to the pane of the passenger side window, still firing questions at me. I remained stoic, my gaze focused straight ahead, my only thought being to keep my composure.

Finally, we were free of the crowd and managed to pull out of the parking lot. My hands trembled. I didn't know what to do with them.

"Who was that, Mrs. Morgan?"

"My sister-in-law, Charlotte Morgan Douglas." I brushed my tremulous fingers to my lips, unsure if it was the freezing cold or Charlotte's wrath causing them to shake. My stomach clenched. Hot, metallic saliva flooded my mouth. "She and my husband were close."

Joss tapped a nail against the steering wheel. "I'm assuming you don't want to press charges. Not a good look."

"No. It's—it's—" I swallowed and fanned myself, my eyes screwing shut.

"Mrs. Morgan?"

One hand flailed in her direction, the other fumbled for the door latch. It was coming.

"Oh, God. Pull over. Pull over, pull over, pull over."

"What—?"

I pawed at the door, frantic to get it open. Joss screeched to a halt as I yanked on the handle, pushing the door open. I bolted from the car, barely ahead of the rainbow of vomit that surged from my mouth.

5

Joss PULLED to a stop across the street from my house, right behind a maroon sedan streaked with salt. Potts and Travis stood next to the driver's side door, their conversation coming to a halt once they realized it was me. Strings of black and yellow tape ringed the alternating patches of green grass and inlets of snow populating my front yard. Battalions of Winnetka's finest stood guard against the glut of cameras and reporters clogging the sidewalk at either end of my circular driveway. I stared up at the two-story brick colonial, majestic and traditional, typical of the North Shore of Chicago, and of our little burg of Winnetka. Our marital home, the only one Charles and I had ever shared. It was like a stranger to me in this moment.

Joss cut the engine and faced me. "Are you all right?"

I swallowed over the grit of vomit, my throat burning. "I'm fine."

"Okay. This is fairly standard procedure. They just want you to walk through what you told them last night, make sure there aren't any discrepancies between that and what's at the scene." She studied my face. "Will there be?"

"Will there be what?"

"Discrepancies?"

"No," I said. "None."

She pursed her lips. "Okay. Now. Only answer the questions you're asked. No elaboration, no rambling answers. Short and sweet. Yes or no when possible."

"I understand. Let's just get this over with."

She nodded and opened her door. I took a deep breath and did the same, pummeled by the punch of bitter December cold. As soon as the assembled media throng spotted me, they beelined. I pointed my head down as the detectives rushed me toward the house, lifting up the crime scene tape to lead me up the driveway, empty of any cars. I frowned.

"We impounded your car," Travis said, reading my mind. "We impounded all the cars."

"You did what?" From the corner of my eye, Joss shook her head slightly and I clamped my mouth shut.

The detectives took off their leather gloves, replacing them with latex ones. Travis opened the front door, which was unlocked, and motioned to someone inside. I couldn't see what was going on. A young man bearing a black digital camera emerged from my house.

"All right, Mrs. Morgan, let's start from the time you pulled up to your house last night," Travis said.

I nodded as I waited for them to do their official statements of identification for the camera, white clouds of breath obscuring their faces. I glanced over my shoulder at the assembled media, still shouting questions, their own cameras rolling.

"Whenever you're ready," Travis said.

I froze for a moment as I stared at the empty space where my car should have been, then back at my front door. The tips of my ears burned and my nose tingled. My mind flashed to the night of Charles's arrest and the photo I'd anonymously texted to him of the envelope containing the knife I'd used to kill his slut, propped up against the front door.

"Mrs. Morgan?" Potts asked.

I snapped back, my head wobbling around as I remembered

where I was and what I was doing. The young man trained his camera on me.

"Yes. My apologies." I cleared the sour phlegm from my throat. "I pulled into the driveway and parked behind Charles. His car had been here since he was arrested, so it wasn't unusual. The house was dark."

"Then what?" Potts prodded.

Charles sitting there. Waiting. Burning to confront me for my crimes.

"The house was dark," I repeated. "I unlocked the door, walked in and I heard a noise. A creaking, a squeaking on the stairs. It's our landing."

Travis pushed the door open a little wider and invited me to step inside. I hesitated before mentally urging myself to cross the threshold.

My house was teeming with strangers clad in strange uniforms, pawing through my possessions. Dusting, examining, recording, writing, murmuring. A few of them glanced at me. Most of them didn't notice me, or if they did, they didn't let on. Camera clicks echoed around me, accompanied by bursts of flash. The room smelled of metal and the taste of it filled my mouth.

From across the room, I could see it.

The tape outline.

Charles.

It was a crude figurine of black tape splattered with dried blood. It didn't account for his trim physique, developed through his childhood of touch football, swimming, track, and tennis, maintained through golf and squash. It didn't record the feathery blond hair, the blue eyes, the golden tan. The wry laugh, the easy smile.

An outline of tape on the living room floor. That's what was left of my husband.

The soft chatter of voices receded. Heat flooded through me and more nausea swirled in my stomach. My knees began their inevitable buckle.

"Mrs. Morgan?" Potts asked, grasping my elbow as I swayed.

"All right, Detectives, that's it," Joss interjected. "I told you, my client is in no shape—"

"If I could ... a glass of water—" I turned in the direction of the kitchen.

Potts planted himself in front of me. "I can't let you go in there. It's all part of the crime scene."

"My kitchen?" I asked, incredulous. "Nothing happened in my kitchen."

"We only have your word for that," he said.

"Detectives—" Joss tried again.

"I've got a fresh bottle of water in my bag," the young cameraman offered. "You can have that."

I nodded feebly. Travis indicated he would retrieve it, telling the young man to keep the camera rolling. He pressed a lukewarm bottle of water into my hand, which I slurped down greedily, ignoring their stares and Potts's impatient shuffling.

"Ready to continue?" Travis asked as I sucked down the last drop of liquid.

"Yes." I screwed the cap onto the bottle. "I'm ready."

"Take it slow," Joss whispered in my ear.

We walked through the living room and I recited everything I'd told them last night. I clutched the water bottle in my hand, the crunch of plastic echoing around the room, annoying more than one person, if their irritated looks in my direction were any indication. I avoided looking at the outline of Charles's body, instead concentrating on the details of my story. My confidence grew with each utterance, though I was careful to remain solemn, commanding the tears to flow sporadically. It was good that I'd kept my story simple. That's what tripped people up in situations like this. Complicating matters.

The detectives took copious notes, rapt with attention over my every word. Joss was a silent, hulking statue, taking her own occasional notes, but mostly, trapping me in her steely gaze. The young man with the camera trailed me like an earnest puppy, documenting my every move. Pivoting when I pivoted. Stopping when I stopped. Shuffling when I shuffled.

"When did you call 911?" Travis flipped through the pages of his notebook.

"As soon as I realized it was Charles."

Travis nodded as though contemplating this. "Hmm," was all he said.

"You said earlier that as soon as your husband hit the floor, you realized it was him," Potts said.

"Yes." I nodded. "That's right."

"How exactly did you realize it was your husband?" Potts asked.

"I'm afraid I don't understand."

"Just that," he said. "How did you realize it was your husband?"

What had I said last night?

You didn't say anything. What you said was as soon as he hit the floor, you realized it was him. Well, now you have to come up with something. He's looking for an inconsistency. What's logical? Did he call out my name? Did I recognize him? It was dark, so probably not. Not from that distance, anyway. No. Once I realized what I had done, I screamed and ran over to the body. And that's when I saw it was Charles.

"As soon as I fired, I screamed," I said. "I was—I was horrified. Stunned. I ran over and immediately realized it was Charles. And then I called 911."

Travis nodded again, while Potts pursed his lips. I forced myself to look away from the rudimentary tape outline.

"Anything else, Mrs. Morgan?" Travis asked.

"I don't think so, no."

"You planning to stay with your friend?" Potts asked.

"If you need to reach Mrs. Morgan, you can call me." Joss flicked a card in his direction. He rolled his eyes as he took it from her, shoving it into the breast pocket of his jacket without even looking at it. "When will my client be able to return to her home?"

"Another couple of days," Travis said. "We'll let you know."

"In the meantime, don't leave town," Potts said.

"She wasn't planning on it," Joss snapped.

"We'll be in touch," Travis said as he adjusted the smooth, tight knot of his tie.

"Francine." I looked around, it dawning on me she wasn't with us. "She said she would follow behind us, meet me here," I said more to myself than them.

"She's probably waiting for you outside," Travis said. "The officers wouldn't have let her come in."

"Actually, I'll drive you," Joss whispered in my ear as Potts and Travis turned their backs on us to put their heads together. "As I mentioned, we have a lot to discuss."

"I'm exhausted," I said, returning her hushed tone. "Can this wait?"

Joss twisted her mouth around before she pulled me over to the foyer. "All right, we'll pick this up tomorrow. In the meantime, don't talk to anyone, don't say anything."

I could only nod again, fatigue swooping across me, pulling at my joints and muscles. "I won't."

"I'll call you first thing in the morning."

I palmed the outside of the borrowed tracksuit, frazzled. "I—I don't have my phone. I don't know where it is."

"It's probably in evidence. I imagine you'll get it back in a day or two. I'll get you through Francine."

"Oh. Okay."

She took a deep breath. "Ready?"

I nodded. She slowly opened the front door and within seconds—less than seconds—the horde snapped to attention, screaming questions at me from beyond the perimeter of the crime scene tape. She locked her hand around my elbow and I bowed my head as we hurried down the driveway, the mob engulfing us once we were in the street, shouting the same probing queries from just a few hours ago. Had that only been a few hours ago?

Joss opened the passenger door of Francine's car, squeezing my hand before I climbed inside, shutting the door to the noise. Through the back window, I could see Joss plow through the crowds before she got into her car.

"You all right?" Francine asked.

"Yes, let's just leave. Please."

She nodded and put the car into gear, inching forward as the horde returned to encircle us. I folded my hands across my chest and looked out the driver's side window at the passing sidewalk. A lone man stood apart from the crowd.

No camera.

No phone.

No notepad.

I popped up in my seat, looking behind me to get a better view. He was black. Chubby. Beyond that, I couldn't get a handle on his features. He was too far away. We were picking up speed. He took a few steps, his hands shoved into his coat pockets.

Staring.

"What's wrong?" Francine asked.

I shook my head and focused my gaze out the windshield.

"Jillian?" she pressed.

"Nothing. I'm just tired. It's been a long night." I took a deep breath. "I need to call the boys later. I'll need all my strength for that."

Francine nodded and I slumped down in my seat, unnerved, but couldn't say why. Something about the way that man stared after me pumped me full of apprehension.

I looked over my shoulder one last time, but he had vanished from view.

6

"JILLIAN. PLEASE. HELP ME."

"Just let go, Charles. Let go. There's nothing—"

"You fucking bitch. You'd just let me die here, like this?"

"Yes, Charles. I would."

I bolted up in bed, clammy sweat raining down my skin.

"You'd let me die, Jillian? You'd let me die?"

I looked around Francine's guest room, draped in darkness.

"Jillian."

"Shut up," I hissed. "Just shut up."

"Jillian."

I pushed away the heavy comforter and ran for the bathroom. I splashed water across my face, the heat crawling across my skin instantly subsiding. I took the squat drinking glass wedged into the corner of the countertop and held it under the faucet, taking hearty gulps. I turned to go back into the bedroom and hesitated, afraid. I closed my eyes. Charles was dead. He was dead and he wasn't coming back.

I edged into the unfamiliar bedroom, my nose wrinkling involuntarily at the bulky oak sleigh bed, armoire, and matching nightstands, each housing a gold and glass lamp. I flipped one on and the room flooded with light, awash in gold leaf wallpaper. I blinked several times as my eyes adjusted. I went to the window, peeking past the pastel yellow curtain. Streaky daylight was struggling to break free from the darkness.

Daylight.

Daylight?

I picked up the face clock on the bedside table. Seven a.m. No, that couldn't be—

The events of yesterday morning came racing back. Charlotte. Throwing up on the side of the road. Walking through the crime scene. That strange man staring at me. Francine tucking me into bed with tea, toast, and a sleeping pill. That had been yesterday morning. Early. I flopped onto the bed.

Had I really slept almost twenty-four hours straight?

I ground the heels of my hands into my eyes, pawing at the cobwebs of my brain for what next, what now. I had intended to call Chase and Gabe yesterday. I was supposed to talk with my attorney.

My eyes fluttered open and I noticed another of Francine's velour tracksuits resting on the twin butter-yellow ottomans at the foot of the bed along with a fresh package of underwear. I craned my neck to see if my phone and purse had landed anywhere in the room.

"I—I don't have my phone. I don't know where it is."

"It's probably in evidence. I imagine you'll get it back in a day or two."

I jumped off the bed, my heart racing.

Evidence.

It hadn't registered when Joss said my phone was in evidence.

Evidence.

My phone. Dear, God, my phone. It was a treasure trove of evidence. Apps, text messages, e-mails—

Except it wasn't. I'd done a factory reset of the phone literally the day before Charles was released from jail, spending the afternoon rebuilding my contacts and the like. I sank to the floor, relief warming me. All of the apps I used to send Charles text messages and, e-mails, to track his phone, to torture him into confessing to my crime—gone. I had erased everything. The police would find nothing to link me to the little game I'd been playing with my husband.

I pressed my hand against my chest, commanding my heart to stop its frenetic beating.

I would walk away. Clean. Unscathed.

Still, I wanted my possessions back. I wanted my house back. I wanted to put this unpleasantness behind me and move on with my life without Charles.

Whatever that meant.

For almost thirty-two years, it had been the two of us. I hated him as much as I loved him. Despite his betraying me with the tawdry cocktail waitress, despite my having to slit her throat and frame him for it, despite all of it, Charles was my soul mate.

I missed him.

And yet, I was glad to be rid of him.

Funny how that works, no?

My stomach rumbled as I took a shower, washing the past few days from my hair and skin. I blanched at the wan imitation of a woman staring back at me when I wiped the fog from the mirror, longing for color in my cheeks, a swipe of pale pink gloss, a wedge of soft brown eyeliner across my lids to bring me back to life.

No. I could use this ravage to my advantage. There should be no "looking well." No looking hale, no looking hearty.

Play the part.

I smoothed moisturizer from the jar on the countertop across my damp skin and stepped into the robin's egg blue tracksuit and grabbed fluffy white house slippers from the closet before I eased the door open, my ear cocked for sounds of life.

Smell was the first sense to come alive as I inhaled the rich aroma of coffee drifting up the stairs. I could hear the low murmur of a television and the rustle of newspaper, Francine and Raymond's voices droning underneath.

"Oh, Jillian, honey, you're up," Francine said as I appeared. She rinsed out an empty carton of blueberry yogurt in the sink before tossing it into her recycling bin. "Coffee?"

"Tea would be wonderful," I said and she winked as she put on the kettle. I nodded at Raymond seated at the kitchen table, his steel gray eyes, a perfect match for the thatch of white hair and deep olive skin, boring into me. "Raymond. Good morning."

"Jillian," he said, his voice stiff with effort.

Ah, Raymond. In the camp of, "Jillian, what the hell did you do?"

I slunk into a chair across from him, clasping my hands together because I couldn't think of what else to do with them.

"Honey, I spoke to your mother," Francine said. "She and your father will be here tonight. Joss called a few times. She wants you to call her back right away. I talked to your mother-in-law—and Chase—yesterday, and Celia said they would come straight here with the boys to see you. They should be here soon. I tried to tell Celia you were sleeping—"

"Don't worry about it. Celia can be quite determined." I paused. "How—" Tears sprouted from my eyes at the thought of my boys. I wiped them away with the sleeves of my jacket. My dear, sweet boys. "Chase. How did he seem to you?"

The tea kettle whistled and Francine pulled a black mug and tin of tea bags from the cabinet. She shrugged. "Well, he already knew, of course. Had seen the news, talked to Charlotte."

Francine's voice hitched around my sister-in-law's name. Even with all my gifts, I'd always been a touch in awe of the hard-driving businesswoman with the independent streak and corporate savvy. Charlotte and I had always been so close, the sister the other never had.

Still, Charles was her brother. Thick as thieves they were. I already knew she'd never forgive me.

Another casualty in my war with Charles.

I took the mug from Francine, relishing the chamomile-scented steam. "I have no idea what to say to them," I whispered.

"You shoot him on purpose?" Raymond asked.

"Ray," Francine said, exasperation and disappointment lacing her words.

My head snapped up, tears spilling down my face, ready to respond, when I saw Charlotte's talking head on the TV over Francine's shoulder. Her eyes were rimmed red and her normally lush blond hair was the same greasy, disheveled mess it had been the other day. She stood in front of her house, her daughter, Chelsea, plastered to her side, her arms locked around her mother's waist. Charlotte's husband, Rex, stood behind them, stoic, his lips pursed, both hands resting on his wife's shoulders. Microphones hovered beneath them, the bright lights of the cameras reflected against the glass of the front window of their house.

Out of habit, I looked around for the remote. "Turn it up," I said to Francine, fluttering one hand in her direction.

"Are you sure?"

"Turn it up," I repeated. "Please."

Francine complied and Charlotte's voice filled the room.

"The loss of my brother, Charles, is a wound from which I doubt any of us will ever recover. I will miss his wry wit, warm smile, and gregarious nature. There will never be a time the phone will ring and I won't wish it's him. There will never be a time I won't miss my brother dearly. I can only hope justice for my brother is swift and certain and that his soul only knows eternal peace. Thank you. That will be all."

Rex opened the door and the family turned, disappearing into the house. The camera swerved to a reporter, shellacked to perfection even at this early hour, the large black oval of her microphone perched beneath her lips.

"An impromptu statement this morning by Charlotte Morgan Douglas, about the death of her brother, Dr. Charles Morgan, who was fatally shot on the twenty-eighth by his wife, Jillian Morgan. According to police, Jillian Morgan alleges the shooting was accidental, that she believed her husband to be an intruder. The Morgan family, being, of course, one of the most prominent old money families in Chicago, the driving force behind the Chicago History Library, administrators of the Morgan Family Foundation, and the Morgan Group, a global conglomerate comprised of the C.B. Morgan luxury hotel chain, beer companies, and banks, of which Charlotte Morgan Douglas is president and CEO. The distraught Charlotte Morgan Douglas confronted her sister-in-law a few days ago in the parking lot of Evanston Hospital. It is not known if she and Jillian Morgan have spoken since."

The TV cut to yesterday's ruckus, including Charlotte's slap. Involuntarily, I jumped, almost as though I were being hit all over again.

The reporter was back on camera. "As you'll recall, Dr. Morgan was himself recently arrested for the Halloween night murder of Rogers Park resident, Tamra Washington, with whom he'd allegedly been having an extramarital affair. Dr. Morgan had been released on bail the afternoon of December twenty-eighth and according to his attorney, Bernard Reynolds, had returned to his Winnetka home to retrieve some personal items before checking into a hotel. Police say they are continuing their investigation into Dr. Morgan's death and that so far, Jillian Morgan has not been charged and she is not in custody. Her current whereabouts are unknown. Reporting live from Lincoln Park, I'm Patty Pennington. Mel, back to you."

The anchors in the studio uttered a handful of inane, practiced platitudes before transitioning to traffic and weather.

"Are you okay?" Francine asked quietly.

I threw my shoulders back. "Charlotte is entitled to her feelings." Frankly, the less I antagonized Charlotte right now, the better.

"Jesus, I hope nobody figures out you're here," Raymond said as he scooted back from the table, carrying his mug and plate into the kitchen. "The last thing I want is a bunch of vultures in my driveway."

"If it's too much trouble, I can go to a hotel."

"You won't—" Francine glared at her husband. "He didn't mean that. You'll stay here until you can get back into your house."

Raymond dropped his plate into the sink, porcelain crashing against stainless steel. "Here's what I want to know. What in the *hell* were you doing with a gun?"

"I can't—"

The doorbell interrupted.

My in-laws.

My sons.

7

"Jillian."

My mother-in-law, Celia, held out her arms, swallowing me into a Chanel No. 5 embrace, the blond tips of her classic bob peeking out from beneath her mink headband, her matching coat silky and warm against my skin. We held onto each other for a few moments before she pulled back, cupping my cheeks with both gloved hands. The fine patrician features of her own face were drenched in tears. As I thought about it, this might have been the first time I'd ever seen tears from her. She shook her head as we stared at each other, two women locked in two very different emotional strains.

Over Celia's shoulder, Clayton stood, tall, aristocratic, not a strand of that soft white flap of hair out of place, his tan wool coat and plaid scarf stiff as ever. He looked troubled, his lips sealed into a thin line, his eyelids heavy against his wrinkled face. He reached out to place a papery hand on my shoulder, patting it over and over without uttering a word.

"Oh, my dear. I am so sorry." Celia pulled me to her again, whispering into my hair. "I'm sorry for everything."

"How are you, Jillian?" Clayton rasped.

I broke from Celia and grabbed his hand. "In shock. Still trying to understand it all." From the corner of my eye, I could see Raymond and Francine retreat into the living room, standing awkwardly by the couch.

My in-laws. It didn't entirely surprise me they were being so genial. It was the Morgan way. Circle the wagons and all that. At best, Charles had an ambivalent relationship with his parents. As much as I got on with Clayton and Celia, at times I did find their treatment of him an abomination. Celia was brittle and haughty—much more than myself, which was saying something—prone to chipping away at practically every word that came out of Charles's mouth with little to no justification. Clayton was such a pompous hypocrite, I often wondered how he got through doorways with that enormous ego of his. I never understood what seemed to be their profound disappointment in Charles. I suppose it was like Charles had always said, that Clayton bitterly held onto his only son's rejection of the family business in favor of medicine. I didn't know why. Charlotte was far better suited to the boardroom. Of course, Charles had been the Golden Boy, excelling at sports and academics with equal ease. He'd gone to Northwestern and Harvard, married a Main Line debutante no less. Became a respectable doctor with a thriving private practice, had a beautiful family along the way. He did everything right. Yet, for some reason, it never seemed to be enough for them.

Still, he was their child.

And he was dead.

Murdered by his wife in cold blood.

That had to pluck something.

I let my gaze sweep over Chase and Gabe, startled still, startled always, by these two beautiful, magnificent creatures who belonged to me. Two things Charles and I had done right.

I opened my arms. A sobbing Gabe fell against me, his face swollen with grief, his glittering blue eyes awash in pink veins. As shock and disbelief shuddered through his lithe body, I stroked the smooth, lush strands of his hair and murmured what I hoped were soothing words.

Parents always say they don't have a favorite child, but we all know that's about the most unequivocal lie to ever pass from a mother or father's lips. Just as I was my father's spoiled little princess and my mother hovered over my baby brother the moment his gurgling pink form and curious blue eyes came bouncing into this world, if you have more than one child, one of them is your favorite.

Gabe was mine.

Don't misunderstand—both our boys were flawless specimens, in both mind and body. Kissed by the Morgan athleticism and golden good looks and the Vaughn intellect and gentility, there wasn't much room for compromise for either of them. But while Chase was Charles's mirror image, down to the boyish lick of flaxen hair across their foreheads and carefree countenance that masked a sometimes ruthless competitiveness, Gabe was my doppelganger. Blond and lanky. Quiet and introspective, he possessed a sensitivity that eluded most of us mere mortals. Always observing, never saying much, but managing to drop a nugget of incisiveness that left everyone agape. Always scribbling or doodling in the endless journals that had been glued to his palm since he was five. He'd always shown such propensity for sketching and painting, I hoped he might become the artist I never did. Alas, journalism won out as his college major.

Gabe was also a difficult pregnancy, necessitating bed rest for most of my last trimester, which still wasn't enough to stave off the premature birth or his prolonged confinement to the NICU. I prayed every moment of those long tortuous days for God to bring me another healthy, beautiful baby. As rough and tumble as I had allowed both my boys to be, Gabe's welfare always made my heart lurch just a little bit more.

I pulled back and cupped his cheeks in my hands. Looking into that handsome, guileless face, innocent of sin, my heart fractured. Lousy father though he had been, Charles *had* been their father. No matter the circumstances, it was a loss.

"Are you okay, Mom?"

"Oh, sweetheart, please, don't worry about me. I'm fine. Really. How are you, my love?"

Gabe shrugged, his gaze floating to the floor. "Okay, I guess."

"You know, Gabe," I said, lifting his chin with the hook of my index finger. "It's okay to not be okay. It's okay to be mad at me."

He threw himself against me once more, a fresh round of tears flooding his eyes. I looked over at Chase, standing off to the side, his hands shoved into the pockets of his black wool coat, the stoicism etched in his face showing no signs of crumbling. He placed a hand on his brother's shoulder, giving it a soft tug.

"Hey, Gabe, why don't you go get a glass of water or something?"

Francine popped up from her unobtrusive perch on the arm of the slouchy brown leather couch and rushed toward Gabe. "Come on, honey, come with me," she said guiding him by the shoulders to the kitchen. She flicked her head at Ray, indicating he should join them. He sighed and complied and the three of them exited to the kitchen.

Chase stared at me, his jaw squirming beneath the concrete of his face. "So, tell me what happened, Mom," he said.

"I—"

"You walked into the house and what, just shot Dad?"

"Chase—" Celia snapped.

"No, Celia, it's okay. He has a right to know what happened to his father."

"So?" Chase folded his arms across his chest, still staring at me. Waiting. "What happened?"

I ran my palm across the top of my head and sat down on the couch, leaving the rest of them to stare down at me like redwoods. Joss had warned me not to say anything to anyone. However, I couldn't keep this from Chase.

I took a deep breath before relaying in a shaky voice my version of events. Celia and Clayton eventually sat down next to me, offering soft, reassuring pats on my shoulder. Chase remained standing, his jaw continuing to crank so hard, I had the momentary fear he might break it.

"So, wait, Mom," he interrupted me, palms upturned. "Why did you even have a gun to begin with?"

Celia and Clayton's heads swiveled toward me, waiting.

"Well, son, to tell you the truth, for protection. I was alone a lot—your father working all the time, Gabe leaving for school. Me, alone in that big house. It made me feel better to have it."

"When did you get this gun? How long have you had it?"

"Not long—"

"How long is not long?"

"A few months—"

"So, did you go to a shooting range to learn to shoot or what?"

"You know I did clay shooting in England when I was younger. I guess I thought of it as picking up an old hobby."

"You haven't done that in years. You're telling me that all of a sudden, you just woke up one morning and decided to go back to *this* particular hobby?"

Ah, Chase. The future lawyer. Leaving no stone unturned. Pressing forward in the pursuit of every detail, no matter how minute. Truth, justice, and the Chase Morgan Way. He'd be quite good at his chosen profession.

"Calm down, son," Clayton said. "This must be very difficult for your mother."

Chase scoffed, but obeyed his grandfather, leaning against the banister, hands in his pockets, his eyes narrow slits.

"Yes, and especially with all that business with Charlotte." Celia tsked. "Front page of both newspapers. Lead story on all the newscasts. Impromptu press conference this morning. All of it, all over the Internet."

"I'm so sorry about that, Celia," I said. "She and Charles were so close, I understand why she's upset."

"You shouldn't be apologizing, my dear." Celia drew up. "Charlotte has always had trouble handling her emotions. Look at how she stormed out of the house at Christmas."

"I'll have a word with her," Clayton said. "Very unbecoming. Very bad for business."

"Clayton, that's really not necessary."

"Oh, my dear, I wish you would have called us," Celia said, wresting the conversation from her husband, as she was prone to do. "You could have stayed with us, if you really felt alone—"

I grabbed her hand. "I appreciate your saying that."

"I'm just so disappointed in Charles," she said. "All of that sordid business with that woman and getting arrested. Beyond distasteful."

"We let you down, Jillian," Clayton said. "If we'd somehow done better with Charles, perhaps he wouldn't have—"

"All right, you know what? Stop it," Chase boomed.

"Chase—" I held up my hand.

"Yes, all right, Dad did some shitty things—"

"Young man!"

"Some stupid things," Chase plowed ahead, modifying his words only slightly in response to Celia's admonition. "But he was a good dad, gave us a good life. He's not on trial. He's dead." His voice wavered. "He's dead. For God's sake, let him rest in peace."

Clayton cleared his throat and Celia adjusted the collar of her coat several times. The low hum of Francine and Gabe's voices floated out from the kitchen.

"I'm sorry," I ventured in a meek voice. "I'm sorry for all of this. If I could go back—"

"We'll get you the best lawyer—"

"I have a lawyer, Celia—"

"Who?"

I gulped over the cotton of my mouth. "Her name is Joss Hamilton."

"Joss Hamilton?" Celia grimaced. "I've never heard of her. Who is this person, Jillian? Do you know who she is, Clayton? Have you heard of her?"

"No, no, I can't say that I have," he said. "No matter. We'll call Lawrence. He can recommend someone."

"I promise you, she's quite sharp." I was crumbling, coming apart grain by grain. I wasn't going to be able to stand them much longer. I grasped Celia's hand. "Really, please don't worry yourselves with this. I can handle it."

"Hamilton, you say?" Clayton asked, groping for his phone in his pants pocket. "We'll have Lawrence do a background check on her, see just what her story is."

If I could have physically shoved them out the door, I would have. Instead, I purposely stifled a yawn. *That ought to get them moving.*

"Oh, dear you must be exhausted," Celia said. "Well, you can sleep in the car on the way to Fairmore."

"I'm staying here," I said.

"Nonsense. You'll stay with us. We're behind that big gate, no one can get to you," she huffed. "Besides, you should be with family during a time like this."

"Chase, go and fetch your brother," Clayton said, getting to his feet.

"No, really, I'm fine to stay with Francine and Raymond." I licked my lips. "I *want* to stay with Francine and Raymond."

"Gabe and I are going to stay with Aunt Charlotte for a few days. I already texted her, she said it's fine," Chase said.

"Oh." Celia frowned, obviously disappointed. "I suppose ... well, I mean I just assumed you'd—"

"Chase, did I just hear you say you were going to stay with your aunt?" Francine asked as she came in from the kitchen, Gabe following behind. Raymond apparently had no compunction to join us. Though Gabe's tears had stopped, he remained solemn, shrouded inside his blue and yellow ski jacket.

"Yes, Mrs. Ladd. Obviously, we can't stay at the house since it's still considered a crime scene," Chase said.

No mistaking who that was meant for.

"And we don't want to impose on you—" he continued.

"Oh, honey, we've got plenty of room, if you want to stay here with your mom."

"Jillian, dear, you should really come home with us," Celia said.

"I'll stay here," Gabe piped in. "With Mom."

I smiled weakly at his show of support and he offered me only a furtive glance in return.

Chase shrugged. "Yeah, okay, whatever. Grandma, Grandpa, if you can drop me at home so I can grab my car." He looked back at Francine. "Thank you for the offer, Mrs. Ladd."

"Oh—Chase, I'm sorry, but they've impounded all of our cars. Because they were part of the crime scene," I said.

He scoffed. "You're kidding, right? What, you ran Dad over with the car, too?"

"That's highly uncalled for, young man," Clayton said, shooting my son one of his most disapproving looks. "You stop all this nonsense. Right now."

"It's only for a few days," I said. "You'll probably have it back by tomorrow or the day after."

"Jesus. All right, I'll just grab an Uber into the city then," he said. He hesitated a moment as he stared at me, unsure it seemed, as to how he should proceed with me. "I'll talk to you later, Mom," he said, opting for polite distance. He pulled his phone out of his pocket, swiping and tapping in search of his Uber before hustling out of the house, intent on collecting his bags and getting as far away from me as possible.

I said my goodbyes to Clayton and Celia and there was talk of coming together the next day to discuss funeral arrangements and the like. I could only nod, agreeing to whatever they wanted, in no mood to make contributions. Despite having slept for nearly twenty-four hours straight, I was ready for another round.

Gabe grabbed his suitcases and Francine settled him into the other guest room. He declined talking in favor of his own nap, quietly shutting the door on me. I kept my ear pressed to it for the sounds of muffled sobs, but heard nothing.

Francine motioned to me from the stairs and I followed her into the kitchen.

"How are you holding up, honey?" she asked. "Really."

I sighed. "Drained."

"Dealing with your in-laws is trying on a good day, much less—" She shook her head. "Anyway. I have to run out for a few hours. I forgot I've got this stupid planning meeting this afternoon for a luncheon next month and I can't get out of it. You be okay here for a little while?"

"Oh, yes." I ran a hand over my face. "I'm going to lie down and likely by the time you're back, I'll be a bit more refreshed."

"You should try to call Joss back before too much time passes. Her card is on the bulletin board in the kitchen."

My hand flew to my forehead. Bits and pieces and words and phrases and memories and lies swirled across my brain, threatening to explode. I nodded feebly instead. "Right, yes, I'll give her a call."

"Ray's going to that indoor driving range he can't seem to get enough of and then meet his daughter in the city for dinner, so it will be the three of us tonight."

"Raymond's not quite sure what to make of all this, is he? Of me?" My voice was quiet. Melancholy almost.

"Oh, honey, he's just trying to process everything." She squeezed my hand. "Try not to let it bother you."

"Of course." I nodded.

"All right, well, make yourself at home, help yourself to whatever. I'll be back this afternoon."

"Thank you again, Francine. For everything. I truly don't know what I'd be doing right now if I didn't have you to lean on."

"What are neighbors for?" She smiled. "What are friends for?" She patted my hand before she grabbed her purse from the kitchen counter and set off on her mission.

I yawned heartily as I heard her pull out of the driveway. I'd take a short nap then call Joss. I fixed myself another cup of tea, sipping it slowly as I made my ascent up the stairs, when the doorbell pealed, stopping me in my tracks. Had the media figured out I was here?

Or maybe it was Chase, coming back to smooth things over with me. That thought propelled me down the stairs.

I opened the door and my heart dropped.

Vanessa.

8

She smiled.

"Hello, Jill."

"Jillian," I said, twisting the doorknob in my hand. "I prefer to be called Jillian."

"Oh. My apologies," Vanessa said. "Jillian."

"How did you know I was here?"

"Well, I'd heard Charles mention his good neighbors the Ladds on occasion." She shrugged. "I took a guess."

I cocked my head to the side, alternating between annoyance, and if I were being honest, a modicum of fear. I hadn't considered what to do about her. An oversight I hoped wouldn't come back to bite me. I wanted to slam the door in her face, but bees and honey and all that.

"Won't you come in?" I said as I stepped aside.

She smiled and breezed past me, smugness mingling with whatever low-rent perfume she bathed in, the squeal of her hot pink vinyl boots making me cringe. "I drove by your house. The media have completely taken over."

"Yes, I know."

"How long will you be here?"

"A few days. The police are still processing the house as part of their procedure."

She pursed her lips. "Well, sure. Being a crime scene and everything."

Vanessa Shayne. If anyone could blow me out of the water, it would be Vanessa Shayne. She knew enough to be dangerous, but not enough to know what she was doing. A slippery slope.

Vanessa Shayne. A successful cardiologist. My husband's practice partner. His wannabe paramour. My wannabe co-conspirator. A busty pinup girl who wiggled around in tight clothes and innuendo. Savage strawberry blond waves and seductive green eyes barely concealing a pathological need to throw herself at any living, breathing, speaking body who might show her even an ounce of affection.

Vanessa Shayne. The very embodiment of desperation.

She'd tried with Charles and failed. To be honest, I was surprised he hadn't taken her up on her offer. Not that she was his type—slinky blue-eyed blondes had always been his preference. Still, wasn't the point of an affair to try something different? Perhaps he ultimately found Vanessa as unbecoming as I did.

I guess it was about a year or so ago when I first noticed a ripple between her and Charles. It was at one of those boring awards dinners I had allowed myself to be dragged to nearly every week during the early years of our marriage, but in the ensuing decades, had managed to maneuver out of with my patented grace. I still went on occasion to keep the peace, but I'd just as soon stay home and pull out my eyelashes one by agonizing one.

The look that flashed between my husband and Vanessa was just that—a flare—but it told me volumes. She was hopelessly in love with him, romanticizing him as much as I had years ago, wondering how blatant she should be in her pursuit of him. Would she be content as the long-suffering mistress or was the stature of wife a more apt fit? He was mildly amused, intrigued even, no doubt feeling the first tingles of the inevitable slide into the knowledge he was growing older. He must have sensed a mild, nagging panic about just how long those preternatural good looks would hold on, how many more years of a full, abundant head of blond hair were ahead of him. If those weekly squash games would continue to beat back the drooping gut that had felled his contemporaries. If that year-round tan would turn to papery leather, and age spots would sprout overnight across the backs of his hands like nagging weeds.

So, yes, I thought if anyone, it would be the brazen and hopeless Vanessa Shayne who Charles would deign to cheat on me with in order to fulfill his tacky midlife crisis.

It would have been better for him if he had.

"Can I get you anything? Tea? Water?" I asked, ever the gracious hostess.

"Oh, no, I'm fine," she said, fluffing out her hair as she did a slow scan of the living room's country lodge décor—brown leather couches and ottomans, knotty pine coffee table, burgundy Jacquard print wallpaper, oversized brass pots stuffed with towering green plants—almost as though she were casing it.

"Can I take your coat?" I asked, eyeing the white faux fur monstrosity.

"Thank you." She slipped out of the coat to reveal sausage-casing blue jeans and tight, plunging hot pink sweater, all to match the hot pink vinyl boots that stretched just over her knees.

"Have a seat." I gestured to the soft brown leather couch as I laid her coat across one of the ottomans. I flinched at the whiny crunch of those hideous boots as she sat down. I took the oversized matching chair, draped with a brown zebra print throw, opposite her.

"So, how are you, Jillian?" she asked. "Really."

"A bit numb to be honest." My hands were loosely knotted in my lap as I waited for her to get to whatever it was she wanted.

"I can imagine. To accidentally shoot and kill your husband." She shook her head. "You must feel as though you woke up in some sort of nightmare."

"Yes, something like that."

"It was such a shock to get the news," she said as she fingered the knotted strand of her pearls, the only demure aspect of her gaudy ensemble. "I'm still reeling."

"Yes, I would imagine so."

"I have to admit, Jillian, I do feel a bit of remorse, a bit of responsibility about all of this."

As you should. After all, you were the one to blab to me all about my husband's extracurricular activities.

She'd been the one to insist on a dignified lunch after spotting Charles and his tramp fondling each other at a restaurant in Lake Geneva, after he'd lied and told me he was spending the weekend in surgery. She'd been the one to slyly suggest we team up to take him down. She'd been the one to send him taunting e-mails, in the beginning anyway, probing about whether his wife knew about his trollop.

Oh, yes, Vanessa should feel responsible.

She'd set this whole thing in motion.

"Oh?" was all I said instead.

"I just—well, if I hadn't been the one to see him with ... *her* that night and then told you about it." She sat up like a puppy panting after a treat. "Did you tell him I told you? Did you tell him I saw the two of them together in Lake Geneva?"

"To be honest, no. I didn't think it was important for Charles to know how I found out. After all, what did it really matter?"

"I'd want to know." She huffed, indignant. Put out. "It's human nature."

"What I mean to say is, he asked, of course, but I didn't think it fair to put you in that position."

"Oh." A dark cloud floated across her face. "So, he didn't know it was me, that I was the one—"

"As I said, Vanessa, I didn't think involving you in this was prudent. After all, you were colleagues. I mean, to tell Charles about the information you shared with me ... well, I assumed it was in confidence..."

"No, no, you're right. Of course. There was no need for Charles to know anything about my role in this," she said.

Vanessa Shayne. So desperate to be relevant. To be in the thick of it.

Sorry to disappoint, dear. My husband's last thoughts weren't of you and your big mouth.

She cleared her throat. "So, please, continue. Tell me what happened last night. I mean unless your lawyer has instructed you not to say anything."

"Lawyer?" I tilted my head to the side.

"I just assumed you'd gotten a lawyer."

"Really?" I smiled. "Is that what you assumed?"

Scarlet—shame? Frustration? Anger?—flushed across her cheeks. She wanted so badly to get under my skin. Rankle me.

Keep trying, Vanessa. How far do you think you'll get?

"Sure. Yes. I mean not that you have anything to hide. It's just that people who get lawyers in this situation, it's usually because they have something to hide, right?" She cleared her throat again. "You know what, if you're not up to talking about what happened, I completely understand."

"Oh, I don't have anything to hide, Vanessa." I perched on the edge of the couch. "But you're right, I do have a lawyer."

"I figured as much. I mean, of course you do. Have a lawyer. Someone like you would have a lawyer."

She was babbling now. I cocked my head to the side, narrowing my eyes slightly. "Someone like me?"

The red of her face deepened. "You, someone of your stature, of your, well with someone in your position—"

"We are all entitled to a defense," I said. "The constitution is quite clear on that point."

"Yes." She threw her hands up. "That's exactly right. The constitution."

"At any rate, yes, you're right, I can't discuss what happened. Per my lawyer."

"Of course." Her voice softened. She was back on familiar ground. Without warning, she leapt across the room, the vinyl of her boots squealing, and slid her arms around my shoulders, rocking me from side-to-side. She couldn't see the look of disgusted surprise on my face.

"Oh, Jillian. Jillian, Jillian, Jillian. You poor, poor thing," she murmured. "Even though I know you can't talk about what happened, I read in the paper this morning that you mistook him for an intruder, that you didn't know he was coming home?"

"I really can't talk about it."

"This whole thing is just so awful." The fine point of her chin found its way into my scalp and she held me tighter. "When I told you what I knew, deep down, I hoped you'd allow me to be a friend to you. To help you."

"I see now you would have been a good friend to me," I said, continuing my charade. "In my time of need."

"Yes, there's that. There's definitely that. But that's not the only thing I meant."

I froze. She knew something.

Or she thought she did.

I held my breath, waiting for the other shoe to drop.

"I'm not sure I understand what you mean," I said carefully.

"You know, Charles really wasn't well those last few months," she said. "I mean it was obvious he was coming off the spool. All that rushing out of the office all the time. Distracted. And he looked terrible."

"Yes," I said. "Charles was clearly under severe strain those last few months."

"Hmmm. Clearly. Do you know what was most curious of all?"

"No, I'm afraid I don't."

She pulled back, looking at me, her green eyes dancing with ... something.

"Vanessa? Is there something you want to say?"

She smiled and patted my hand. "It'll keep," she whispered. "You look so tired, Jill. Jillian. You should rest."

Fury detonated inside of me. Vanessa Shayne. I should have seen her coming.

"You know what? You're right," I said. "It's been an excruciating few days and I'm afraid I must go and lie down. Please, excuse me."

"Of course." She patted my shoulder. "You really should get some rest. You look terrible."

"Thank you again for your concern," I said, getting to my feet.

"What are friends for?"

I rolled my tongue along the inside of my mouth, an attempt at keeping my ire in check. "Indeed."

"And I do hope you feel better soon." She stood and grabbed her purse from the couch as I handed her the monstrosity of her coat, the twin engines of anger and fear revving in my veins. "The sooner you do, the sooner we can ... chat."

"Yes," I said, my blood boiling. "We really should get together again soon."

"At any rate, I'm glad we had a chance to spend even a little bit of time together," she said as we walked to the front door. She turned around and looked at me. "I do hope you're able to pull yourself together."

I offered her my best fake-party smile. "Of course. So lovely of you to drop by and check on me."

"Can't wait to see you again," she said as she breezed out the door. "I'll be in touch."

I wanted to slam the door behind her, but didn't want to give her the satisfaction of displaying my rage. I walked slowly into the living room, my arms folded across my chest, steam roiling inside me. Tears of fury stung my eyes as I stalked across the room, the anger swelling with each step. Had Gabe not been upstairs slumbering, had it not been someone else's house, I would have thrown something. Screamed. A primal, bloody scream of anger and frustration.

Damn her.

Damn Charles.

Damn his slut.

I wiped my nose with the heel of my hand as I carried my teacup into the kitchen, swapping it for a cold glass of water, guzzling it down in two hearty gulps. I slammed the glass onto the counter, oddly fortified. Focused.

So, Vanessa Shayne wanted to toy with me.

All right.

Game on.

9

THE BARS of early morning sunlight, the first we'd seen in nearly a week, streamed through the curtains of my guest room, slashing my skin as I paced across the Oriental rug. I craved a cigarette and it struck me I hadn't had one since *that night.*

Sleep had been impossible. Vanessa's little drop-in yesterday afternoon had left me pulled tight as a piano wire. After an evening call with Joss, I'd gone to bed early, for all the good it'd done. I'd tossed and turned all night, finally rousting myself out of bed around four to shower and change into yet another Francine Ladd tracksuit. I finally decided she must own stock in the company.

Of course, tracksuits were the least of my worries.

What on earth could Vanessa possibly know? With her, guessing was futile. Snake that she was, there was no telling what she had slithered into.

I tapped my nail against my tooth, scouring my brain for the possibilities. Could she have seen me exiting the slut's apartment on the occasions I let myself in to study the layout, all part of my plan to murder her and frame my husband? Seen me tromping through the dumpster to retrieve the incriminating evidence Charles had tossed?

Speculation was useless. Until I knew what I was dealing with, I couldn't formulate a plan of attack. For all I knew, she was blowing smoke, speculating on her own.

The doorbell pealed from downstairs. I rubbed my wrist, missing my watch, missing the chunky silver bracelet I'd worn practically every day since my Aunt Biddy had given it to me for my Sweet Sixteen. I looked at the clock on the bedside table. Eight. Nothing good could come from a doorbell ringing at eight a.m.

I peeked through the blinds and out the window, which faced the front of the house. The salt-encrusted maroon sedan from the other day sat on the street, snug against the end of the driveway.

The police.

Fear scurried through me. I froze as I waited for the inevitable knock on the door and tinkling of handcuffs. My eyes flashed around the room, as though an exit would miraculously materialize.

"Get a grip," I whispered. I took several deep breaths and closed my eyes. They were police. Idiots. The dimmest bulbs in every box. Child's play.

I flew to the bed, grabbing the book Francine had lent me from the nightstand before fluffing up the bed pillows behind me. Just as I opened the book, there was a knock on the door. I swallowed.

"Come in," I said.

The door crept open, an ashen Francine peering through the crack. "Honey, I'm sorry, the police are here."

I closed the book over my finger. "Oh. That was the doorbell, then."

"Listen, I'll call Joss, tell her they're here—"

"Quite all right, Francine." I set the book on the bed and stood up. "I'll keep it simple. Answer yes, answer no. No more, no less."

"Honey, I'm not sure that's a good idea," she whispered.

I patted her arm. "I'll be fine," I said before I floated down the stairs, grateful now for the restless night and accompanying bloodshot eyes. Potts and Travis watched me without a word, no hint of their mission this morning. Even at this early hour, Detective Potts looked like he might have slept in that salt-stained Buick, while Detective Travis was as dapper as always, his coat open to reveal a dark wool Armani suit. He must have had some family money somewhere, or been an executive or something in a former life and was now fulfilling his childhood fantasy of cops and robbers.

"Cocky to the end, aren't you Jillian?"

"Detectives." I squashed Charles's voice into some unknown corner. "Francine said you wanted to see me."

"We've got a few more questions for you, Mrs. Morgan," Travis said.

"As I recall, you're to speak to my attorney."

"We're going to need you to come down to the station," Potts said.

"Is she under arrest?" Francine asked from over my shoulder. "If she's not under arrest, you can ask your questions right here."

"Your attorney can meet us down at the station," Potts said. "This shouldn't take long. Just need to clarify a few things."

"It's okay, Francine. If you'll call Joss—"

"Jillian, are you sure about this?" she whispered as she tugged on my arm. "You're sure you don't want to wait?"

I didn't say anything, turning to face Potts and Travis. "I'm ready when you are."

10

I LOOKED down at the gunmetal gray table, resisting the urge to tap the edge of my red lacquered fingernail against it. The gray-green cinder block walls beneath the dim fluorescent light above me seemed to grow grayer and greener as the minutes ticked past. Sweat burned against my underarms as cramps pulsed against my legs, begging to be walked out. Upon our arrival at the police station, Potts and Travis had deposited me into this stuffy box and promptly disappeared. The ancient face clock over the door told me that had been almost an hour ago. As if they could get me to crack. As if I might resort to relentless pacing, nail-tapping, and heaving sighs.

Oh, no. I could and would continue to sit here quietly and demurely. The model of calm and collected. The Ice Queen at her finest.

There'd been no sign of Joss Hamilton. No matter. As I had said to Francine, I would keep it simple. There would be nothing they could do to trip me up, no matter how valiantly they tried.

The door swung open and Potts bumbled in, followed by Travis. Potts held a manila folder filled with papers in his stubby, grubby fingers. He slapped the folder down on the table.

"Sorry to have kept you waiting, Mrs. Morgan," Travis said, smiling, flashing a set of expensive veneers. Yes, he definitely had money stashed somewhere. Maybe he had married well. Or was a trust fund baby.

"Seems like your attorney got lost." Potts flipped open the folder, shuffling through the papers, while Travis extracted a notebook from his shirt pocket along with a pen.

I didn't say anything, just waited.

Stick to the facts.

"We've got a few questions for you. Some things we need to clear up," Potts said, still rustling through the papers in front of him. I flicked my gaze toward the papers, wondering what I might be able to catch a glimpse of, but wasn't able to discern anything beyond a flash of words and charts. Potts extracted a sheet and cleared his throat.

"Mrs. Morgan, remind us again what time you arrived home on Friday night?"

"Seven forty-five."

"Right. After dinner with your friend, Suzette Nichols."

"Yes."

"Uh huh. Ms. Nichols said you and she went to Avli. Do you normally go there?"

"We don't have a set place."

Travis nodded as he scribbled this down in his notebook. Potts just stared at me.

"How sure are you about the time, Mrs. Morgan?" Travis asked.

"I looked at the dash of my car right before I walked into the house."

"Okay." He stopped writing and looked up at me. "And your husband's car was in the driveway when you arrived home, right?"

"Yes."

"Where were you the night your husband was arrested?" Travis continued.

"At his sister Charlotte's fiftieth birthday party. It was at her home in Lincoln Park."

"Charlotte Morgan Douglas. The one you just had the little run-in with," Potts said.

"Yes."

So far, so good.

"It's my understanding you weren't actually home when your husband was arrested," Potts said.

"I was still at Charlotte's, yes."

"All right. Let's get back to the night you shot your husband." I winced inwardly as Potts licked the point of his pencil. "You arrive home at seven forty-five and the house—were your outside lights on?"

"No. Normally they operate on a timer, but the timer was malfunctioning. I had an electrician scheduled to come out next week."

Good detail to drop in. And the truth. Easily verifiable. Credible.

"Huh. Okay. And no lights on inside the house?"

"No."

"Mrs. Morgan, where was your husband?"

I scoured my brain to remember what I had told them in the hospital and later when they'd questioned me at home.

You heard a noise. The creaky step. The landing.

"I walked into the house. It was dark. I heard the noise on the steps. The boys were out of town with their grandparents, Charles was still supposed to be in jail. I didn't know what to think except no one should have been home."

Travis nodded, dutifully filling his notebook with these details. "So, you heard the noise on the steps. Which step was it?"

"The landing."

"Okay, so you hear this creak from the landing of your staircase. How many steps is that from the bottom?" he asked.

"I don't know."

"If you had to guess?"

I shrugged, flummoxed. "Ten, fifteen, maybe?"

"And you didn't hear any footsteps?" Travis asked. "Nobody running down the stairs?"

"Well, not running no, but footsteps. I heard the noise—the squeak—and then footsteps, but again, my first thought was an intruder."

"Huh. Okay. And you said there were no lights on in the house. Right?"

"Yes."

"We talked to your husband's attorney, Bernard Reynolds and according to him, he dropped your husband off at six twenty, which was a good hour and a half before you arrived home. He wouldn't have turned on at least one light?" Potts asked.

"Well." I chuckled sadly, allowing a few tears to spring forth. "My husband could be a bit tight with the dollar. Always one for saving electricity—running behind us, turning off lights, that kind of thing."

Again, all true. Details, details, details.

"Huh." Potts tapped the blunt edge of his index finger on the table, the thud reverberating around the room. "So, you're saying it wouldn't be unusual for him to be sitting in a dark house."

"Not at all."

"Huh," Potts said again. "Interesting."

I cleared my throat and waited. The second hand of the clock thundered above us.

"It looked like your husband had packed a suitcase. We found it, upstairs in the bedroom," Travis said.

"I had no idea," I said.

"Doesn't your bedroom face the street, Mrs. Morgan?" Travis asked.

"Yes."

"He didn't have a light on in the bedroom? While he was packing, I mean," Travis said.

I shrugged. "He could have been on his way down to the kitchen for a glass of water. He definitely would have turned off the bedroom light to do that."

"And he didn't call out or anything when you walked in the door?" Potts asked.

"Not a word." I paused, tensing my neck muscle. The tears flowed on cue. "I wish he had."

Travis extracted a sparkling white linen handkerchief from his pocket and slid it across the table toward me. I was impressed by the whiff of Laundress tickling my nostrils. I dabbed at my tears and took a few deep breaths before nodding that they could go on.

"When was the last time you talked to your husband?" he asked.

"I visited him once in jail. I can't remember the exact day."

"What'd you talk about?"

I blotted the skin around my eyes. "About his arrest. His affair. That I planned to file for divorce."

They both looked at each other as though some new nefarious motive had bloomed. I knew our little jailhouse conversation had been recorded. I was surprised they hadn't unearthed this little tidbit yet. On the other hand, perhaps they had and this was their pathetic attempt at trying to trip me up.

"Had you filed?" Potts asked.

"I planned to after the holidays."

"So, it's fair to say you and Dr. Morgan hadn't really left things on a positive note," he said.

"No."

"Gives you plenty of motive."

"What are you saying, Detective Potts?"

"I mean, Mrs. Morgan, you have to admit, the timing on this is pretty convenient."

I leaned forward, tears in my eyes. "I promise you, if I had known that Charles was home, I never would have shot him. Was I angry, humiliated by all of this? Of course. What wife wouldn't be? But was that enough to drive me to shoot him in cold blood? No. Never. Absolutely not."

Exactly the right amount of hysteria co-mingled with steadfastness and remorse. A potent combination.

Travis clasped his hands in front of his mouth as Potts leaned back in his chair, that same skeptical yet smug look on his face.

Potts was the first to break. He hunched over the table and took one sheet of paper from the top of his stack. He tapped the sides of it with his index finger for a few moments, frowning at it.

"Mrs. Morgan, let me ask you something." Potts ran his tongue along his bottom lip. "Why did you purchase this gun back in September?" He flicked the paper in front of me, a copy of my registration application and receipt. I picked it up, giving it a cursory glance before calmly putting it back down on the table.

It was all I could do to keep from laughing at his supposed *gotcha!* moment. Instead, I cleared my throat and met his gaze.

"I have a bit of a confession to make," I said. I could see their eyes light up. Charles always used to say I had cartwheels spinning in my eyes. I could just about see the twirl of one in Potts's milky brown iris.

"Go on," he said, all but licking his lips and rubbing his hands together.

"As any doctor's wife or significant other can attest, you're alone. A lot." I let my gaze linger on Potts. I wonder if he realized he rubbed his ring finger. Obsessively so. Divorced, most likely. A fed-up wife who could no longer endure the lonely days and nights. "My nest was empty. As you noted the other day, I have a big house and I suppose I wanted some measure of protection." I leaned back in my chair, making sure yet again to fold my hands in my lap. Demure. "At any rate, I've been clay shooting in England many times and I elected to take up an old hobby, so I signed up for lessons at the North Shore Range in Highland Park."

They each deflated like balloons. No smoking gun as it were. Potts sighed.

"Did you take lessons from any particular instructor?" Travis asked, a ribbon of disappointment running through his question.

"William Ronson. Mondays and Wednesdays."

"We'll be sure and check that out," Potts said.

"Of course," I said.

Fumes of frustration rolled off both of them. I wanted to smile, but kept my calm, cooperative, slightly dazed demeanor front and center.

Potts closed his manila folder, defeat seeming to pull at his jaw, while Travis stared at his trusty notebook, his hands a tent over his face.

"Is that all?" I asked.

"For now," Potts said. I almost detected a snarl.

"I was wondering when I might be getting my house back."

"We can probably get some of your property back to you today," Travis murmured. "House and cars, probably tomorrow, day after."

"Thank you. I appreciate it. Perhaps one of your officers would be kind enough to call me a taxi."

"Actually, Mrs. Morgan, I did have another question for you," Travis said.

"Yes?"

"How many cigarettes do you smoke a day? On average."

I went stiff, unease squirming across my insides. He was fishing for something. I couldn't even guess what.

"I guess I've been going through a pack a day."

"A pack a day?" Travis asked.

"Maybe a little less. Why?"

A mysterious smile tugged at one corner of his lips. "No reason."

My heart somersaulted down my ribcage. My cigarettes. Me smoking. What could that have to do with anything? I searched that handsome face for a glimmer of what he was trying to trap me with. His expression remained blank.

"I'll go see about getting you some of your property." He pushed back from the table, and it shook a little as he stood. Potts didn't look at me as he followed his partner out of the room, slamming the door behind him.

I quivered in my seat, fear hammering my insides, sweat gushing into the fibers of that horrible tracksuit. My fingers trembled as I crossed them in my lap and jagged little bursts of air masquerading as breath rushed from my lips.

The door swung open and I blanched a little as Travis swooped in, bearing plastic evidence bags. He dropped them in front of me.

"Your purse and phone." He cut the tops of the bags off with a pair of scissors and nodded at me, indicating I was free to stick my hand inside and extract the items. I pushed the reset button on the phone, but the screen stayed black. There were dried streaks of some sort of chemical across the screen and cover. I pawed through my purse, mentally picturing everything that had been in there a few days before: wallet, one hundred dollars in cash (four twenties, a ten, and two fives), hairbrush, two compacts, one for powder, one for blush, tube of Pink Blossom lipstick, tin of Altoids, two Gold Cross pens, hand cream, hand wipes, pack of Kleenex, rollerball of Shalimar.

And my silver lighter and near-empty pack of cigarettes.

"I had a watch and bracelet." I paused. "My wedding ring. I'm assuming they're with my clothes."

"We're still processing the clothes."

"I don't think I'll be wearing those again," I said quietly.

"Right," he said. "I'll see if we can turn the watch and jewelry back over to you."

I waited, itching to extract a cigarette, to just hold it, roll it around. Instead, I looked up at the ceiling, mentally counting to one hundred.

Travis returned, this time bearing my bracelet, ring, and watch. He plunked a second bag down in front of me. "Your husband's wallet, phone, wedding ring."

Bile rose in my throat at the sight of Charles's possessions encased inside all that plastic. We repeated the cutting-of-the-bag ceremony and I put all of his things into my purse, not wanting to look at them, barely wanting to think about them. Slipping the silver bracelet onto my wrist was a happier experience. It calmed me, somehow. I was less naked now. I quietly palmed the wedding ring and dropped it into my purse.

Travis slid a piece of paper in front of me. "I need you to sign this as a form of receipt for your property. We'll get your house keys and cars back to you in another day or two."

I plucked one of the pens from my purse and signed, hoping the wobble of my fingers wouldn't be noticeable in my signature. It was a relief to see my name smooth and authoritative on that black line.

"Thank you," I said, gathering my things.

"Officer Rose will give you a ride back to the Ladds'," he said. "We'll be in touch."

I nodded and followed him out to where the officer was standing, waiting to ferry me back to Francine and Raymond's. The officer deposited me into the backseat before he slid behind the wheel. I chewed on my nail, my tooth sinking deep into the red lacquer of my polish.

"You should have listened to me about the smoking. It's like I always told you, a nasty habit that will only bring you misery."

"Shut up," I whispered. "I can't deal with you right now."

"I'm sorry, ma'am, did you say something?" The officer's eyes queried me from the rearview mirror.

My head jerked up, surprised he'd heard me.

"Nothing," I said, my cheeks burning. "Something I had forgotten about that just occurred to me."

He nodded, shifting his eyes back to the road in front of him. I went into my purse, pulled out my pack of cigarettes and fingered them, wondering just what trouble they were going to get me into.

11

THE STREET below my guest room window was quiet. Still.

Of course, the suburbs were always quiet. Charles had despised it. He craved noise, stimulation, sights, smells. When Chase was in high school, the mild itch for city life grew into a raging infection. It permeated every conversation. He wanted us to downsize to a condo once Gabe left for college. Become empty-nesters! The theater! Restaurants! Gallery openings! Own one car! No car! Taxis!

The notion held little allure for me. I loved our home. The stream of sunlight from our picture windows splashed across the wood floors, the cozy reading nooks, spacious and airy kitchen. Our backyard deck, which had accommodated countless parties. The formal dining room, host to Thanksgiving every year. Our street cloaked in trees. Our tranquil neighborhood, punctuated only by the occasional barking dog or the muted, faraway bell of a commuter train every thirty minutes to an hour. The short walk to the shores of Lake Michigan. The predictability of our neighbors—Monty Finch's endless home improvement follies, the light show of dancing pumpkins the Gerners put up every Halloween, the two weeks Ben and Bethany Savitch spent in Door County every July—provided a measure of contentment. I loved Winnetka with its brick walkways, quaint little shops, and homey restaurants. I loved the fresh air, the peace. The Children's Fair at the Village Green, which I took the boys to for years, marking the unofficial start of summer. The Winter Carnival every January. I enjoyed meandering walks through the neighborhood without worry of muggers, rapists, and would-be killers springing from the bushes to wreak havoc on my person.

Except tonight the quiet was too quiet.

The soft knock on the door broke my trance. I swiped a hand through my hair and said to come in.

Francine poked her head into the room. Chestnut curls bounced around her face, her lips shimmered red, her eyes framed with a hint of eyeliner and mascara. The minuscule black sequins of her dress glittered in the half-light of the bedroom and her perfume—Jungle Gardenia, if I didn't miss my guess—wiggled in ahead of her.

"Ray and I are leaving," she said as she came to stand in front of the ottomans at the foot of the bed. "You're sure you don't want to come with us?"

"You're a dear to ask, but I'm simply not up for it. Besides, under the circumstances, I don't think it's advisable for me to be participating in revelry."

"It's just a quiet dinner at the club, nothing outrageous."

"Oh, no, I realize that. Still, I'm not up for it."

"Well, we can cancel, stay home and order pizza or Chinese or something," she said. "Watch the ball drop."

"No, please, Francine, go and have a wonderful time ringing in the New Year."

"I feel a little bad, leaving you here alone, especially with Gabe gone."

"He's better off spending the night with Thad." I held up my book. "And I'm happy to spend the night concentrating on something besides myself."

She sighed. "All right. You'll call or text if you need anything?"

"Of course. I'm going to read, have a little glass of wine and some of that lovely salad and salmon you made for lunch today. I'll probably be in bed well before midnight."

"We should be home around one thirty, two. Somewhere around there." She came over to me and we embraced briefly before air kissing each other's cheeks. "Happy New Year, honey."

"Thank you. And Happy New Year to you, too."

She smiled and squeezed my hand before leaving. The low rumble of her and Raymond's voices slid under the door briefly before disappearing outside. Even from the driveway below, I could still hear them talking as they got into their car. Within seconds, Raymond backed into the street and off they went for a night of champagne and confetti.

New Year's last year. What had Charles and I done? Oh, yes. Walter, Charles's other practice partner and best friend, and his wife had rented out a space downtown, a room in a private club high above Lake Michigan to celebrate her birthday. It was actually an enjoyable evening. Charles had been in a good mood, his scotch consumption limited to only two tumblers that night. He'd been charming, witty, jovial. Per my usual when it came to parties or vacations, I'd had a bit too much to drink and as I looked at Charles over the rim of my glass, liquid heat surged through me. Our lovemaking that night was ferocious. Alcohol always put me in an unusually amorous mood and Charles was all too happy to oblige me. I woke up that first morning of the New Year, dewy and anticipatory. I would make a sumptuous breakfast, suggest a drive to North Utica for the day.

Instead, Charles had disappeared, first to the same indoor driving range Raymond liked to frequent and then to his office to work. Nothing but a terse text message not to hold dinner for him, that he'd grab a sandwich on the way home.

No well wishes for a Happy New Year. No "I love you's." Just the pile of wet towels in a corner of the bathroom floor and smudges of butter, boysenberry jam, and crumbs from his toast on the kitchen counter, accompanied by a winding trail of coffee grounds.

I stuck my index finger between the pages of my book to hold my place and quietly eased open the door of my room. The house was quiet. Lifeless. Gabe was gone. Raymond and Francine were making their own memories.

Leaving me alone to ramble.

I snapped on the TV in the kitchen, quickly changing to the classic movie channel. I poured myself a glass of wine as I heated up the leftover poached salmon and tossed a handful of field greens, cherry tomatoes, Kalamata olives, and feta cheese in some lemon vinaigrette. I didn't even know what movie was playing. I was just grateful for the noise.

I carried the fish and salad to the kitchen table and turned up the volume on the movie before taking three bites of salad, two of the salmon.

Thump!

I froze, the fork falling from my hand, my heart pummeling the inside of my chest as my head whipped around in search of the direction of the sound.

Thump! Thump!

I grappled for the remote, slowly turning down the volume, my ear cocked for more noises.

My eyes scurried around the kitchen, landing on the heavy bottle of wine on the counter. I raced over to grab it, the glass cool and slippery in my hand. Calling the police flashed through my head. With everything going on, I doubted they would take me seriously.

Better to take care of this myself.

I crept into the living room, scanning every nook and cranny, examining every shadow. I looked up at the ceiling and the sturdy cord affixed to the skinny rectangular door leading to the attic.

No, no, no, no. There was no one in the attic. That noise came from outside.

I edged over to the front window, my grip on the bottle slipping from the condensation. I wiped my hand on the sage green velvet of Francine's tracksuit and clutched the bottle again.

Thump! Thump! Thump!

Someone was knocking—banging—on the front door.

I obviously wasn't expecting anyone. Gabe would have texted me to let me know if he was coming back. I doubted even Vanessa would trek out to the suburbs at this time of night. Francine and Raymond would have used a key and they most definitely weren't expecting anyone.

Thump! Thump!

My breathing was loud and jagged. I ducked down to the floor before peering through the blinds in the direction of the front door. I could make out a hulking figure, hands shoved into the pockets of a puffy coat as he hopped from foot to foot to keep warm, his breath a stack of smoke out of his mouth.

I squinted, trying to suss out some sort of recognition.

Thump!

I jumped, panic tearing through me. I pressed my palm against my chest in a feeble attempt to slow my heartbeat down, but it continued its relentless *bu-bum-bu-bum.*

He looked around, exasperation smeared across his face.

I straightened up.

The man from the other day.

The man standing on the sidewalk, apart from the throng of reporters, a malicious stare on his face as he watched me roll by.

I frowned. Who on earth was he?

And what did he want?

He let out one final sigh and turned to leave. I ducked my head out of the way, hoping he hadn't seen the curtain flutter. Within seconds, a car started up and drove off into the night.

I slowly rose from my perch on the floor and meandered back into the kitchen, the salmon cold, the salad warm. I pushed the plate away, my appetite ruined, my mind racing.

I poured another glass of wine and tossed the salmon and salad in the trash. A new movie chattered softly on the TV. I turned it off and carried my book, wineglass, and bottle of Chardonnay upstairs, regretting there wasn't a lock on the bedroom door. I slightly parted the curtains covering the window and looked down.

Quiet.

As I sank into the bedroom chair, I kept staring out at that dark, cold night.

And I watched.

And I waited.

12

THE NEXT TWO days passed in a haze of funeral arrangements, well-wishes, and non-stop news coverage of the sordid "Morgan Family Tragedy," as the media had christened it. Not that I'd subjected myself to actually watching anything. However, it wasn't hard to miss the headlines splashed across the front of the Ladds' daily newspapers, or the white noise of the cable news shows Raymond watched.

I had to tolerate a tongue-lashing from my attorney for talking to the police without her. Never mind she'd been tied up in court, Francine unable to reach her. Chase communicated with me through Gabe, Charlotte still wasn't speaking to me. Celia phoned nearly every hour it seemed. My parents arrived late in the day, my normally affable, wisecracking father stunned into whimpering silence for the first time in his life, bursting into tears every time he looked at me. Charlotte and Celia conspired to plan Charles's funeral. I merely agreed with whatever arrangements were relayed to me. It didn't seem proper to offer up any opinions on the matter. My younger brother, John, and his family planned to wing their way east in time for the service. Raymond avoided me, while Francine continued to play the role of congenial hostess. When he wasn't with Thad, Gabe kept to the guest room, emerging only for meals.

In the midst of the madness, Vanessa was an unwelcome presence in my thoughts. I hadn't heard a peep from her since her little visit and I continued to swat at the veil of her threats, racking my brain for what she possibly could have had on me.

I had to push my ruminations on Vanessa aside for the moment, because I was finally going home.

It was eleven p.m. A police detective had come to the Ladds' earlier to deliver my house and car keys, letting me know they were through processing the crime scene and that I could pick up my navy BMW whenever I was ready. We thought it prudent to wait until a late hour when it was likely there wouldn't be any media camped out front, before attempting to sneak back into the house. I almost didn't care if they did see me. It was my home. They weren't going to keep me from it.

Francine pulled up to the house and fortunately, there were no media to be found, though I doubted it would stay that way. She turned to me. "You're sure you and Gabe don't want to stay one more night, honey?"

I grabbed her hand. "We need to start getting back to normal. Gabe will be going back to school soon—"

"I'm not going back," he said from the backseat.

I twisted around. "Excuse me?"

"I'm not going back to school. I'm going to stay here with you."

"Oh, Gabe." I kneaded my forehead and sighed. "Sweetheart, this is not up for discussion. You're going back to school."

He shook his head. "No, I'm not. It's final."

I looked at Francine, as though she held the solution to my problem. Her lower lip drooped in sympathy.

"We'll talk about this later." I opened the passenger side door. I would have to lean on Chase to help me with this. Or worse, Clayton.

Gabe didn't say anything as he flung his own door open and bolted for the house, dragging his suitcase behind him.

Panic slashed through me as I jumped out of the car. I couldn't let Gabe be alone the first time he saw the spot where his father had been murdered.

"Francine, I'm sorry, I—Gabe, wait!"

"Go, go, it's okay," she said. "Let me know when you want me to take you to pick up your car."

I nodded and threw a frantic wave in her direction, slamming the door as I ran after my son, who had ignored my pleas and unlocked the front door of the house. He skidded to a stop as he slowly walked toward the living room. I caught the knob in my hand and shut the door, flipping on lights so we wouldn't be in darkness. My mouth went bone dry and my chest tightened. Gabe stood in the middle of the living room, grief and sadness seeming to tug at his face as he slowly scanned the room. I edged closer to the threshold then stopped.

"Afraid to go inside?"

A few days ago, it had been a room teeming with poking, pawing strangers. Now it was a room I no longer recognized. It was a room in shambles. Large swaths of the area rug were cut. A chunk of the wall was missing, as were portions of the wood floor. My new couch was in shreds, rectangles of fabric sliced from it, almost like checkerboards. What little was left of the couch pillows were strewn across the sofa as an afterthought. The coffee table was wedged into one corner, all the coffee table books, once fanned decoratively across the surface, were stacked haphazardly to one side, the glossy covers missing. Chairs were overturned, artwork, sculptures, our family photos, scattered—nothing was where it was supposed to be.

Gabe stared down at the still visible outline of tape from where his father's body had thudded to the floor after I'd shot him. I swallowed over the hard lumps in my throat.

"What did you do, Jillian?"

"Is this where—?" Gabe stopped himself and pursed his lips. "Is this—Dad?"

"Sweetheart, you should really go upstairs and get some sleep. We'll talk about this in the morning."

He pointed to the faint tape outline. "Is this where Dad died? This spot, right here?"

I looked down, my own tears pushing out of my eyes. "Yes," was all I said, all I could say.

A sob exploded from Gabe and he darted toward the stairs, taking them two at a time. I ran after him, calling his name as he escaped to his room, never turning back once to look at me. He intended to slam the door shut, but I was too quick for him, catching the doorknob in my hand. His room was also upturned, but he didn't care, as he shoved aside the clothes and books piled on top of the bed and flung himself onto it facedown, anguished cries choking his body. I reached out to him, not sure what to say.

"Gabe."

"Leave me alone."

"Please, talk to me."

"I said go away."

"Whatever it is, please, sweetheart, you can tell me. If you're angry with me—"

He flipped over, hate and confusion marring his features. "How could you shoot Dad? How could you kill him?"

I flew to him, catching him in my arms, rocking him back and forth as he cried, his tears filling up the reservoir between my collarbone and shoulder.

"I'm so sorry, sweetheart. I'm so, so, sorry," I said as I stroked his hair.

"What did you do, Jillian?"

Gabe stiffened in my arms and pulled away, slumping down to the bed, his back to me. "I'm tired, Mom," he said, his words swallowed up by his pillow.

I sighed. "All right, son. Let me know if you need anything." I touched a strand of his hair, my heart splintering. "I love you."

He didn't respond, and despite the warning flags telling me not to do it, I bent down to kiss his wet, salty cheek. He didn't stir and I backed out of the room.

I padded down the hallway to my room, commanding my teary gaze to stay straight ahead, not letting it drift over the banister to the living room.

"What the hell are you doing with a gun?"

"Shut up," I whispered as I opened the door to my room, in the same state of bedlam as the living room. Bedsheets stripped from the mattress, my lilac duvet in a heap on the floor, the drawers spilling out from the dresser, clothes yanked off hangers, perfume bottles turned over, black smudges of fingerprint powder coating every surface.

I worked through my tears to quickly instill some semblance of order. I adorned the bed with fresh linens, swapping out the duvet for a clean one from the closet, hung up the clothes, put all the drawers back where they belonged. I'd have to worry about the various smudges and stains later.

"You'd really shoot me, Jillian? Just like that?"

I turned away from his voice, too tired, too shell-shocked. The only think I wanted was a long, steamy bath and a large sleeping pill.

I ran hot water into the Jacuzzi tub, dumping in bubble bath, lavender Epsom salts, and bath oil before stripping out of Francine's tracksuit, hoping I'd never have to step foot into another one again, eager to slip back into the Jillian Morgan uniform of skinny black pants and crisp white button-down.

As I sank beneath the froth of bubbles and inhaled the steamy lavender, I let the warm water thread through my fingers and cascade down my arms. My eyes drifted shut and I laid my head against the inflatable pillow, Charles's voice silenced, Vanessa's threats somewhere over the long horizon, facing Gabe tomorrow a distant worry.

It felt good.

I continued to take deep breaths, peace settling around me as I thought about climbing into my own bed, the clean, crisp Egyptian cotton sheets calling my name. Just a little while longer. I'd leave the serene cocoon of the bathtub in a few more minutes to settle in for the night.

"*You forgot something, Jillian.*"

"Shut up," I whispered.

"*You're supposed to be so smart, Jillian. Stupid, stupid, stupid.*"

My eyes popped open. I frowned and looked around the bathroom, confusion worming its way across my brain.

Forgot.

Forgot what?

Nothing was coming to the fore. I gave a careless wave of my hand. Put Charles back in his box and—

I bolted upright, a massive swell of water smacking my face, spilling out of the tub, a tidal wave crashing against the floor.

The box.

I forgot the goddamned box.

13

I SPLASHED around my bathtub like a drowning woman, wide-awake now. Water sloshed wildly across the floor, creating massive lakes. My foot slipped on the lip of the fiberglass tub as I struggled to get out, skidding again as I lunged for my robe hanging over the towel rack. It slid through my fingers right into the water, but I didn't care. I hastily wrung it out and threw it on, the silky material plastered to my drenched and heated skin. I beelined for my nightstand, yanking out the drawers I'd just replaced, dumping the contents onto the freshly made bed, my hands clawing through the sparse belongings, my heart sinking as I did so. I raced to Charles's side of the bed, doing the same, coming up empty, before I dropped to my knees, whipping up the edges of the duvet to search under the bed. I scoured the closet, fumbling through shoe boxes and garment bags, quaking with the knowledge that it wasn't here, the damn thing just wasn't here. I paced across the room, tearing through my brain for what had happened to the box.

A little black wooden puzzle box with elaborate gold foil etchings covering all four sides.

A little black box that I'd filched on my way out of the slut's apartment the night I'd murdered her.

A spontaneous little souvenir.

A deadly little black box that could bring all of this crashing down around my head.

I came home, Charles was sitting in the dark living room. We talked. He stood up, dropped the box in my lap.

"What did you do, Jillian?"

I picked it up, turned it over. Played with it. Then let it fall out of my lap.

Living room. The box was in the living room.

I leapt for the bedroom door, nearly tearing it off its hinges as I flew down the stairs, ignoring the snap of cold stealing the heat from my skin, the sopping silk bathrobe heavy as a chain across my body.

I flung books, pictures, candles, sculptures out of my way, goose bumps giving way to prickles of flop sweat. I pushed and pulled couches, chairs, and tables every which way until I'd created a new maze of furniture in my living room, accentuated by the bathwater dribbling from my robe, creating a whole new batch of puddles. Panic saturated my insides as I sank to the floor.

That damn puzzle box. Charles had found it in the drawer of my nightstand, likely looking for a Kleenex.

And now, the police had it.

Evidence.

Evidence against me.

"So, so stupid, Jillian. Why would you keep it?"

Why would I keep it? Why would I take it?

An ill-gotten souvenir. A memento.

A memento that could be my undoing.

Except, Charles would have had it. Charles would have taken it as a souvenir. The police thought he'd murdered her. It would make sense for it to be in his possession.

"Your fingerprints are on it, Jillian. I dropped it in your lap, you *picked it up, played with it. And how many times did you fondle it before that, so proud of yourself?"*

Damn it. There was no way I could explain that little fact of DNA.

"Mrs. Morgan, why did we find your fingerprints on a puzzle box belonging to Tamra Washington?"

"I found it," I whispered. "In my husband's bedside drawer. Why did he have it? I don't know. I really couldn't say. Why was it downstairs? I don't know. Maybe he'd brought it down earlier."

A ridiculous explanation. It clanged against my ear like tin. I'd have to come up with something, some plausible explanation as to why my fingerprints were on that box.

Dear God, why didn't I throw it away when I had the chance? I'd had months to get rid of it.

"You won't get away with it, Jillian."

"Oh, I will, Charles. You better believe I will. You and your tramp will not be my undoing. I promise."

"Mom?"

I gasped and whipped my head around to see a sleep-rumpled, tear-stained Gabe staring down at me, confusion further blotting his features. I hurriedly slicked back the wet strands of my hair and struggled to my feet, shivering now in my soggy bathrobe.

"Yes, sweetheart, what is it? Can I get you anything?"

"Who are you talking to?"

"Who am I. . .?" I looked around, laughing. "Oh, nobody, sweetheart, nobody. I—I was just talking to myself. Trying to figure out what to do about this mess the police left behind."

"Are you okay?"

"I'm fine, darling, just fine. How are you? Feeling any better?"

"Why's your bathrobe all wet?"

I looked down at the puddle of water dripping from me courtesy of my drenched robe. "It fell in the tub."

"Why'd you put it on?"

I shrugged, frustrated, on the verge of tears. "I don't know."

"I heard you moving furniture or whatever down here and talking, so I wanted to see what was going on."

"I came down to look at the damage, think about how to handle it. I suppose I'll have to call in a cleaning crew, an organizer or someone to help me get everything back in order."

"Okay," he said, not seeming all that convinced.

"I'm fine, I promise, sweetheart. Really. I took a nice long bath and I'm just going to crawl into bed."

"I guess I'll go back to bed then."

"You're sure you don't want anything? A little snack? I can't remember what's in the refrigerator, but—"

"I'm not hungry," he said, his voice disappearing down the hallway toward his bedroom, the angry click of the door following immediately after.

I waited a few moments before climbing the steps back to my room. I stripped out of my robe and hung it up to drip in the shower before flopping onto the bed, naked. I flung my arm across my closed eyes.

"What are you going to do now, Jillian?"

Indeed.

What in the hell was I going to do now?

14

PLAY DUMB.

Play dumb and point the finger.

That was what I finally decided after a night of listening to rain tap gently against my windowpane while I stared up at the ceiling as though an answer to my problem would drop down from above.

I would plead ignorance and blame the whole thing on Charles.

I'd never seen it before, didn't know what it was. He must have been holding the box when he came downstairs. Where was it from? No idea. I had no idea he even had such a thing. I never knew him to be one for puzzles, much less puzzle boxes. Games, yes. Puzzles, no. Perhaps it was a gift. He must have dropped it when I shot him. In the frenzy of those chaotic moments, I must have moved it or touched it, hence why my fingerprints were on it.

The more I turned it over in my head, the more sense it made. Play dumb and place the blame on Charles. After all, he couldn't dispute my account.

I closed my eyes, fatigue pulling at every pore, every bone, every joint. How desperately I wanted to sleep today away. I let the rain lull me for a few more minutes, wishing I could snuggle in the comfort of my dark room and cool soft sheets all day.

Except, I had a role to play today. Grieving widow. Aggrieved trigger woman. Consoling mother. Vulnerable daughter. Contrite daughter-in-law. Weepy woman.

I had to bury my husband today.

Strangely, murdering Charles had brought me no comfort. In hindsight, I didn't know if I'd kill him again. It was true that initially, when I got confirmation of his ticky-tacky little affair, I did want to murder him. Deep down though, there was an infinitesimal part of me that did want him back, that wanted to figure out a way to rebuild some semblance of a life together. Overwhelmingly though, I wanted him to pay and pay and pay and pay. Enter the hapless Tamra Washington. Now her ... I felt no compunction about slitting that cow's throat. No more than if I'd stomped on an ant. I'd do it again.

I was still naked, not having bothered to put on a nightgown, the Cesarean scar from Gabe's birth, red smudge of birthmark on my thigh, and mangled nail of my left baby toe, all on stark, ugly display. I slipped off the bed and padded into my closet, pulling down a tasteful black Donna Karan suit. I went through the motions of a shower, makeup to conceal the dark moons of flesh beneath my eyes, a severe bun at the nape of my neck. I finished with a few spritzes of Shalimar before slowly opening the bedroom door and heading downstairs.

Even in the drab gray of day, it was still a shock to see the jumble of my normally beautiful living room. I'd have to call my designer, Elaine, tomorrow, see if she could help me restore order. My in-laws would be hosting the after-service program at their house. Even if I didn't have this mess to contend with, it wouldn't have been appropriate for me to host, anyway. Murderess offering a plate of sustenance to the assembled mourners. Quelle gauche.

Gabe wasn't down yet and I proceeded to the kitchen to make myself a cup of tea, not sure I could manage much else.

Unlike the rest of the house, the kitchen was relatively

unscathed. All the plates, glasses, and mugs that had been removed from the cabinets now rested on the counter next to the silverware. The pantry shelves remained mostly intact. I filled my kettle with water and set it on the stove and quickly washed a mug for tea, putting the rest of the dishes in the sink. I'd load them into the dishwasher later.

I sat quietly at the kitchen table, sipping my tea as my mind groped ahead to the day. It would be excruciating. Well-wishing mingled with stares and uncertainties about what to say, how to proceed. Though I wasn't under arrest, that cloud of suspicion would hover over my head nonetheless.

Celia would stay glued to my side, Clayton a spigot of platitudes. My mother would be her usual arrogant, judgmental self. My father would pat my head to his shoulder and encourage me to cry, like I was still his little girl. Any softness or warmth I possessed was courtesy of him. It was my mother who'd made me tough. Mostly because she had resented my beauty and delicateness, such a contrast to her husky simplicity. A button nose, dimpled chin, and fresh-scrubbed ivory cheeks had been the only attributes to rescue her from total homeliness in her youth. Plain, with a subtle edge of crust. What my father ever saw in her, I'd never know. He could have married anyone, he was such a handsome man. Strapping. Jaw of steel. Wavy blond hair, chiseled muscles, bawdy jokes forever hovering on his smiling lips. Unfortunately, drink had decimated his looks. Much like Charles, he'd always been one for scotch, and had always been able to handle it. Through the years though, likely the only way he'd found to cope with my mother the harpy, was with scotch. I knew it wouldn't be long before his liver sputtered and died. He'd find a transplant undignified somehow. I also knew he'd rather go out on a wave of Glenlivet than give up his daylong nightcaps.

Like Clayton, my brother, John, would look uncomfortable through it all, offering stiff, awkward banalities in a grim attempt to comfort me. His wife would be a sobbing, frenzied disaster. In general, I liked her, but Renata was utterly useless in a crisis.

And Charlotte. I couldn't begin to predict what she would do. Antagonizing her would not be smart. I would avoid her if possible. Even if she spit in my face, which she was quite likely to do, I would be conciliatory if we were forced to face each other.

I heard Gabe's door open from upstairs and the light tread of his footsteps on the stairs. His wet blond hair was slicked back from his face, which burned bright red. His body spray filled the kitchen as he came loping in, dark suit hanging on his lanky frame, red print tie swinging lightly.

"Gabe," I said gently. "How are you?"

"Fine."

I chewed on my bottom lip as I watched him wash one of the bowls and a spoon in the sink and pull down a box of cereal from the pantry. The frosty flakes cascading into the bowl was the only sound in the room.

"The milk might be bad," I said.

Without looking at me, he went into the refrigerator and hauled out the half-full jug of milk, removing the top to take a whiff. Apparently, it passed muster, as Gabe carried the milk over to the counter where his bowl sat.

"Have you heard from Chase?"

"He said he'd meet us at the church," Gabe said as he drowned his cereal in milk. He parked himself at the table, hunching over to lift sopping spoonfuls of more milk than cereal to his mouth.

"Sweetheart, do you—"

"I don't feel like talking much right now, Mom."

I clamped my mouth shut, stunned by his abruptness.

"You murdered his father, you bitch. Do you want him to throw you a fucking parade?"

Charles was right. What did I expect? I took a sip of my tea, wincing at its iciness. I topped it off with hot water from the teapot, sneaking looks at Gabe, who remained resolute on his cereal. The clinking of his spoon against the porcelain and the slurp of cereal and milk, the tears I could see him blinking back made me ache. I wanted to throw my arms around him, beg for mercy and forgiveness.

Instead, I quickly finished my tea. He'd said nothing when I excused myself upstairs. Within the sanctuary of my bedroom, my own tears pricked my eyes and within seconds, I had dissolved into a full crying fit, not unlike the one my sister-in-law would likely treat us to in a few hours. Hiccups soon followed and I had to breathe deeply to calm myself down.

"Boo hoo, Jillian. Nobody feels sorry for you. Especially me."

I yanked my cigarettes out of my purse, hoping a quick smoke would soothe me.

"What did I tell you about the cigarettes, Jillian? You and those cigarettes."

I crushed the cigarette in my hands, the grains of tobacco floating through my trembling fingers to the floor, Detective Travis wending his way through my head.

"How many cigarettes do you smoke a day?"

Ignoring the voices, I went into the closet and pulled down one of my small and tasteful cocktail clutches. Much more appropriate for a funeral than my everyday Louis Vuitton tote. I rummaged through my bag, extracting only the essentials. My wedding ring tumbled onto the bed. I picked it up, examining the round cut diamond flanked by baguettes on either side. It would feel strange not to wear it, as it had adorned my finger for three decades. I slipped it on. Perhaps I'd squirrel it away in my jewelry box sometime in the future, never to be seen again. For now, though, I would wear it.

I resumed foraging through my bag. Charles's wallet poked out of the inside pocket. I fished it out and sank onto the bed, inhaling the rich smell of leather. I ran my fingers across its bumps and ridges before flipping it open. Three credit cards, the color of Olympic medals, a neat stack of receipts paper-clipped together with a small yellow Post-it on top with "Fred" (our accountant) scrawled across it in blue ink, a few of his business cards, seventy-five dollars in cash (three twenties, two fives, and five singles), the family picture of us from last year's Christmas card. His driver's license. I liberated the small square of his license and stared at his picture before lifting it to my lips and kissing it.

"Farewell, Sweet Prince," I whispered. "Good riddance, Sweet Prince."

I picked up his phone, turning it over in my hands, the battery long since petered out. Gabe knocked on the door and I called for him to come in.

"Grandma just texted and said she and Grandpa will be here soon."

"Okay. Thank you."

"That's Dad's phone," he said.

I looked down at it still in my hand. "Oh. Yes. The police gave it back to me the other day and I just now remembered I had it."

"Can I have it?"

I frowned. "Why?"

He shrugged. "Dad was always taking pictures of stuff. I don't know. Maybe there's something on there I want."

I hesitated. I could only imagine what was on that phone. Well, nothing that could connect me to torturing Charles in those last months of his life. Nothing that could connect me to murdering him. Still, I wouldn't want Gabe stumbling into a possible trove of pornography starring his father's slut.

"Sweetheart, if you wouldn't mind, just let me take a look at it, make sure there isn't anything that ... well, might not be appropriate for you to see."

He clenched his jaw. "Whatever it is, I can handle it."

"Gabe, I don't think—"

"I think it's my father's phone and I think I'd like to have it." He paused. "It's the least you can do."

My breath hitched in my throat. We were locked in a standoff, my son and I. Uncharacteristically, I blinked. Haggling with Gabe over a phone of all things just wasn't worth it. Besides, I couldn't protect him forever.

"All right, Gabe." I handed it to him. "It's yours."

"Thanks," he mumbled, running his hands over it.

I glanced at Charles's wallet still on the bed and picked it up, extracting the stack of paper clipped receipts. "Perhaps you'd like this as well."

He took the wallet off my hands, shoving both into his pocket. "Thanks," he repeated.

"Gabe." I reached out and touched his arm. "If you do find anything ... disturbing, on the phone, I hope you'll come to me so we can talk about it."

"Yeah, fine, whatever," he said as he turned on his heel and exited my room.

I stood rooted to my spot, watching his retreating back as he loped down the hall toward his bedroom. The doorbell rang from downstairs, which meant Celia and Clayton were here. My shoulders sagged and tears sprouted from my eyes. I blew my nose and quickly splashed cold water on my face, deciding not to do any touch-ups on my makeup, lest it look like I was trying too hard.

Just play the role today.

Grieving widow. Aggrieved trigger woman. Consoling mother. Vulnerable daughter. Contrite daughter-in-law. Weepy woman.

15

OF COURSE PEOPLE said wonderful things about Charles. They didn't have to live with his indifference. His slavish devotion to his work. The long, lonely nights.

His tawdry affair.

A parade of friends, patients, colleagues, and comrades stood at the altar to share their misty-eyed reminiscences about my husband. They were all careful not to look at or address me directly, using the generic moniker of "his family."

Gabe and Chase, gentleman that they were, escorted me up the aisle of St. James, allowing me to hold my head high and provide some shield from the ripple of whispers and tentative gawking. My heart lurched at the sight of the oversized photo of Charles perched at the altar: perfect, paper-white smile, feathery blond hair, twinkling blue eyes, rich, golden skin mocking me. Walter and his wife, Tina, both offered me sympathetic smiles. Vanessa, of course, managed to maneuver herself near the front. I ignored her as we marched past.

As predicted, Celia fastened herself to one side of me. Gabe sat on the other. I noticed his longtime on-again, off-again girlfriend, Brynn, hovering in a back pew with her parents, her face bright red with tears. Chase sat on the other side of Gabe. Next to him sat Jacqueline, the tall, blue-eyed, magazine-cover blonde from Greenwich, Connecticut he'd brought home at Thanksgiving, who he said was "the one." My parents sat next to her, my father sending me silent, solemn encouragement. My mother, well, my mother looked suitably contrite, though was no doubt gearing up to unleash some tirade of disapproval on me when we were alone.

Chase delivered the eulogy—masterfully, of course. He had an extraordinary gift for public speaking. You couldn't teach what he had. He plucked each of the assembled mourners from the pews and laid them carefully in his palm, leaving everyone rapt with attention. He shared tender memories of his father—teaching him to ride a bike, how to tie a tie at the young age of five, the year Charles bought him his first set of golf clubs, and all the Saturday afternoons they'd spent tossing the football around or playing catch.

No mention of the missed Little League games, birthday parties, or total lack of interest in grades or girlfriends. I guess we all have to pick and choose what memories to cherish and which to discard. It's the only way to cope, I suppose.

The rain stopped during the processional and as we made our somber trek across the slick grass of the cemetery, our feet slipping on the thick batter of mud, Gabe gripped my hand as we navigated toward the burial site. As we settled into our seats, my heart continued to ram against my chest, the gaping black hole of Charles's final resting place staring back at me, almost inviting me to fall in and join him. I was alternately euphoric and saddened that Charles was going into it. I looked down at my lap, tears slipping out of my eyes. Almost in unison, Chase and Gabe each took a hand, holding on as much for me as themselves.

The words of the bishop floated somewhere over my head, one or two dropping into my ear. Cold, damp wind battered us, whipping the tarp around the burial site. I snuck a peek at Celia, surprised to see tears staining her fine patrician features. Clayton's bottom lip trembled and I wondered if he would break down in private later.

Charlotte sat stone-faced, her arm around Chelsea, who sobbed brokenly, Rex holding his wife's hand. Charles told me Chelsea had expressed interest in going pre-med when she went away to college in a few years, asking if she could go on rounds with him once in a while. Her being so industrious surprised me. Not because she wasn't intelligent. She was obnoxious. A spoiled, incapable brat. Perhaps her mother had put her up to the request.

The gleaming mahogany coffin began its descent into the ground. Pain stabbed me as I tried not to think about all that earth wrapping around Charles for eternity.

"Feeling bad, Jillian?"

Celia and Clayton ambled over to us, my mother-in-law hugging the boys then me, my father-in-law gripping my shoulder, interrupting Charles's taunting.

"You did a fine job on the eulogy, son," Clayton said to Chase. "A fine job."

"Yes, your father—" Celia sobbed, looking away and pressing her handkerchief against her face. "Your father would be so proud."

Chase looked over at the casket, his face drooping. "I hope so," he said quietly.

"Well." Celia straightened up, shoulders squared, the Grande Dame of the North Shore firmly back in control. "We should be getting back to the house. Get ready to greet our guests."

"It was a lovely service," my mother's voice chirped behind me.

I turned to find her, my father, and brother, John, at my elbow. Daddy nodded at me and I knew he would allow me to weep privately on his shoulder later. John offered me an awkward, Old Spice hug, while his wife, Renata, grabbed at my arm, forcing me into her own perfume cloud. My two nieces and nephew stood discomfited off to the side until Chase and Gabe sidled over to reconnect with their cousins.

"We should be going," Celia repeated, clutching my arm as she addressed us. "We can't keep our guests waiting."

She tugged me along and I trailed behind her, numbly, having decided I would demurely follow her lead. It was the only way I could manage to fumble through the rest of this day. I would nurse a cold glass of white wine and accept the uncomfortable platitudes that would soon wash over me. I would crawl into bed late tonight and cry myself to sleep from the sheer emotion of it all.

I dabbed at my eyes as we made our way to the black limousine that would ferry us to Lake Forest and Fairmore, the Morgan family home.

And then I saw him.

The man standing outside my house the other day. The man who thumped on the Ladds' door on New Year's Eve.

He was clearer to me now, this man.

This smirking, sneering, overweight man, hands shoved into the pockets of a puffy gray down coat.

Staring straight at me.

I did a slow scan around me, searching for another recipient of this man's burning gaze.

His eyes remained pinned to me.

I looked away, my heart thumping. My palms itched inside my leather gloves.

Was he the police? Some new detective, though no less slovenly than Potts, assigned to rattle my cage?

No, no, no. He would have been inside the house with the other detectives a few days ago, not outside. Besides there was something ... *common* about this man and his countenance. No authority.

I allowed myself to recede into the crush of conversation around me, to ignore the man's gaze. My head swam with words. My eyes drifted shut for a moment.

Before I folded myself into the limousine, I looked behind me once again.

He was gone.

16

THE RUMBLE of whispered conversation had finally died down with the departure of most of the mourners. "Tragedy." "Can you believe?" "What's she going to do now?" "Do you think she'll be arrested?" followed me along with awkward, perplexed stares. People weren't sure if they should console or condemn me.

I had spent the better part of the afternoon awkwardly tucked into an unobtrusive corner of the cavernous, dark-paneled, high-ceilinged living room, nursing my single glass of Pinot Gris, twitching every time the doorbell rang, relentlessly inspecting the room for signs that the mysterious man (stalker?) might have slipped in unnoticed.

While I didn't see him, my eyes continually fell on Vanessa, surprisingly attired in a tasteful, long-sleeved black knit with a Peter Pan collar. At the moment, she was deep in conversation with Francine. She flashed her eyes at me, letting only the hint of a smile tug at the corner of her lips. It figured Vanessa would try to stay until the bitter end, even though she had no earthly reason to be here other than to torture me.

My parents had returned to their hotel, my mother pleading an encroaching migraine and my father approaching sloppy drunk. My in-laws were somewhere in the bowels of the house being soothed by well-wishers. My brother's family had also made their escape. Charlotte had made an appearance, avoiding me in the process. It would be fair to say that heads swiveled between us in anticipation of another altercation. Rex kissed my cheek while his wife wasn't looking, and Chelsea remained sullen in a corner, shooting daggers in my direction until the trio finally left.

I stood near the French doors, which led to the veranda, stroking the hard shell of my black clutch, yearning for one of the cigarettes trapped inside. One smoke. I would stand off to the side of the house for one quick smoke. I would extinguish the butt in one of the puddles left by the earlier rain and wrap it in a Kleenex, which I would tuck into my purse and go about my business.

I took a quick glance around to make sure no one was watching me. I eased the door open and slipped around the corner of the house, obscuring myself behind the shade of a soaring hedge, scrambling to retrieve the nearly empty pack of cigarettes from inside my purse. It took a few tries with the lighter, but finally, I was able to light up and take a long, smooth inhale, my eyes rolling into the back of my head from the ecstasy.

"Jillian."

I gasped at the rumble of the deep baritone and the featherlight touch on the small of my back.

"Oh, my goodness." I turned around to see the burly Walter towering over me, the gold button of his navy jacket straining at his midsection, the matching slacks giving him more room. I was momentarily lost in the rich ebony gloss of his skin, dark brown eyes, and wavy black hair. I had always found the hulking, awkward Walter attractive in an odd sort of way. "And here I thought no one had seen me sneak out."

"I saw you slip outside and thought it would finally give us a chance to talk." He sighed. "It's been a hell of a day."

I blew a cloud of smoke over my shoulder. "It certainly has."

"How are you?" he asked, shading his eyes from the sudden burst of late afternoon sun with one hand.

I tapped my ash to the ground and shook my head. "I'm not sure how to answer that."

"You know despite whatever may have happened ... in the end ... Charles loved you."

I let Walter's words hang between us for a moment as I looked across the vast expanse of trees, shrubbery, and rolling green as far as the eye could see. The tops of the wrought iron gate at the end of the long, winding driveway were barely visible.

"Did you know?"

Walter blanched a bit before nodding. "I did."

I took another inhale, letting the smoke roil inside of my mouth for a moment before blowing it out.

"Well," was all I could say.

"I want you to know that I begged him—*begged him*—to stop all of this running around, all of this lying and for whatever reason he couldn't or wouldn't. I don't know. But despite all of that, like I said before, he did love you. That much I know."

I bent down to dip the butt of my cigarette into one of the shallow puddles near the edge of the veranda. "I appreciate you saying that."

"Listen, Tina and I would love to have you over to dinner some night."

"That sounds nice," I said. "Really lovely. Thank you."

"It's sincere now, okay? I'm not saying 'Hey, come to dinner some night' to be nice, all right? We really would love to spend time with you."

"I promise I'll call or e-mail to set something up."

"If you don't, I will." He grasped my shoulder and nodded before pulling me into another embrace. When we broke apart, tears shimmered in his eyes.

I shoved my cigarette butt into a pack of Kleenex in my purse. "I should probably get back inside. Celia will send a search party after me."

Walter nodded and guided me back toward the house. We both jumped back a bit as the French doors flew open to reveal Vanessa.

"Hello, Walter," she said, all but purring as she smiled at me. "Jill. I wanted to offer my condolences to you."

That Jill business again. "That's very kind of you, Vanessa."

I could see Walter's wife signal to him from inside the house and he excused himself, leaving me alone with Vanessa the Viper.

"I must say, Jill, you're looking well."

"Jillian."

"I'm sorry?"

"You called me Jill. As I told you the other day, my name is Jillian."

She stared at me blankly for a moment before bursting into laughter. "You did mention that, didn't you? Oh. I've insulted you. My apologies."

I gave a nod of my head, an indication I accepted her shallow act of contrition.

"I've been wanting to call you, but I've held off," she said. "I figured you probably had your hands full."

"It has been a busy few days, yes."

"Any word from the police?" she asked with feigned sincerity.

I gave her a tight smile. "No."

"Well, that's a relief. No news is good news as they say. It would be terrible if the police came barging in here to arrest you."

Good God, this was exasperating. I was mere seconds from walking back inside and leaving her gaping and grasping.

Play it cool. Suss out what she wants.

"Yes," I said. "Quite."

"You seem to be holding up remarkably well under the circumstances." She smiled. "Really. How do you do it?"

I folded my arms across my chest. "Don't be fooled, Vanessa. The circumstances are very trying."

"Yes ... the circumstances." She fluffed out the ends of her hair.

"Speaking of, I'm interested in discussing *your* circumstances further."

Finally. We were getting to the meat of it. My *circumstances*. My antennae crackled with anticipation.

"Oh?"

"Yes. In fact, I'd like to invite you to lunch for just that reason."

Lunch. How this whole thing had started. Fitting that's how it should continue.

"Yes," I said. "Let's have lunch."

"I'm free tomorrow."

"Friday is better," I said. "There's so much going on right now. That will be my first opportunity to take a little time away."

"Friday." She brightened. "I'll clear my schedule. Blue Door? Like last time?"

"Yes," I said. "Just like last time."

"I think it will be an illuminating conversation."

I narrowed my eyes, debating how I should respond. Thankfully, Celia motioned to me from inside the house. "Well, Vanessa, thank you again for coming today," I said, stepping around her to indicate I was headed inside. "And for your condolences."

"Anything for the Morgan family," she said, following me. "And I look forward to Friday."

"Jillian, sweetheart, I need to borrow you for a moment," Celia said, commandeering me as soon as I stepped through the French doors.

"Of course," I murmured.

Celia turned to Vanessa, her face faltering a bit at first as she struggled to place her face, turning on a dime as she remembered this was her son's practice partner.

"Dr. Shayne—"

"Please. Vanessa."

"Thank you so much for coming today." Celia squeezed my hand. "We appreciate all the support we can get during this difficult time."

"I wouldn't be anywhere else." Vanessa looked at me. "As I was just saying to Jill—Jillian—anything for the Morgan family."

"I'm sure Jillian appreciates your being here to offer succor." Celia slid her hands across my shoulders. "Isn't that right, dear?"

"Yes, it's important to have a strong network of support during a difficult time."

Vanessa placed a hand on my arm. I went cold at her touch. This might be more dire than I could fathom.

"Anything I can do to help, I'm happy to do it," she said.

"Well, thank you again, dear," Celia said as she placed her own arm around Vanessa and steered her toward the front door. I stifled a laugh. There was more hushed chatter between them before the door finally slammed shut. Good old, Celia. A master at banishing hangers on.

"Well," she said, all but smacking her hands together as though she'd just taken out the trash, which in a sense she had. "Now that the last of the mourners are gone, we can relax."

"It's been a long day," I said.

"Indeed it has. In the hubbub, I wasn't sure if you'd been notified, but Charles's attorney reached out to Charlotte. The reading of his will is to commence tomorrow morning."

I frowned. "Why would he contact Charlotte and not me?"

"Oh, dear, who can say why lawyers do the things they do. Ours is not to wonder. At any rate, tomorrow morning, ten sharp. Why don't you and the boys stay here tonight? We can all go in together."

"Thank you, Celia, but Chase told me earlier he and Jacqueline will stay with Charlotte, and I think Gabe and I'd better take our leave, if Jones wouldn't mind giving us a ride. As I said, it's been a long day and I'd just like to go home and sleep."

"Really, it's no trouble. God knows we have the room."

"You know how it is, Celia. Sometimes you just want the comfort of your own bed."

She sniffed. "Well, I suppose that makes sense."

I reached out my hand to hers, squeezing it. "Gabe and I will see you in the morning."

"Of course, dear. You just get a good night's sleep. Put today behind you."

I smiled feebly, Vanessa's face floating across my mind, that strange man accompanying her.

"Yes. Tomorrow is bound to be a better day."

17

GABE and I avoided each other's gaze as we rode up the elevator to the seventieth floor. I looked straight ahead at the mirrored doors. He looked down at his shoes. I reached over and put my hand on his shoulder.

"Are you okay, sweetheart?"

"I guess."

"I'm sure this won't take long," I said. "Very much a formality."

The doors dinged and slid open. I walked ahead of Gabe into the plush lobby, Michigan Avenue teeming below the floor-to-ceiling windows spanning the entire wall.

"Gabe and Jillian Morgan here to see Edmund Dawson," I said to the receptionist.

"Have a seat." She directed us to a bank of chairs pushed up against the wall next to her. Gabe plunked down, his legs sprawled in front of him, his upper body slumped against the cushions. This was quite out of character. I frowned and shook my head and he immediately straightened up.

"What do you expect, Jillian? Nothing will ever be the same for him again."

I closed my eyes against Charles's needling and sat back, crossing my legs, declining the receptionist's offer of coffee. We watched stressed-out lawyers bustle back and forth through the lobby, stacks of paperwork under their arms, eyes rimmed red, ties askew, even at this relatively early hour. They likely all had ulcers. Or at least drinking problems.

"Jillian." Edmund appeared in front of me in an impeccable suit, tie, and freshly pressed shirt. Unlike his colleagues, he looked tanned and well rested. I rose and shook his hand and Gabe did the same. He motioned for us to follow him through a maze of hallways.

"Has anyone else arrived?" I asked.

"You and Gabe are the first," he said. "Can I get you anything? Coffee?"

"Your receptionist was kind enough to offer us something, but we're fine, thank you."

"We'll be meeting in our main conference room." He pushed open a heavy glass door and gestured that we should have a seat. I walked all the way around the massive glass table to take a seat facing the door. Gabe sat a few chairs down, groping in his pocket for his phone, scrolling through whatever was on the screen to occupy himself.

"I just have to run to my office for a moment," Edmund said. "Make yourselves comfortable."

"Take your time," I said. "We'll be here."

He nodded, smiled and departed, leaving Gabe and me alone.

"Gabe, make sure you turn the ringer off," I murmured.

He glanced up and nodded, swiping and tapping until I presumed he had complied. I adjusted the collar of my suit and tucked a stray piece of hair from my low ponytail behind my ear. From down the hall, voices floated toward us and it didn't take long to realize one of them belonged to Charlotte, chatting with the receptionist. She froze momentarily when she saw me, before marching over to Gabe, hugging him, stroking his hair, and peppering him with questions about his emotional state and entreaties about staying with her. Rex looked momentarily stricken, his loyalty tested, obviously wanting to be gracious toward me, but mindful that Charlotte was watching his every move. In the end, his wife won out, as she should have. He followed behind her, coming the long way around to hug Gabe and offer me a helpless nod. I nodded back, offering a blink-and-you-miss-it smile of understanding.

I looked for Chase, my heart skipping when he appeared in the doorway behind the receptionist, but ahead of Celia and Clayton, who offered limp hugs and dry kisses. Chase avoided me, heading straight for Gabe, drawing him into a bear hug. My heart ballooned at the sight of my boys. Brothers. Leaning on one another. Taking care of each other. They would get each other through this.

"You still murdered their father, you bitch."

"Chase?"

He cleared his throat. "Mom."

"How are you, sweetheart?"

"The police questioned me yesterday." His face and voice were stiff, as though he were trying to contain an outburst.

An arrow shot clean through my heart. "After the service?"

"They were waiting for me at Aunt Charlotte's. Asked me all kinds of questions about you and Dad." He looked at Gabe. "They want to talk to you, too."

"About what?"

"Same thing. What was Dad like, what's Mom like." Chase glanced at me. "They want to make sure they aren't missing anything."

"I'm so sorry, Chase," I said, my voice shaking. "I had no idea the police would badger you—"

"I don't really want to talk about this right now." He backed away from me, flicking a business card toward Gabe that he'd extracted from his jacket pocket. "They want you to call them today."

Gabe shrugged listlessly and put the card in his pocket.

"Chase." I reached my hand toward him. "Perhaps we can have lunch or dinner sometime this week?"

He shoved his hands in his pockets and focused his gaze on his feet. "I'm pretty busy."

"Well ... think about it. Please?"

He didn't say anything, turning on his heel and taking a seat next to Charlotte. I threw all of my concentration into doing my haughty best to keep my head high through that small, but oh so potent humiliation and get on with this. At least it would all be fairly routine. Trusts for the boys, the bestowal of certain personal items, various business arrangements to be handled by Charlotte. Everything else to me.

Edmund returned, a sheaf of papers in his hands, a young woman behind him. He assumed his place at the head of the table, the young woman taking a seat next to him, and nodded solemnly at all of us, dressed in black for the occasion.

"Thank you for being here this morning," he said as he pulled wire-rimmed reading glasses from the breast pocket of his jacket, perching them on his nose.

We all murmured our pleasantries and waited. Clayton and Celia dignified as always, Chase's jaw grinding beneath his skin, Gabe's arms folded on the table in front of him, eyes downcast. Charlotte, looking much how I presumed she looked in board meetings or tense negotiations—ramrod straight, ruby-red lipstick, stark black eyeliner, face a concrete mask warning she would take no prisoners. Rex comfortable. Not surprising as he'd likely been to countless of these in his own capacity as an attorney.

"Let's get right to it." Edmund licked his thumb and flicked the top page of his stack over. He cleared his throat and took a deep breath. "I, Charles Andrew Morgan, being of sound mind and body..."

I tuned out for a bit as Edmund droned on in a tangle of legalese about revoking all previous wills, the settlements of debts and such. There were mentions of the Charles Morgan Trust, established after Chase was born, amended following Gabe's arrival, meant to benefit our sons, including their support, education, and medical care. His gold Rolex and collection of cufflinks to Chase, golf clubs to Gabe, books, clothing, and various knickknacks split between them however they decided, his medical journals donated, the rest to charity or disposed of as they saw fit. His shares in The Morgan Family Foundation, the Morgan Group, ownership in various Morgan family homes across the country, divided between them equally.

"Should I precede my wife, Jillian Elizabeth Vaughn Morgan in death, she shall be entitled to the marital home residing at 640 Tower Road, Winnetka, Illinois. Should Jillian Elizabeth Vaughn Morgan retain the home, she shall assume all debts and maintenance associated with it. She shall also be entitled to sell the home should she choose and be entitled to all its proceeds."

Chase and Gabe glanced at me and I smiled at them briefly. All as I expected.

He then switched to Charlotte, granting her his ownership stake in his medical practice, directing her to confer with Walter and Vanessa. I winced at the mention of the viper's name.

Edmund plodded on, referencing insurance policies, stocks, bonds, trusts, various other business interests, and the like, most under Charlotte's domain, some divided between our sons. I lightly rubbed my temple, waiting for Edmund to come back around to the personal assets.

"With regard to my personal assets, excluding the aforementioned marital home, I hereby appoint Charlotte Morgan Douglas as the sole and legal executor of my estate. Acting in the best interests of my sons Chase and Gabe, Charlotte Morgan Douglas shall have sole authority over all individual personal checking and savings accounts in my name, including half of any joint bank accounts between myself and Jillian Elizabeth Vaughn Morgan, and all stocks and bonds in my name. These assets are determined to be in excess of twenty-five million dollars. Aside from her half of any joint accounts, Jillian Elizabeth Vaughn Morgan is entitled to zero dollars. Signed December twenty-sixth, 2016." Edmund set the paperwork down and removed his glasses.

A spear of disbelief punctured my chest. December twenty sixth. He'd just done this. Two days after I'd visited him in jail. The one time I'd visited him in jail. To tell him I knew. To berate him for humiliating me. To tell him I planned to file for divorce.

I closed my eyes and leaned forward, my head wobbling in disbelief. "Edmund, just to make sure I understand this correctly, are you saying Charles effectively cut me out of his will?"

Edmund sighed, no longer looking tan and rested, but ashen and strained. "Charles called me while he was incarcerated and indicated he wanted to make a change. It was obviously all very sudden. I never dreamed a few days later ... well, that's why we keep our affairs in order. Plan for the inevitable."

"What paperwork do you need me to sign, Edmund?" Charlotte all but tap danced on the table. Had she known about this? Had Charles made her privy to his plans? Probably. Thick as thieves those two were.

Sweat prickled inside my sedate black suit. Charles hadn't done this to leave me penniless.

He'd done this to put me in my place.

"Like I told you that day, you're not getting a goddamned thing from me."

"There are a number of documents I'll need you and Chase and Gabe to sign," Edmund was saying. He glanced at me briefly before shuffling papers, loaning pens, handing documents to the young woman to be notarized. I could only sit there, numb. Glued to my seat.

Finally, I forced myself up, touching the sleeve of Gabe's jacket. "I'll be in the ladies' room. I'll wait for you in the lobby."

"Okay," he said and turned back to signing the voluminous stack of papers in front of him.

I walked out of the room with as much dignity as I could muster, my head held as high as I could make it. I all but stumbled into the ladies' room, grateful no one was there. I slumped against the countertop for a moment before splashing cold water against the red flush of my cheeks.

I jumped as the door swung open and Charlotte stormed in. I instinctively shrank away, visions of more stinging slaps across my face.

"Did my brother tell you he was cutting you out of his will?"

"No, of course not." I drew up. "I'm assuming he told you of his plans?"

She smirked. "Not at all."

"Well, I'm sure Charles had his reasons for ... this."

"I wonder what the police will say when they find out."

Unconsciously, I tugged at the hem of my jacket, while silently cursing myself for this lack of control. "What does that have to do with anything?"

"People tend to murder for three things—sex, love, and money." She powdered her already matte nose and applied a fresh layer of lipstick before looking me in the eye. "You murdering my brother doesn't seem so accidental anymore. Does it?"

She swept out of the ladies' room, leaving me alone.

18

I ADJUSTED my sunglasses against the sun's early morning assault as I looked over my shoulder to make sure no one had seen me. I had snuck out the back, carefully squeezing my way out of the gate, passing the Finches' backyard to reach the street one block behind my house. Over a week since I'd killed Charles and reporters continued to clog the sidewalk out front, hoping for a glimpse of me through the curtains, shouting questions at my scant visitors about how I was doing and who they were and what we were going to talk about. Gabe had opted to spend time in the city with Chase and Charlotte to escape the harassment. I can't say I blamed him, but I missed him terribly. His absence made the house that much emptier, that much more haunting.

I'd finally broken down and driven to Skokie late last night to the twenty-four-hour grocery store to shop. I continued to wait for the next story to come along and sweep me off the front page, but the fascination seemed unyielding. The house was less of a mess at least, as I'd hired a crime scene cleanup company on the advice of my designer to scrub away the bloodstains and stubborn black fingerprint powder. My lawyer had informed me that, so far, all of the evidence supported my story, so she doubted there would be any charges forth-coming, which made the media's fixation on me all the more puzzling.

Still, I couldn't be too put out.

After all, I was getting away with it.

It was quiet as I headed toward the path leading to the lake. Few people were out, so I effectively had the beach to myself. The air was cold, damp. Fresh. I took voracious gulps of it, glad to be out of the house and away from its grim reminders and secrets. For a little while anyway, I could free myself from the pervasive thoughts of Vanessa the Vile and the lunch I was being forced into with her tomorrow. Not to mention, my head was still spinning from the humiliation of Charles's will. I didn't need the money. I was a multi-millionaire several times over, courtesy of exceedingly generous trusts from both sets of grandparents.

Still ... any way he could find to stick it to me. Even in death. A prick to the end.

The soles of my tennis shoes sank into the sand, frothy bits of lake lapping against the shore. It was cold, but the wind was silent, making for a pleasurable, sunny stroll. I continued down the beach for a good thirty minutes, avoiding eye contact whenever I encountered the odd jogger or elderly couple out for their own brisk march.

I looked at my watch and turned to make the trip back home, feeling refreshed. Clear. I took off my sunglasses and rubbed the hem of my top against the lenses to wipe away some of the morning mist. When I went to put them back on, I saw him.

Standing at the far edge of the beach.

Just staring at me.

Had he seen me leave the house? Had he followed me?

The gratitude for no early morning company dissipated as I calculated the distance home. It would be quicker to head directly to my street—and smack into the media throng. Would he—whoever he was—dare confront me with so many witnesses? It hadn't stopped Charlotte, so why should it stop him? He was robust, bordering on obese. I could easily outrun him if it came to it.

But he *was* bigger. Likely stronger. If he got close enough, he could handily tackle me to the ground.

But only if I let him.

I swallowed, keeping my face a mask of stone, refusing to acknowledge his presence. He was still far enough away that I had a good head start on him in case I needed to break into a run.

Silently, I kept walking, fighting the urge to whip my head around to see if he was still watching me.

I quickened my pace, my footsteps tapping rapidly against the pavement.

I stole a glance over my shoulder.

He was gone.

I gasped as I swiveled my head left then right.

I didn't see him.

I gulped and walked faster, pushing a stray tendril of hair behind my ears. Should I run? Keep walking?

I clutched at my throat, the soft pink spandex material of my top suddenly a furnace against my skin. I looked around again.

Where was he?

I turned one more time, my eyes darting between the cracks of the tastefully appointed mansions, behind the towering trees, and next to the hulking SUVs.

There he was. Emerging from behind the beech tree in a corner of the Savitches' front yard, his eyes boring into me as he marched forward, his arms swinging by his sides like a cross-country skier, his own steps accelerating as he attempted to close the gap between us.

I broke into a run.

He did the same.

The cold morning wind rushed past my ears, stinging the tips. My lungs welcomed the guzzles of oxygen as I grunted and whimpered. I could cut through the Pattersons' yard and slip past the Finches' and from there, mere steps to my house.

What if he tries to break a window, kick in the door?

I dared to take another look behind me. He was hobbling and clutching his side. I whipped my head back around.

And went flying.

I didn't know how long I was airborne. Seconds. My feet popped up off the ground as a groove in the sidewalk reached up to grab the point of my tennis shoe and send me soaring.

I gasped as I skidded across the pavement, crying out as skin ripped away from my hands and forearms, revealing pink flesh and streaks of blood. My knee knocked against the sidewalk and for a horrifying moment, I thought I heard a crack. My sunglasses flopped down across my nose at an angle and I ripped them from my face, shoving them into my jacket pocket. I shook my head to get my bearings. I looked up to see he was gaining on me. I crawled backward, the heels of my hands digging into the rough concrete.

He was getting closer.

Getupgetupgetupgetup.

I grunted and pulled myself up, not taking time to assess the damage before adopting my own hobbled run. I sucked in my breath as pain crawled up my leg, ears ringing, the exposed skin of my forearms stinging with gravel and cold.

Even with my tumble, he still hadn't gotten close enough to me. I slipped past the Finches' yard and limped to my gate, firmly shutting and locking it behind me. I dragged my leg behind me, still glancing over my shoulder, half expecting him to scale the fence or ram his shoulder against it in an attempt to get the wood to splinter and crack.

I fumbled in my jacket pocket for my key, my fingers numb and red, my forearms burning.

The latch on the gate rattled. I gasped and flung myself around to see the gate jerking back and forth. I gripped the frame of my back door, shoving my key into the lock, finally managing to get it open before throwing myself inside. I collapsed against the door, locking it. I peered through the blinds, my heart cannonballing, blood pulsating in my ear canals.

He's going to break in. He's going to bust through the back fence and storm the house.

I looked around the room, my eyes wildly searching for weapons. Nothing.

When I actually needed my gun, it was being held hostage at the police station.

So, if you can't use your gun, what can you use?

A knife.

I limped toward the kitchen, my hands flailing in front of me as I groped for the knife block on the counter. A long blade found its way into my hand and in my haste, I knocked the block over, causing me to jump back in anticipation of a cavalcade of knives cascading to the floor.

They stayed put, only slipping a little from their snug slots.

I gripped the knife in my hand and peered out the window again, half expecting to see the sinister leer of his face plastered to the pane.

The doorbell rang.

I jumped, the knife skipping from my hand and clattering to the floor, the horrible metallic echo thundering across the kitchen. I clasped my neck, hot and slippery beneath my fingertips, my pulse hammering against my palm.

"He wouldn't dare. Not with all those reporters out front. All those witnesses. He wouldn't dare march up to my front door," I murmured, aware of the tinge of madness lacing my words.

But he might. Whoever he is, he might want to put a bullet in your brain with the whole world watching.

The doorbell pealed again and I slowly drew out another knife, not sure if I would be able to get back up from the floor if I attempted to pick up the other one.

I took several deep breaths. The handle of the knife slipped against my sweaty, throbbing, bloody palm and I tightened my grip around it, afraid of it slithering out of my hand.

The doorbell rang in two quick successions, followed by a knock.

I edged closer to the door, the knife out in front of me, my other hand reaching slowly for the knob. I closed my eyes for a moment and slid the knife behind my back. There was a blip of sunlight through the peephole. I would look through it, quickly. Just a second. No more.

He wouldn't dare put a gun up to the peephole. Not with all those people watching.

Except he might.

All right. I wouldn't look through the peephole.

I would have to chance it and hope my reflexes were quicker than his.

I opened the door.

19

"Mrs. Morgan?"

I squinted at Detective Travis, my jaw slack, my heart stopping, then shocking itself back into action.

"What?"

Potts and Travis glanced at each other before looking back at me.

"You all right there?" Potts asked.

"Yes," I said quickly. "Why?"

His gaze flicked over me. "You look like you took a tumble. You're all skinned up. Bloody."

I looked down, as though I was seeing the wreckage for the first time, which, I suppose I was.

"Oh. Yes." I peered over their shoulders, my eyes searching the crowd, looking past the flashbulbs, for my stalker.

Vanished again.

They exchanged glances once more. Potts rubbed the back of his neck, frowning. "Can we come in?" he asked. "We have a few questions to ask you."

The knife. What are you going to say about the knife?

I considered slamming the door in their face, but thought better of it and stepped aside to let them in, palming the knife to the outside of my thigh so they couldn't see it. I looked out at the crowd of gawkers again, all of them staring at me, a few shouting out questions, cameras trained on the fleeting, precious glimpse of the reclusive Mrs. Morgan. I swiveled my head right, then left, in a vain search for some sign of his puffy coat. His malicious grin.

Gone.

I slowly closed the door, wincing at the creaky hinges. I planted my back against it, my hand still twisted around the knob. Both men stared at me.

"Does my lawyer know you're here?"

"We understand your husband's will was read yesterday," Travis said.

"What?"

"Your husband's last will and testament?"

I blinked, trying to focus. Over Potts's shoulder, something fluttered in the backyard. I gasped.

He'd gotten in after all.

"Mrs. Morgan, is there something going on that you'd like to tell us?" Travis asked as both men continued to stare at me.

I gulped and craned my neck for a closer look out of the window, squinting as I dipped down, flinching as my knee reminded me it needed tending to.

"Mrs. Morgan?" Travis repeated.

"I—" It was on the tip of my tongue to tell them to check the backyard, to go out there and chase the boogeyman away. I opened my mouth again when I realized the flutter was a bird flying out of a tree.

"Mrs. Morgan?" Travis reached for his hip. Going for his own gun, no doubt. Was today my day for getting my head blown off?

"You've caught me at a bad time."

"What's going on, Mrs. Morgan?" Potts asked, his wisecracks seeming to take a turn toward alarm. "Do you need medical assistance?"

"What? No."

They exchanged another quick glance. "Are you sure?" Potts asked.

"I went for a walk this morning and tripped on the sidewalk and —my lawyer doesn't want me talking to you without you—I mean her —without her present, so if you'd like to call her to make an appointment to speak—"

"Maybe you want to go and clean yourself up then we can talk," Potts said.

"No." I hadn't moved from the door, the knife planted against my thigh, out of their view.

"It's our understanding that your husband cut you out of his will," Travis tried again.

I blinked again, my equilibrium slowly tipping back to balance. "And?"

Charlotte. She'd blabbed, no doubt.

"Did you know your husband had cut you off without a dime?" Potts asked.

I straightened up, still glancing over their shoulders out the window. The only sounds were the chirp of birds and faint rustle of leaves from the wind. I bent around a little more.

The gate was still closed.

"Mrs. Morgan, did you know your husband planned to leave you with nothing?" Potts repeated.

"Nothing?" I asked, looking at him.

Potts shrugged and looked around, his hands in his coat pockets. "Nothing but this house as we understand it."

"Oh," I said. "I see. You think because my husband left me nothing in his will that I killed him."

"Did you?" Travis asked, his face blank, his voice flat.

"No, I didn't know about the changes my husband made to his will. No, I'm not destitute. I have plenty of my own money. Please, feel free to check." I paused. "As I'm sure you will. If you have anything else, please call my attorney." I fumbled for the knob behind me and flung open the door. All this time, I'd managed to keep the blade suctioned to my thigh and out of sight.

Potts pursed his lips and Travis narrowed his eyes at me. However, they both complied and formed a single file line toward the door. The frenzy reignited as cameras clicked and questions sailed through the air in our direction. I looked around one last time in search of my stalker, but he was gone.

"We'll be in touch," Potts murmured as they moved past me and stepped outside.

I didn't say anything but closed the door after them, catching myself at the last minute from slamming it shut.

As soon as the door was closed, the knife slid from the grimy, bloody clamp of my hand, crashing to the floor. I fell against the door, eyes closed, my hand over my chest. The heaviness of my breath fought for attention over the furious boom of my heart in my ears.

A branch scraped across the roof and I gasped, having to remind myself that same branch had been scraping against our roof for over thirty years.

I stayed slumped against the door, my eyes locked on the window overlooking the backyard. Before long, I could see the top of Monty Finch's head over the fence, hammering away at one of his infinite home improvement projects, could hear Amelia Finch open the back door to let their miserable looking Shar Pei frolic in the melting islands of dirty gray snow crisscrossing their yard.

I was safe.

For now.

20

I YAWNED THEN FINISHED the last of my white wine, my eyes flicking to the front of the house for the tenth time in as many seconds. I looked at my watch. Vanessa was fifteen minutes late. Enjoying the thought of my squirming, no doubt, and knowing there was no way I would leave without indulging in this little tête-à-tête.

I rubbed my eyes. I was exhausted. The last thing I wanted to do was subject myself to Vanessa. After the police had left yesterday morning, I'd cleaned myself up, dousing my wounds with peroxide, patching them up with monstrous Band-Aids and packing the swollen violet of my knee with Ziploc bags of ice. All the while, every noise made me jump, every cast of a shadow made my heart race. I had to cancel with my designer, Elaine, for I was in no shape to think about paint chips or fabric swatches. I was relieved when Gabe came home late in the afternoon, before the sun sank into the horizon and darkness descended. I couldn't stand the thought of being home alone. Having him there was some measure of comfort. We had a pleasant, if somewhat strained dinner of delivery Thai and all talk of leaving school ceased. Likely via Chase and Charlotte's influence.

Still, sleep eluded me. Between the anxiety of today, yesterday's chase, the police's unexpected drop-in, and the pain from my scrapes and bruises, all I could do was lie awake, waiting for morning.

"More wine, Madame?" my server queried.

My eyes flipped open and I stared at him for a moment before it registered what he'd asked me. "Yes, that would be lovely. Thank you," I said as I looked again to the front door. Thankfully, the restaurant was half-empty and none of the few diners seemed to recognize Jillian Morgan the Murderess.

My heart jumped when the front door swung open, flooding the host stand with cold sunlight. I caught a glimpse of the blustery crown of red hair.

Vanessa.

I straightened up in my seat a little, wincing from the throb of my knee, willing my server to hurry back with my fresh glass of wine. Vanessa all but floated toward me, pale pink wrap dress suctioned to the curves beneath her white wool swing coat, fire-engine red lipstick slashed across her mouth like fresh blood, a cadre of thread-thin, waist-length gold chains bouncing against her breasts. Her cheap perfume engulfed me as much as it did her.

She tossed her coat onto the empty seat beside her before she slid into the chair across from me. I picked up my just replenished wine, grateful to have something to hold onto.

"Jillian." She smiled. "See? I got it right?"

"I'm much obliged," I said.

"You're looking well," she said. "And smelling good as always."

"Thank you."

"And for Madame?" the server asked.

"I'll have what she's having," Vanessa purred, her smile wider now. It didn't hide her motive. Of course, maybe she didn't want it to.

"I was beginning to think you wouldn't show," I said.

"My apologies." She folded her hands on the table in front of her. "I had an emergency with a patient that I had to respond to. Besides. I wouldn't miss this for the world."

I resisted the urge to fiddle with my earring. It would show weakness. Fear. I couldn't let her smell it as I waited for her to drop whatever shoe she thought she was holding.

"So, Vanessa," I said, carefully setting down my wineglass and meeting her eyes, intent on holding her gaze, determined not to be the one to flinch. "You, of course, have my curiosity piqued as to why you wanted to have lunch."

"Would you excuse me?" She held up her hands. "I just want to dash into the little girls' room to wash my hands."

I clucked my tongue. "By all means."

She smiled and dashed off to the ladies' room while I gritted my teeth and took comfort in my wine while I waited. She returned within minutes, her lipstick a little shinier, her nose less so. She dropped her napkin into her lap and took a sip of water.

"Don't you just love it here?" She looked around. "So charming."

I nodded as I glanced at the whitewashed wood shelves and tables, the display of blue and white porcelain dinnerware against the champagne colored wall, and wrought iron cages housing lanterns hanging from the ceiling. "Yes. The very epitome of French Country chic."

"Well, as I started to say, I wanted to check on you, see how you're holding up during this terrible time."

I cocked my head to the side. "How thoughtful."

"And how are the boys?"

"Fine. They'll be going back east soon."

"You know it really struck me at the funeral how much Gabe favors you," she said. "And Chase is, as my Aunt Verna would say, the spit of Charles."

The hairs on the back of my neck shot to the ceiling. Was that what this was all about? Chase? Harboring a demented schoolgirl fantasy of seducing my son as some sort of consolation prize for not being able to sink her hooks into his father? I picked up my wineglass, hoping to would quell my urge to leap across the table and stab her.

"Yes, he does resemble Charles quite heavily." I took a sip of wine. "People have always commented on it."

"Yes." She paused. "I suppose they always will."

The server interrupted, requesting our order. My stomach was a madhouse, rumbling and churning so much, I was surprised no one could hear it. Food was the last thing I wanted. Nevertheless, I ordered a spinach salad, something I could choke down with minimal damage. Vanessa, ever the follower, ordered the same, though she asked to add roasted chicken.

She handed her menu to the server. "Well, now that we've got that out of the way, we can get on with our lunch." She held up her wineglass. "Cheers."

"What are we toasting?"

"To a long and fulfilling friendship," she said. "I think we should become friends. Don't you?"

Even under the best of circumstances, Vanessa was the last person on earth whose existence I wanted to dignify with my presence.

Still, I had to play along. Keeping enemies close and all that. I held up my glass and clinked it with hers.

"To friendship," I said.

"To friendship," she echoed, taking a hearty sip of her wine. "And I do hope you'll let me be a friend to you, Jillian."

"Well, one can never have too many friends, can they?"

"Not at all." She ran her index finger along the rim of her wineglass, her gaze locked onto me. "I really do think you need a friend who understands you and just how difficult these past few months have been for you."

"Of course," I said.

Any day now, Vanessa.

"Someone who knows things from both sides. Your side, Charles's side..."

Finally. We were getting closer. I shifted in my seat, my spine prickling with the anticipation of what was about to spill forth. "Yes, I suppose you do have a unique vantage point. All things considered."

She took another gulp of wine. "You know Charles was really a mess those last few months. He was usually so cool. Unflappable. I can honestly say I don't think I'd ever seen him so discombobulated as this past year."

Yes, juggling a slut and your wife will do that.

I smoothed down the front of my suit. "It's true Charles certainly was distracted those last few months. I did try to get him to talk to someone, but he rebuffed my efforts."

"Doctors do make the worst patients."

"I certainly learned that firsthand."

"However, I do think there was something else bothering Charles," she said.

"Oh?" I leaned forward, frowning, as though I was concerned. "Was there something specific you noticed?"

She poked one finger through that nest of red waves and scratched her scalp, looking flummoxed. "As a matter of fact, there was something."

Spill it, Vanessa. Let's get this over with.

Our server arrived bearing two plates piled high with greens, laced with warm bacon dressing, sprinkled with chunks of goat cheese, candied pecans, and tart green apples. Vanessa's requested chicken huddled to one side of her plate. I forced myself through the pleasantries of thanking the server for our meal and refusing anything else. I refrained from picking up my fork and digging in, lifting my wineglass to my lips instead.

Vanessa showed no such restraint. She attacked a chunk of chicken and goat cheese with her fork, dipping them into the puddle of dressing atop the bed of spinach.

"Oh." She rolled her eyes in ecstasy. "This is absolutely delicious. I swear they make the best spinach salads."

I poked at a leaf, nibbling daintily before smiling and nodding, but teetering on the knife-edge of impatience and fear. "Yes, indeed, they do make a delicious spinach salad."

She finished chewing then drained her wineglass, motioning to our server attending to the table next to us that she needed another. I ventured a few more sparse leaves, my hands shaking ever so slightly. She was so wrapped up in her salad, I don't think she noticed.

I cleared my throat and picked up my napkin to dab at the corners of my mouth. "You were saying, Vanessa?"

"Hmm? Oh, right. Charles. Yes, there were some odd things going on with him at the office. Very odd."

"Such as?"

She set her fork down and looked me square in the eyes, all the cutesy pretense and taunting innuendo sliding from her face, replaced with some concrete, irrefutable knowledge that she intended to blow me away with.

"All of those funny little packages he kept getting at the office," she said.

And there it was. Her little bombshell. Something she could nail me with.

Or she could try.

Not that I was any good at it, but I decided to play dumb. "Packages. What kind of packages?"

"Let's not play that game, Jillian. I know. I know what you were doing."

"Vanessa, I really don't know what you're getting at." *Play dumb. Play cool.*

"You were tormenting him. Sending him those little gifts to torture him."

My stomach fluttered. "Excuse me?"

She picked up her fork again, scooping up the dregs of her salad. "I was walking past his office one day. On my way to the kitchen for something, I can't even remember for what now. It was late and he didn't see me, but I could see a jack-in-the box sitting on his desk. And he was sweating profusely. I mean, I don't think I've ever seen anyone so drenched in sweat from just sitting."

I gripped my fork. "I imagine a jack-in-the-box would send anyone into a tizzy. I'm not fond of them myself."

"It was really bizarre. Before I could go in and ask him about it, he swept it off his desk and into a drawer. My curiosity was piqued, naturally, and I made a big pretense of saying goodbye to him as I left the office. And I waited until I saw him leave and I went back in."

And went rummaging through Charles's desk. You're a nastier piece of work than I'd imagined.

"You mean to say you went rifling through my husband's desk?" I asked.

"Under normal circumstances, of course, I would never do that," she said, mock indignation stamped across her face. "Still, we did all have keys to each other's offices for emergencies and such. You have to understand, Jillian. Charles was my practice partner. If he was coming unhinged, it was my right as an equity partner in the practice to know what the hell was going on with him."

"Of course," I murmured. "Self-preservation."

"Exactly." She leaned back in her chair, seemingly relieved someone understood her furtiveness. "I was doing my duty."

"So," I said, signaling our server for another glass of wine. A cab or an Uber was possibly in my future. "You mentioned gifts. What gifts? And what do you think these gifts had to do with Charles's state of mind?"

She leaned close once again. "Did you know we keep a log book in our office of all deliveries?"

"I was not privy to all of the minutiae of your office."

She laughed. "Of course. What a silly question. You wouldn't know. You'd have no idea. At any rate, I got curious about all of these little packages being delivered to Charles. So, I decided to do a bit of investigating."

Deliveries. I paid them handsomely. Anonymously. She's stumbling around in the dark. She doesn't know anything.

"Oh?"

"I looked through the log and noticed these deliveries weren't our usual service. Still, it was curious, so, I went to this delivery service, this *different* delivery service and I found a little canary who would sing for the right price."

I pursed my lips and set my fork down. I looked her square in the eye. "And what did this little canary sing to you?"

"I'm sure I don't have to tell you, do I?"

I ran my tongue across my teeth, aware my breath was quickening, that my palms were damp. *Play cool.* "Please. Enlighten me."

She chuckled and shook her head. "I have to give it to you, Jillian. You have quite the poker face. Really, you're good."

"Vanessa—" I lifted my shoulders, nonplussed. "I do wish you would tell me what it is that makes you think these gifts had anything to do with my husband's state of mind. As you say, there is such a thing as a right to know."

"At first, I didn't get what they were. A pair of fishnets. A tiny shovel. None of it made any sense. Then after Charles was arrested for murdering that poor girl, I read some of the stories and it all started to come together."

"I'm still not following." Just because she had put on her detective cap didn't mean I had to confirm the answers she thought she had.

"Oh, for God's—" She leaned toward me, dropping her voice. "I know it was you. You were the one sending him those little mementos. To let him know you knew about the affair. You were trying to drive him insane."

"Trying to—?" I laughed. A hearty laugh. Turn this around on her. "I'm sorry, did you say I was trying to drive Charles mad with ... trinkets?"

"It does sound a little nuts, doesn't it?" She laughed. "Whoops. Poor choice of words."

I leaned back in my chair, taking another sip of wine. "Well, I am floored, absolutely floored you would think this about me."

"Oh, come off it. You were trying to drive him wacko." She wound her index finger around in tight little circles near her ear, laughing. A crazed little laugh. A vicious little laugh. "You know it and I know it."

I wiped my mouth with my napkin before folding the white linen into a neat little square and placing it on the table. "Is that what you think?"

"Yes," she said. "That's exactly what I think."

My pressure began to recede. She didn't have anything. Like the Bad Cop Squad, she thought she could trick me into spewing my secrets.

Guess again.

I picked up my fork and dug into my salad, my appetite creeping back ever so slowly. "What an interesting theory you've posited."

She sneered as she reached down to the floor for her pink Coach tote, pulling out a manila envelope. She extracted a slip of paper and plunked it down on the table. I glanced down at it.

It was me. Or rather me in disguise. A grainy photo from a surveillance camera of me at the counter of this so-called anonymous delivery service. Still, despite the dark wig, oversized sunglasses, and dowdy clothes, it was most definitely me.

She'd played her ace.

"I'm a woman of science, Jillian. I never 'posit' a theory unless I can prove it," she said, her lips curling into a malicious smile.

Her meaning was clear. She meant to put me in a corner. She had a plan for me.

I scratched at the skin under my eye with my middle finger and leaned forward, my blood boiling. *Play cool.* "All right, Vanessa, what do you want?"

"A moment of truth, finally?"

"I'll ask you again. What do you want?"

"What do you think the police will say about this?"

"I can't imagine. I'm sure you'll feed them a theory."

She fluffed out her hair. "Oh, I don't know, the police are pretty smart. I'm sure I won't have to connect too many dots for them."

"And what is your theory? Exactly?"

She fell silent for a moment, biting her bottom lip as she looked me up and down. "I don't think it was any kind of accident that you killed Charles. I think you had a plan for him all along. I think you murdered him in cold blood. I think you were pissed about his affair and you wanted revenge. And I think you got it."

"My, my, my," I said. "For a woman of science, you certainly have quite the active imagination."

"You know what I admire about you, Jillian? Your coolness. I mean, most people, when faced with something like this would cower. Whimper, beg, and plead. Scratch at the door like a dog waiting to be let out. Not you. You just take everything in stride. Cold as ice."

"So, I suppose your intention is to take this little fantasy of yours to the police, leading them to all sorts of conclusions they can jump to, leaving me to defend myself against baseless charges?"

"Where there's smoke there's fire." She grinned. "And I bet there's a raging fire somewhere out there."

I folded my hands on the table in front of me, strangely calm. "Name your price, Vanessa."

"And what would you be paying me for exactly?" she asked, her voice spun sugar.

"You're a smart woman. I'm sure you know what you would be getting paid for."

"That's true enough," she said.

"Your price?" I repeated.

"Oh, Jillian." She shook her head, tsk tsking. "I don't need money. I've got plenty of that."

I cocked my head to the side, waiting, the cork keeping my fury and fear bottled inside me dangerously close to blowing.

"All right then, tell me. What is it you need from me to make this all go away?"

"Well, like I said, I've got plenty of money." She licked her bottom lip, her eyes drooping into half-drowsy slits. "What I don't have enough of is someone to keep me warm at night."

If it weren't so absurd, I'd laugh. Was she actually proposing an affair? With me? She ran her finger along the neckline of her dress, indicating that yes, she was quite serious.

"Vanessa, I—" I scoffed to myself, sinking into my chair, my eyes fluttering closed. "You'll have to forgive me, but I was under the impression you were straight."

She shrugged. "Sexuality is fluid, isn't it? I've always believed that anyway."

I scoffed again, my head spinning. "I was also under the impression you were madly in love with my husband."

"Oh, don't get me wrong. Charles … yes, I admired him tremendously. We had amazing chemistry. We could have had something real. Something true." She dropped her voice to a whisper. "But Charles isn't here anymore, is he?"

I looked down at the debris of my salad, wilted and waterlogged. I pushed the plate away and hunched over the table, still trying to put together the puzzle of what was in front of me.

"You couldn't have my husband, so you see me as some sort of consolation prize?"

"Not exactly." She laughed. "You are an exceedingly beautiful woman, Jillian. I am quite attracted to you. I think we could be mutually beneficial to each other."

"How so?" I asked, flummoxed.

"As I said at the outset, you could use a friend. A protector. And I could use a little companionship. It's been some time and a girl does get lonely."

"I can't believe I'm hearing this," I said more to myself than her. I flagged down our server and tapped my wineglass, resisting the urge to have him bring a bottle.

"Jillian, if you think about it—really think about it—it's magnificent. Truly. I keep this big, fat secret to myself, therefore keeping the police from knowing too much about your extracurricular activities. And we build our friendship. Our relationship." She ran her index finger around the rim of her wineglass. "We could have a very nice time together. I'm certainly better than a cold prison cell."

"You certainly present an interesting proposal," I said, not sure what else I was supposed to say. Our server appeared with a fresh glass of wine for me. Suddenly, it repulsed me and I pushed it away, disgusted.

Had it really come down to *this*?

She grinned. "I did promise you an illuminating conversation."

I had to get out of there. I couldn't take one more minute of her vulgar countenance, her leering, her threats.

"You've certainly given me a lot to think about," I said. "Though I suppose that was your aim."

"Take your time." She paused and giggled. "What am I saying? Yes, you can have some time. But not an infinite amount of time. A girl can get impatient. Twitchy. Talkative."

"Yes. Of course." I signaled to the server for our check as I pulled out my credit card, resisting the urge to jump out of my seat and run far, far away.

"Oh, no, Jillian, please, I asked you to lunch."

"I couldn't possibly," I said, handing my credit card over before the server had a chance to scurry away. "Besides. I wouldn't want to be in debt to you in any way."

"That's so funny." She shook her head. "I remember Charles saying the exact same thing that day at the airport. Remember? When we ran into each other last fall?"

"What a good memory you have."

She'd been beyond insufferable that day. If only I'd known she could sink much, much lower.

"Thank you for lunch, Jillian. It was truly an enjoyable afternoon."

The server came back and I indicated he should wait while I scrawled my signature across the receipt before handing it back to him. Surely, she wasn't expecting me to agree. Instead, I smiled and stood up, bracing myself for a wobbly exit. Surprisingly, I felt stable.

"Yes, it was quite the interesting meal," I said. "I should really get going."

"I'm just going to stay a few moments to finish my wine." She pressed her wineglass to her bottom lip. "I look forward to hearing your answer to my proposal."

"Yes, I—I will be back in touch with you soon," I said.

"I hope it is soon."

I gave her a curt nod, slipping my coat from the back of the chair before I strode out of the restaurant, my body flush with fear and anger, wondering if she was watching me leave, if she was cackling to herself that she had me right where she wanted me.

I slid behind the wheel of my car, my mind racing, processing what she'd said, watching her wave that manila envelope in my face. Finally, I pulled out of the lot, my steering wheel in a death grip beneath my fingers. When I was far enough away, I turned into an alley and shut off the car.

And I screamed, beating the steering wheel until my hands were raw, my throat burning with rage.

After several minutes, I stopped and collected myself, pulling out of the alley and heading home, feeling calmer. Focused.

If that bitch Vanessa Shayne thought I was going to let her come for me, she needed to think again.

21

"The police aren't pressing charges against you."

Joss Hamilton reclined in her leather desk chair. She wore the same blue suit and Hermes scarf as the day we'd met in the hospital. She stared at me, as though she expected I would confess to her in a wild fit of conscience.

Instead, I closed my eyes and breathed a sigh of relief. "Oh, thank God," I whispered. "Thank God."

"Your story matches the evidence so—" She shrugged. "They have no choice but to close the case. Move on to the next thing."

"This is such a relief. I mean, I know how these things can go and I—well, thank you for all of your help."

"Right." She handed me a sealed envelope over her cluttered desk. "My bill."

"Yes," I said, slipping it into my purse. "I'll take care of it right away."

"I did hear about your husband cutting you off…"

A short, bitter laugh escaped my lips. "Charles only did that to spite me. Don't worry, Ms. Hamilton. I'm not destitute. Far from it. Your bill will be paid."

"Good." She smiled, seemingly relieved to have gotten this unpleasantness out of the way. "Listen, even though you're not being charged, don't skip town or anything. That'll make you look guilty as hell. Go on about your business, but don't do anything to draw attention to yourself. No scandalous vacations, no boozy girls' nights out. No sleazy pay-for-play media interviews. No trashy tell-alls. The lower your profile, the better."

"I have no interest in—or intention of—indulging in any such activities."

"Glad to hear it." She hunched over her desk and stared at me. "So. What *are* your plans?"

"I haven't thought that far ahead. The truth is, I have no idea."

"Like I said, keep your nose clean," she said as her phone buzzed. "That's my eleven."

We both stood and I held out my hand to her. She gripped it—hard. "Thank you, Joss. For everything."

"Of course," she said, pumping my hand, the fluorescent pink tips of her acrylics digging into my skin. "Good luck."

I unbuttoned my coat as I stepped outside. It was an unseasonably warm January day. Near sixty. Climate change was real. I had a few hours to kill before getting home to meet with my designer, Elaine, to start getting the house back in shape. Besides, I was hardly in a hurry to get home, all so I could ramble around that big empty space, thoughts of Vanessa and portly stalkers invading me from all sides. I still didn't know what to do about her. All I knew was, I had to do something—and it didn't involve the two of us engaging in carnal acrobatics. I'd lain awake all night, racking my brain for a solution and none came forth. I was terrified one never would.

I adjusted my sunglasses as I spotted a Starbucks. Perhaps sitting quietly with a cup of tea would allow me to clear my mind and focus.

I peered inside. The line was monstrous, every table occupied. I'd take a pass.

I walked a few more blocks, my eyes peeled for another little café where I could get some tea, figure out what I was going to do about Vanessa.

I didn't see the collision coming.

"Oh, God—I'm—I'm sorry—"

We pulled back at the same time, our faces each reflecting our shock. Her hatred. My modicum of fear and weariness.

"Jillian," she said, her voice grim, her hair pulled back into a severe ponytail at the nape of her neck, her black Gucci cape coat also unbuttoned. She pushed her Warby Parkers to the top of her head.

"Charlotte. Hello."

She sniffed. "What are you doing?"

"I was just meeting with my attorney."

One perfectly shaped eyebrow lifted in half amusement, half hope. "Well, how about that?"

"She wanted to let me know the police won't be filing any charges against me."

Charlotte shook her head before breaking into bitter laughter. "You're serious?"

"I didn't do anything wrong. I thought I was defending myself."

"I don't believe you, Jillian. I just don't."

"Charlotte. I know how close you and Charles are—were—and I know his death has been devastating. *I'm* devastated every day by this. You have to believe me."

She cocked her head to the side, clicking her tongue against her teeth. "When did you know?"

"Know what?"

"About my brother's affair?"

I looked down at the sidewalk. "When did *you* know, Charlotte?"

"I'm sorry?"

"You and Charles talked all the time. I'm just wondering if he swore you to secrecy about it."

She sighed and glanced over her shoulder. "I didn't know. I suspected, but I didn't know anything for sure. I asked him, the night of my birthday party and he said no, but I didn't believe him."

"I found out the night he was arrested."

"Seriously? See, this is why I don't believe you. I know, *Charles* knew, there's not much that gets past you. I find it hard to believe that you lived with him, saw him every day and had absolutely no idea what was going on."

"He didn't park a red convertible in the driveway or start slaving away at the gym in some feeble attempt at 'getting in shape.' Nothing of note changed. He was gone as much as he always was." I looked away. "I know you don't want to believe this, and I know this is hard to hear, but your brother wasn't going to win any Husband of the Year Awards. He missed birthdays, anniversaries, special occasions too numerous to count. He was consumed by his work. Which made him an excellent physician, but a less than sterling husband and father."

"Listen, I'm well aware my brother was far from a saint, but I also know how much he loved those boys. And you. Despite all the bickering and jabs, he did love you."

We stood in awkward, uncomfortable silence, the honking horns, wailing street saxophone, and groaning buses filling the gap between us.

"I loved Charles, too," I said quietly after a while, actually meaning it. "I'd like to think that despite ... the affair ... we might have been able to work our way back to each other. I'm sorry we'll never get that chance."

"Maybe you are telling the truth. Maybe this whole thing was one horrible accident. For your sake, I hope you are telling the truth. I hope to God you are. I'll tell you this, though. If you mowed my brother down in cold blood, the police may not be able to come up with evidence, maybe you covered your tracks just that well—but if you did this, your justice may not come in a courtroom."

I touched her wrist. "Charlotte, this is harder for me than you know. I'll have to live the rest of my life with the knowledge that my husband is dead by my hand. I can't bring him back and I can't undo what happened. All I can do is ask that you be able to find it in your heart to forgive me one day."

She pushed her sunglasses back down across her eyes. "Congratulations on being free. Little good it does my brother." She edged around me, brushing up against my shoulder, slightly nudging me.

"Charlotte just might figure it out. You know she's smart enough. What are you going to do then, dear wife, when my sister puts all the pieces of the puzzle together? Will you kill her, too?"

"Of course not. Don't be an idiot."

The woman walking past glanced at me and I realized I'd spoken out loud. I smiled feebly before my face fell into a scowl. I resumed walking down the street, no longer concerned about finding a little café, but instead making my way back to my car so I could go home.

It was altogether possible Charlotte might become a thorn in Potts and Travis's side, demanding to know what kind of evidence they would need to bring charges against me. She might hire a private detective. She was chummy with the State's Attorney, having made substantial donations to her past two campaigns. She could press her to look more carefully at the evidence, find something, some infinitesimal something to necessitate hauling me down to the police station in shackles.

So, don't give her anything. Confirm that all of the loose ends are double-knotted and indestructible. Watch your back. Every minute. Every second.

I looked skyward. VBS Tower, where the Morgan Group was headquartered, stared down at me. Charlotte was up there, thinking about me, just like I was thinking about her.

Watch your back.

22

"JILLIAN." Walter smiled, his usual boisterous and jovial manner tamped down for the occasion.

I stepped into the large foyer and he kissed my cheek. "Hello, Walter."

He looked over my shoulder as he took my coat. "Gabe's not coming?"

"Oh, he—he's having dinner with some of his friends," I said. "He heads back to Columbia soon, so he's getting in a little bit of quality time before he leaves."

"Jillian? Jillian is that you?" The sugary sweet southern drawl of Walter's wife, Tina, floated out from the direction of the kitchen. Like her husband, Tina was tall, though like me, she was slender. "Golden Goddess" always came to mind whenever I saw Tina: shiny copper skin, high cheekbones, gold nail polish, gold bracelets, diamonds for days on her long, skinny fingers, and a fondness for swirling, fluttery caftans, in the summer. Anyone else would look gauche. Tina, however, carried off the look with stunning aplomb.

Tonight, she wore a deep purple cowl neck sweater dress and tall black boots accompanied by her usual assortment of bangles and baubles. We did the dual cheek kiss and I handed her a bottle of Sauvignon Blanc swathed in a gift bag. "Happy belated birthday," I said.

"Aren't you sweet. Can I pour you a glass?" she asked and I accepted her offer.

"We're glad you came tonight," Walter said, as Tina disappeared into the kitchen. He picked up his tumbler of scotch from the side table. Charles's favorite. "Really. It's great to see you."

"Thank you for inviting me. I must say, I'm not getting many invitations these days."

Walter sighed, his finger running along the rim of his glass. "I want you to know Tina and I are with you."

"Even though your best friend is dead because of me?" I said, my chin trembling.

"Oh, cry me a river, Jillian. Seriously. Where's my violin?"

"You didn't do it intentionally," Walter said. "It was a tragic accident."

Tina handed me a wineglass, her other hand snaking across my shoulders, bracelets chiming. "Girl, it could have happened to anyone. You know in fact, I was reading about a case in Pittsburgh where a woman did almost the exact same thing—her boyfriend was coming through the door, it was dark, she wasn't expecting him, thought someone was breaking in..."

In spite of myself, I laughed. Just a little. I grabbed Tina's hand and squeezed it. "Thank you for that. I guess ... well, it lends credence."

"Of course it does. I mean, it would have been something else altogether if you'd kept firing, shot him multiple times—"

"Tina." Walter frowned, shaking his head a little.

"All I'm saying is, just like this woman in Pittsburgh, she realized what she'd done, called 911 right away to get him help. She didn't skip town or lead police on some wild chase through the streets. It was a horrible, horrible accident."

"You think you have them all fooled, don't you? What an actress. Truly, your talents have been utterly wasted all these years."

I took a sip of wine, ignoring Charles. "I wish my sister-in-law shared your view. I'm afraid she'll never forgive me."

"Give her time," Walter said. "She's upset. Once she calms down, she'll come around."

"I hope so." I sighed. "I really hope so."

"Do you plan to move?" Walter asked.

"Oh, no. It's my home. The boys' home. Maybe later, I'll downsize. For right now, though, I have no plans to leave."

Tina subtly directed us to a tray of crudités and cheese and crackers on the coffee table in the living room. "So how are Gabe and Chase doing?" she asked as she sipped a martini.

Tears sprouted again. Genuine ones. "Chase is barely speaking to me. Gabe is such a sensitive soul, you know he takes everything so ... well, he's just not the type to bounce back and keep going. I worry about him."

"Should have thought about that before you fired a bullet into me."

"I can recommend some psychologists for you," Walter said. "I know a few out of North Presbyterian."

"That would be wonderful," I said. "Thank you. I appreciate it."

"Of course. I'll e-mail you some names tomorrow."

"Jillian, sweetie, please, have some." Tina edged the tray of crudités toward me.

"Thank you." I took one tiny stalk of celery and a handful of broccoli florets, plunking them into the blue cheese dip. I'd already determined I would nibble tonight—I'd eaten a small chicken Caesar salad at home to curb my appetite. Wolfing down food seemed wholly inappropriate under the circumstances.

"And I'm sure, just like your sister-in-law, once Chase calms down, he'll be all right. Sometimes things have to get worse before they get better," Tina said as she bit into a small wedge of Brie.

"Perhaps we can change the subject to something I hope is more pleasant. How's Bitsy?" I asked.

"Oh, she's never coming back. Real California girl now," Walter said. "And she's met someone. Sounds serious."

"That's wonderful," I said. "I'm glad to hear she's getting on."

And that's how it went. We chattered on over a lovely dinner of lemon roasted chicken, cauliflower gratin, creamy balsamic dressing clinging to mixed greens, and an apple tarte tatin, all of which I ate small portions of. They updated me on their children. I was careful to maintain my veneer of subtle distraction, to pick at the food, not laugh too loudly or too brightly at Walter's bon mots and to have cautious exchanges with Tina about frivolous topics. It did feel good to spend the evening with them. No prying questions. No stares. No discomfiting currents of mistrust crackling in the air. No cloying questions or innuendo. No fluttering, oppressive, unwanted attention.

It was nice.

I even managed to keep a lid on Charles and his infernal commentary.

We'd moved back to the living room for after-dinner tea and coffee. The conversation lingered on about some book Tina was reading that she promised to lend me. I glanced at my watch. Eleven. Strangely, I didn't want to leave.

I felt safe here.

Still, the last thing I wanted was them kicking me out. Terribly unbecoming.

"I should really get going." I set my empty teacup onto the matching light turquoise saucer on the coffee table. "I have some early errands to run tomorrow."

"Oh, sweetie, it was so great to see you." Tina clutched my hand. "You call if you need anything, even if it's just to get out of the house for a few hours. In fact, why don't we have lunch next week?"

"I'd like that. Thank you."

We made our way to the front door and Walter handed me my coat. "I'll e-mail you those names tomorrow for Gabe."

"Thank you so much, Walter. I really appreciate it."

"Anytime. Let us know you made it home safe."

I said I would as I hugged them both while we said our goodbyes. Walter walked me out to my car, making sure I was safely inside before lumbering back to his house. They stood in the doorway, waving goodbye as I pulled out of the driveway, pointing the car toward home.

I glanced at the blurry, bluish-green numbers of the clock on my dash. It was a fifteen, twenty-minute drive at most and there weren't many cars on the road this late at night. A twinge of sadness rippled through me. Charles always drove. Anytime we went to an event, it was he who slid behind the wheel to get us home safely, leaving me free to imbibe as much as I wanted. An unspoken edict in our marriage.

I turned the heat down and gripped the steering wheel, rolling my head around a little to release the cricks in my neck, just as the light turned red. I sighed and turned up the volume on the radio, gently tapping my finger along with Diana Krall.

The light turned green and I lifted my foot from the brake, slowly edging forward. The harsh glare of the headlights from the car behind me momentarily blinded me. I squinted and glanced in the rearview mirror, irritated to realize the car was practically hugging my bumper. We were the only ones on Sheridan, a four-lane road. Why didn't they switch lanes and pass me?

I scoffed and switched to the left lane, pressing harder against the accelerator, the glare of the headlights receding slightly.

The car sped up, those same obnoxious lights slamming against my eyes. I looked in the rearview again, struggling to make out the license plate.

I punched the accelerator again, my gaze flitting across the road. This was all residential. Even if there was a store parking lot to pull into, everything was closed this time of night. Besides, getting out of my car to escape a maniac probably wouldn't be all that prudent.

The car raced to catch up with me, swerving beside me, as though the driver couldn't make up their mind what, exactly, they wanted to do.

The light up ahead was green and from the corner of my eye, the "Walk" sign flashed red blinking numbers. Ten. Nine. Eight.

I eased my foot from the accelerator.

Five. Four. Three.

The car behind me did the same.

Two.

One.

I mashed the accelerator and flew through the red light. In the rearview, I could see them idling at the light as two cars I'd managed to miss sped through the intersection from the other direction. I relaxed a little, perplexed about who and why this person was after me.

Then it hit me.

Vanessa.

Of course. I was sure of it. She'd sicced this thug on me to do her bidding. A brazen attempt to frighten me into submission. It didn't surprise me at all she'd have a hoodlum on speed dial, ready, willing, and able to do her dirty work. The memories of the past few weeks careened through my head—New Year's Eve, the cemetery. Tonight.

I had sorely underestimated the lengths she would go to so she could get what she wanted. I wouldn't be making that mistake again.

The peal of tires and a horn exploded behind me. I gasped, my attention snapping back to present. The car was back to swerving behind me, this time, sidling up next to me on the right.

We were in a drag race. I would punch the accelerator, they'd speed up. I would slow down. So would they.

I reached over to the glove compartment, groping for the little used garage door opener. We rarely parked our cars in the garage. My hand closed around the hard blue rectangle and I dropped it in my lap. I was two minutes from home. I would have to speed into the garage and pray I could get it closed before—

I shuddered, shoving the thought out of my head.

I glanced at the rearview and saw the car was once again mere inches from my bumper.

Instead of stomping on the gas, I stomped on the brake.

The wheels screeched as the car veered to avoid hitting me. I stomped the accelerator and took off, my own wheels squealing and whining.

One minute—thirty seconds—away.

I swerved as I turned down my street. It was late and no media were camped out front. I'd lost my stalker, but it was a matter of time before he caught up. I jabbed the button on the opener, willing it to open. I could see the door up ahead, but it wasn't budging. I ground my teeth and pressed again.

The door trudged open at the speed of slow. I looked behind me. The car was turning the corner. I skidded into the driveway, beelining for the garage, pressing the button to close the door. It was even slower closing than opening.

The high beams shone bright against the wall of the garage. The car stopped. I couldn't hit the button again, as that would activate the door to open.

The slam of a car door caused my eyes to pop open. Beads of sweat ruptured across my skin and my mouth clawed for air.

The bottom of my garage door thumped to the concrete.

I was safe.

Except they could break into the house.

I'm trapped.

I grabbed my phone and flung the car door open, scanning the garage. I rushed toward the first thing I saw, wrestling it from the wall.

My keys tumbled from my trembling hands and I struggled to separate the suddenly cumbersome pieces of metal from one another.

They could be in the house right now. They could have kicked the door in, broken a window. They could be standing on the other side of this door, waiting for me.

I snatched my keys from the floor, shoved the house key in the lock and eased the door open.

Quiet.

I gripped the power saw in my hand. Even with its long black cord dangling beside me, pooling at my feet, with enough force, its heavy metal blades could do damage.

I held the hulking tool out in front of me, slicing the air with it as my eyes darted around the room, plunged in shadows. I flicked my head toward the front door.

Closed.

I did a quick scan of the floor-to-ceiling windows.

Untouched.

I edged over to the window facing the street and poked one eye out around the curtain. The car was idling in my driveway, dust dancing in the bright lights of the high beams. There was a soft click and the car backed out of the driveway, the bottom of the bumper scraping gently against the concrete. Within seconds, the nondescript gray or silver compact sped down the street.

I stood rooted to the window, my breath hard and heavy. Fear glued my feet to the floor and sweat flooded my skin. I wasn't sure how much time had passed before I decided the car wasn't coming back.

My phone bleated from my purse. I screamed, and dropped the power saw, which thudded against the wood. I fumbled for the phone, staring down at the blinking blue light indicating a text message.

Walter. Hoping I'd made it home safely.

My eyes slammed shut as I wilted against the floor. I plunged my face into the damp cradle of my palms. I wondered briefly if I should call the police, deciding against it just as quickly. No. I would handle Vanessa and her goon in due time.

First, I had to make it through tonight.

"It's only going to get worse, Jillian. I promise you."

I shook my head furiously as I crawled toward the power saw. "I won't let that happen. Charles."

"You can't stop it."

I kept shaking my head as I gripped the power saw in one hand and hoisted myself from the floor with the other. I tottered into the living room and plunked the saw onto the cushions before pushing the couch around until it faced the front door. I sank to the edge and picked up the saw, aiming it toward the door.

"I can stop it. I will stop it," I said, rocking back and forth. "Neither Vanessa, nor her henchman, or even you, will take me down. No one will."

23

"Mom?"

I jerked awake at the sound of my name. Chase and Gabe stood over me, frowning. I had fallen asleep on the couch, strings of drool tumbling from my lips.

"Oh." I rose up, disoriented as I looked around, shocked to realize I was clutching a power saw, confused about why the couch was facing the front door.

"What the hell is going on?" Chase asked, pointing at the power saw.

I swiped my hand across my mouth, the events of last night slamming against me. Being chased home. Snatching the saw from the garage wall, standing guard in the living room before the fatigue, a full stomach, and wine pulled me down into a fitful sleep.

"I got home late last night from the Ryans' and I thought I heard something."

Well, it was a version of the truth, anyway.

"Why didn't you call the cops?" Chase asked. "Or one of the neighbors? I'm sure Mr. Ladd would have come over, checked things out."

"I didn't think about that." I swept my gaze over Gabe, who just continued to stare at me, nonplussed. "What are you doing here?" I asked Chase.

"I need to pick up a few things."

"I spent the night at Thad's," Gabe offered. "I just got here, too."

"Oh. Well, perhaps I can make us all some breakfast—"

"Are you hungover?" Chase asked, warming up his cross-examination.

"No." I stood up quickly, swaying a bit as I did. I stumbled backward and nearly tumbled onto the couch. Gabe shot out his hands to catch me.

"You don't look so good, Mom," he said quietly.

"I'm fine. Really. I just need a shower, some tea, a little something to eat." My head wobbled around the room, my eyes landing on the front door, half expecting to see Vanessa's heavy standing in the foyer. I cleared my throat and turned back to my sons, who continued to regard me with wary concern. "I just ... I need to get my bearings."

I took a few steps and faltered again, this time both boys catching me. My knee still throbbed from my tumble on the sidewalk and last night's wine continued to slosh in my stomach.

"No, really, Mom, what is going on with you?" Chase asked. "Why are you limping? Did you hurt yourself?"

"I tripped while I was out taking a walk the other day, that's all. The swelling's almost gone. I'll be fine."

Both boys eyed me warily as I smoothed back the bedraggled strands of my hair and glanced at the front door. "Did the paparazzi hound you much when you drove up?"

Chase shrugged. "There weren't that many out there. So, it wasn't too bad." He looked around the living room. It was his first time seeing it since...

He pulled away from me, shoving his hands in his pockets as he walked over to where the couch used to be and stared down at the floor. Though I'd pulled up the tape surrounding Charles's body, its faint outline was still black against the wood grain. The floor would also be going.

"That's where Dad was," he said, a statement rather than a question.

"Chase, we don't have to talk about this now—"

"Do you think about him at all? About Dad?" he asked.

Tears sprung to my eyes. "Of course. All the time," I whispered. I could see Gabe avert his eyes, his own silent tears cascading down his face.

"I still don't understand how this happened," Chase murmured, still looking down. "None of it makes any sense to me."

"I know this is a lot to process," I said. "I'm still trying to."

"Aunt Charlotte doesn't think it was an accident."

I folded my arms across my chest. "The police think otherwise."

"Did you?" he asked. "Do it on purpose?"

His words hit like a sucker punch. Even though he was right, it still hurt for my own son to think of me as a cold-blooded murderer.

"Absolutely not," I choked out. "As I've told you, I had no idea your father was here and—"

"Who the hell else would it have been?" he exploded, bitterness and anger etched into his handsome face. He crossed back over to me in three strides, his face inches from mine. "Huh? Just who in the hell else would it have been?"

"Chase." My voice was quiet. Simmering. "I can't have you talk to me this way. I *won't* have you talk to me this way."

"Let me ask you something, Mom. Do you think about what it was like to shoot him? Do you think about what it was like to watch him hit the ground, to see that bullet rip into him? All that blood? To watch him die?"

"Chase." I pressed my lips into a thin line and took a deep breath, a pained attempt at keeping him and myself from igniting. "It wasn't like that."

"All right, what was it like? Please, tell me. Enlighten me as to what it was like to murder your husband. The father of your children. Did it feel good? Would you do it again if you had the chance?"

I slapped him. Hard. We both stumbled back from the shock, our eyes locked together in disbelief. I'd never struck either of my sons. Ever.

My hands flew to my mouth. "Oh, God, Chase. I'm sorry. I'm so sorry—"

He shook his head and cradled his cheek momentarily then scoffed. "At least it wasn't a bullet."

He brushed past me and I lunged for his arm. "Chase. I'm—please. I didn't mean it. It—"

"It was an accident, right?" He smiled, and rubbed his cheek. "Always just an accident."

"Chase—"

He flung my arm away as he stormed toward the door, slamming it shut behind him, causing me to jump. Gabe was slumped against the wall, tears staining the front of his long sleeved, sky blue Columbia t-shirt.

"Gabe, darling—"

He, too, wrenched away from me and bolted up the stairs to his room, also slamming his door.

Sobs tore through me, as I looked helplessly first at the front door, then upstairs. From the corner of my eye, the edge of the blackened line of tape that had once hugged Charles's body seemed to rise from the floor, looming over me.

"Jillian, what did you do?"

For the second time that day, rage won out. Without thinking, I grabbed the nearest thing at my fingertips. A heavy blue and white vase. I launched it across the room, satisfied as I watched it shatter against the wall and little chips of blue and white ceramic rained to the hardwood floor.

I sank down, the tears rushing down my face in a violent downpour, unable to stop looking at that black outline.

24

"Hi, you've reached—"

I threw my phone down onto the window sill, the lilac sheers fluttering in response. Chase's voicemail again. I blew a stack of smoke out the open window. I'd taken to smoking at the window, as I didn't want Gabe to see me, though I'm sure he knew. He'd been polite enough not to say anything about it at any rate. He'd left early and I didn't expect he'd be back for some time. I'd been up here all morning, after yet another sleepless night of worrying about Vanessa and stressing about Chase, furtively chain smoking like I was back in high school. Fortunately, there weren't any media out front, so I could incinerate my lungs in peace.

It was odd, this retreat to smoking. I thought I'd stubbed out my last cigarette over thirty years ago, not long after Charles and I had started dating. Being a future doctor, he detested it, all but gave me an ultimatum to prod me to quit. And in those days, I would have done anything for him. Strangely, inexplicably, the day after his arrest, I woke up with the stirrings of nicotine lust I hadn't felt in decades. I'm sure some self-aggrandizing psychiatrist would have a field day with that one.

I picked up the phone, contemplating whether to try Chase again. I'd been calling him nonstop for the past few days, cramming apologies into his voicemail like a lunatic. He had, for all intents and purposes, iced me out. Not that I could blame him. I wouldn't give me the time of day either. Gabe was polite, but cold to me, spending most of his time with his friends, leaving in the morning, creeping into the house late at night.

I stubbed my cigarette into the ashtray and paced the room, the throbbing of my knee having receded to a twinge, the scrapes and scratches rapidly fading into oblivion. Perhaps I would go to Charlotte's and throw myself at Chase's mercy, figure out some way to win him back.

My boys were the only thing I had left. I couldn't lose them. I wouldn't.

"You're only getting what you deserve."

"You're enjoying every minute of this, aren't you?" I said to Charles.

"You have no idea."

"This is a temporary setback. Chase will come around. So will Gabe. You'll see."

"Wait until they find out what you did to their father. What you really did, I mean."

"They won't. No one will. That little secret will go with me to my grave." I laughed. "And yours."

"You're unraveling, Jillian. Look at you. Hardly the fresh-scrubbed Main Line debutante anymore, are you?"

I looked down at my robe and pajamas as I ran my hand through my hair, alarmed at the greasy strands. How long had it been since I'd had a shower? I flipped on the bathroom light and blanched at the interstate of red veins crisscrossing the whites of my eyes and puffy, sallow cheeks staring back at me in the mirror. Charles was right. I was a disaster.

My phone chirped and I raced for it.

Vanessa.

I groaned and threw it down on the bed as it continued to ring. I rubbed my hands up and down the length of my face, my anxiety swelling like a blister. I was running out of time. If I didn't do something soon, she'd sing like a siren to the police and ruin me.

"It wouldn't surprise me in the least if she was the one to take you down. She's got the goods."

I resumed pacing, eyeing the phone as it mocked me with the ding of a voicemail from Vanessa the Vile.

"You won't be able to squirm your way out of this one. She's got you right where she wants you."

"For the love of God, do you ever shut up?"

"Why should I?"

I ignored Charles as I continued my march across the room, sweat tingling beneath my underarms, the walls seeming to close in on me with each passing second.

"I have to figure out a way to get rid of her," I whispered as I walked past Charles's closet, the pristine rows of tailored suits peeking out from inside. I'd been putting off packing up his things to let the boys rummage through everything as they saw fit.

Inspired, I rushed toward the closet, pulling suits, shirts, and ties off the rack in a furor, throwing them in heaps atop the bed. Maybe if I eliminated his presence from the bedroom, he'd leave me alone and I could think in peace. In my haste, my frenzy, I yanked on a batch of suits at the far end of the closet a little too zealously, sending some of the items stacked on the top shelf tumbling down.

And like a manna from heaven, the solution to my problem thudded to the floor next to me.

I looked down at it, annoyed, because it shouldn't have been in there to begin with. But as I stared at it and the possibilities presented themselves, elation followed. A plan—the definitive plan—for ridding myself of Vanessa, took its first stuttering steps toward adulthood. I bent down and picked up this beautiful, bulky answer to my prayers, turning it over in my hands, my heart thundering with excitement. Speak what you want into existence. I clutched the Holy

Grail to my chest as I flew down the stairs in order to do more research.

This could work. It *would* work.

"You honestly believe you can pull this off? You really believe you won't get caught?"

"Oh, Charles." I laughed, hugging my treasure tighter to me. "Haven't you learned by now not to underestimate me?"

25

I TAPPED the contents of a brown, raw sugar packet into my hot tea, followed by a squeeze of lemon. I stirred it as I looked toward the front of Convito Café—Gabe's request—for signs of my son. It was my first time out of the house in some days, holed up as I'd been refining Mission Possible: Eliminate Vanessa the Vile, as I was calling it. I'd even figured out what to do about her goon. Still, coming up for air from all my plotting was unsettling, like navigating a broken sidewalk in two different height heels. There was still so much to do. However, I was grateful for his invitation to lunch before he returned to Columbia tomorrow. Chase was radio silent, having fled to Boston two days ago according to Gabe, no doubt ready to hide behind the grind of his last semester at Harvard Law. I continued to call and text him, all still to no avail. I wouldn't give up, though. I couldn't.

Gabe came loping through the crowded room. I shot my hand up to wave to him, smiling in spite of myself.

"Hi, Mom," he said, sliding into the seat across from me.

"Hello, sweetheart." I cleared my throat and picked up my teacup. "How was breakfast?"

"Good." He unfurled his white linen napkin into his lap and took a sip of water from the glass on the table. "Aunt Charlotte and I had a nice time."

"I'm glad to hear that." I took a sip of tea to avoid having to talk anymore about her. I put the cup back into the saucer. "So, have you packed up everything for school? Do you need any help?"

"I'm good," he said, studying the menu.

"You never told me what you and Chase decided to do about your father's car."

"Chase said I could have it if I wanted it."

"Do you?"

"Can we sell my Jeep?"

"Of course. I can take care of it, if that's all right with you, deposit the money from the sale into your account."

"Maybe you could keep Dad's car parked in the garage until I get home for the summer. Then I can drive it back to school in the fall."

I nodded. "That sounds just fine. Perhaps I'll have Thad's brother start it up for you once in a while. I'm sure he'd like to be seen driving a Mercedes around the block on occasion."

"Yeah, sure. Thanks."

"Have you ... looked through your father's phone yet?"

"Not yet." His voice faltered a bit. "I'm not ready."

"Of course." I smiled. "Take your time. And remember, if you find anything disturbing and want to talk about it—"

"Yeah, I know." He resumed looking at the menu, I suspect to hide burgeoning distress.

"Gabe." I reached across the table. He looked down at my hand, uncertainty scrawled across his face, before letting his hand fall into mine. Tears sprung to my eyes.

"Mom—"

"I just want you to know—"

"I don't want to talk about this."

"Your father loved you so much."

"I know."

"And I love you. More than I can even begin to express. I just want you to know that."

He paused a moment, fingering the edge of the menu. "I love you, too."

I squeezed his hand, my vision blurry with tears. I chuckled to myself and picked up my napkin to dab at my eyes. "I hope I can make it through this lunch."

"It'll be all right."

"I know. You're right. I forgot to tell you that Dr. Ryan has said he would be happy to recommend someone for you to talk to in New York—"

"I don't want to talk to anybody." His face flamed red as he went back to studying the menu.

"You may not *want* to talk to someone, but—"

"Mom, please stop."

"Promise me. Promise me, please, that you will?"

He slumped down in his chair a moment before finally shrugging and nodding. "All right fine. If you want me to talk to someone, I will."

"It really would make me feel better," I said. "Sometimes it's nice to talk to someone who doesn't know you at all."

"Yeah, okay, sure."

I twiddled with the empty sugar packet on the table. "Have you talked to your brother?"

"Yeah, he texted me last night. By the way, Thad and I are going to the movies tonight," Gabe said, deftly changing the subject. "So, I won't be around for dinner."

"When is Thad leaving to go back to Yale?" I finally asked.

"Day after tomorrow."

I took another sip of tea, looking around for our server. It was hard not to notice the stares and whispers of our fellow diners. Some had the decency to glance away as soon as they made eye contact with me. Others weren't so discreet. How many camera phones were detonating at the moment? How long before my simple lunch with my son was plastered across the Internet?

I sighed, perturbed that the young man who'd handed me a menu when I was seated seemed nowhere to be found.

"Do we have a server?" Gabe asked as he pulled a roll from the basket of bread between us. "I'm starving."

"Yes, we—" I spotted the young man making his way around the room and signaled to him.

"Hey. Hi." I flicked my gaze over to the owner of the voice on the other side of me, a smiling young woman in black slacks and matching turtleneck, wisps of dirty blond hair sprouting away from her head. She waved a little in my face.

"Oh. My apologies. I thought our server was a young man. At any rate, Gabe, what—"

"Huh? Oh, no, no, I'm not your server," the young woman said. "I mean, I'm not your server here. I'm having lunch with my mom. Don't you remember me?"

I looked her up and down. "I'm sorry, should I?"

"You're sure you don't remember me? From the Starbucks? In Rogers Park?"

I felt the blood drain from my face. The Starbucks in Rogers Park. I remembered the perky barista now. Always so chatty, always attempting to draw me into conversation. Asking me how my day was, what the weather was like. I offered terse responses, but it didn't seem to deter her. In fact, it seemed to make her only more determined to befriend me.

The Starbucks in Rogers Park. Mere blocks from where Charles's slut lived. The Starbucks where I'd spent my days huddled in a corner, swathed in a dark wig and no makeup, watching his slut totter in with her laptop, dutifully order a Venti Flat White and package of madeleines that she would dunk into a cup of cream and roll around in a pile of sugar on her napkin, while she studiously tapped the keys of her computer. All while I watched and waited and learned.

All so I could make my move.

"Grande Green Tea. With lemon? You haven't come in for a while. I thought maybe something had happened to you. How is everything?"

I wanted to reach out for my teacup, to distract myself, but I didn't trust that it wouldn't quiver in my hand and rattle against the saucer or send hot water sloshing against my skin. Instead, I shook my head, as though I was confused. From the corner of my eye, I could see Gabe's own bewilderment.

"I'm sorry, but you must have me confused with someone else."

"You sure?" she asked, peering closer at me before she crossed her arms over her chest, her own look of confusion muddying her face.

"Oh, quite sure. I don't think I've ever been to Rogers Park, much less a Starbucks in Rogers Park."

"Of course, you do look different. Your hair was darker. Like black. You were definitely dressed differently. Do you have a sister? Like a twin, maybe?"

I chuckled. "No, no, I don't have any sisters, twin or otherwise."

"Wow." She shook her head. "I could have sworn that was you. My bad."

My heartbeat slowed and I felt confident enough to pick up my teacup, grateful the restaurant had been out of Green Tea today and the empty packet of Earl Gray was still sitting on the table.

"Quite all right," I said. "No offense taken."

She gave an embarrassed little wave toward Gabe and an equally discomfited smile at me before slinking off in the direction of the ladies' room.

"That was weird," Gabe said.

I chuckled, hoping to cover my nervousness. "It certainly was."

"She probably saw your picture on the Internet or something and got you mixed up with someone else." He fingered the napkin hanging over the edge of the bread basket. "Your picture's everywhere."

My spine tingled at Gabe's statement. Who else could have seen me near the tramp's apartment? Who else could identify me, place me near the scene?

Who else could put two and two together and go to the police?

"*Who else, indeed, Jillian? How many loose ends have you left dangling out there?*"

I ran my hand across my forehead and cheek, the skin burning beneath my fingertips. I had my hands full with Vanessa and her hooligan. I didn't think I could manage much more than that.

"*You're not as smart as you think, Jillian.*"

"You're probably right," I said to Gabe, my appetite swirling away as the perky little barista emerged from the restroom, taking care to walk far away from our table. "I'm sure it's all one big misunderstanding."

"*Don't be so sure, Jillian. Don't be so sure.*"

She snuck a glance at me and we locked eyes. She frowned again before shaking her head and looking away.

26

I ADJUSTED my sunglasses before I peered out the driver's side window. It was early, seven fifty-nine a.m., one minute until the store opened. Lights glared from the windows and I could see workers doing whatever last-minute tasks needed to be done before the store opened. I suppose I could have followed Francine's suggestion to me last night when she came over bearing flowers and a bottle of Pinot Grigio, and enlisted a grocery delivery service. The truth was, I needed to get out of the house and engage in normal activities like marching down the aisles of Target. Still, the gawks and whispers when I did emerge from my self-imposed exile were nerve-wracking.

"What did you expect, Jillian?"

"Shut up." I leaned against the headrest. Gabe had left yesterday afternoon and I'd been able to busy myself with last-minute packing and getting him off to the airport. I'd even managed to put the perky little barista out of my mind and convince myself nothing would come of our little run-in. There hadn't been any media out front today, prompting this early morning trip. For all I knew, they'd be back in the afternoon, so I had to take my moments where I could.

The clock on my dashboard blinked eight and I swung the door open. The parking lot was virtually deserted, save a few cars tucked far away from the entrance, likely belonging to the employees.

I pulled the collar of my coat tightly around my neck as I hurried toward the sliding automatic doors. The only inhabitants were employees, quietly stocking shelves, wiping down stations, arranging displays. I kept my eyes shrouded behind the dark lenses of my sunglasses as I grabbed a cart, keeping my head down to discourage cheery good mornings or queries about whether I needed help. I loaded up on the essentials: cleaning supplies, barrels of laundry detergent, paper towels, toilet paper, a scrub brush for the bathroom, boxes of Kleenex. There were no shoppers to clog the aisles and only one employee offered a bored, "Good morning."

I tossed a four-pack stack of Tupperware into the basket and rounded the corner of the next aisle, coming to a dead stop when I saw Detective Travis.

I backed out of the aisle, heart booming. I peered around an endcap display, curious about what he was buying.

Knives. He was looking at knives.

"Oh. Did you forget that little detail, Jillian?"

I *had* forgotten that not-so-little detail.

The damned knife I'd pulled from the knife block in my own kitchen the night I'd slit that slut's throat. The one I used to frame Charles for her murder. The one Charles was caught with the night he was arrested.

Detective Travis picked up a box and turned it over in his hands, mumbling to himself. He repeated the action a few more times. I was certain something was bothering him about the knives and he couldn't put his finger on it.

But it would come to him. It might be today, it might be tomorrow, it might be next month, but something would tickle the back of his brain about the knife used to kill Charles's tramp, the one that should have come from her kitchen, not mine. He'd obtain a search warrant, come barreling through my door and straight to my kitchen so he could compare the knives, bursting in with his "Ah ha!" Sherlock moment. Still needing me to provide the rest of the puzzle pieces.

Which would lead to the questions. The long string of questions as he attempted to crack me.

I couldn't let that happen.

I had to get rid of the knife block. Now.

I swung my cart in the direction of the registers, my vision going blurry for a second. I looked over my shoulder to ensure he hadn't snuck up behind me.

"Mrs. Morgan?"

I gasped and stopped short. He'd turned down the main aisle at the same time. Our carts were mere seconds from colliding.

"What are you doing here?" I asked.

Despite the early hour, he looked as elegant as always, though his normally smooth cheekbones and chin sprouted what looked to be overnight stubble and his eyes drooped with red fatigue. He looked down at his cart, filled with its own hodgepodge of odds and ends. "Same as you," he said.

"Well, what I meant was—"

"You wanted to know if I was following you."

I clicked my tongue against my teeth. "Aren't you?"

"Mrs. Morgan, trust me, if I was following you, you'd never know it."

I narrowed my eyes, contemplating if I should respond.

"My mother lives in Northfield," he said, beating me to the punch. "I was sitting with her and she needs a few things before I head home for the night." He scoffed to himself. "Morning."

"Sitting with her?"

"She's recovering from pneumonia. My sisters and I have been taking overnight shifts for the last few weeks until she gets back on her feet, since she keeps firing the private nurses."

The mystery of Detective Travis deepened. A mother in Northfield who could afford private nurses. I was more convinced than ever family money allowed him to strut around in $1,200 suits with custom-made shirts, luxe handkerchiefs, and shiny Italian loafers.

"Well," I said, not sure what else I was supposed to say. The red plastic handle of my cart was sweaty beneath my twitchy palm. "Mothers can be tricky to deal with. Especially sick ones."

"You got that right."

"Yes." I gulped and flicked my eyes toward the front of the store. "Well. I must be on my way. Good day, Detective."

"Actually, Mrs. Morgan, there was something," he said to my retreating back.

Oh, God. I turned around. "Yes?"

He reached into his cart and extracted the box containing a knife block. "Would you buy these?"

My heart stopped. I let a mask of impassiveness slide over my face. "Excuse me?"

"All this other stuff is for my mother, but my girlfriend wanted me to pick up a new knife block and I was wondering if you think this is a good brand."

Was he trying to set a trap for me? Fishing with a hook and no bait? Was he actually toying with *me*? Of all people?

"I'm sure your girlfriend will find them to be satisfactory. If not ... well, that's what receipts are for."

"Good point."

Customers began to stroll down the aisle with their carts, perusing the shelves.

"I really must be going, Detective Travis." I looked down at his cart. "Happy shopping."

"You too, Mrs. Morgan," he said as I turned on my heel as calmly as I could, my heart in freefall.

I couldn't let him see my knives.

"One more thing you screwed up, Jillian. When will you learn?"

I resisted the urge to twist around in search of Travis. I pulled my cart into an empty lane and unloaded it, blood pounding in my ears as I scoured my brain for how to dispose of that knife block.

Mara Sullivan popped in my head. We'd served on a gala board last year and she'd mentioned having to get rid of her knives. The thrift shop. She took them to the thrift shop. No, no, no that wouldn't work. Even if I left them there anonymously, they'd still exist. They'd still be traceable.

I would have to destroy them.

"How?"

"Excuse me, ma'am?" the cashier asked.

"What?"

"I thought you said something."

"Oh." I cleared my throat, embarrassed I'd spoken aloud. This was happening far too frequently.

"Losing it, Jillian?"

I quashed Charles's voice as I fumbled in my purse for my wallet, extracting my credit card, my hand shaking as I handed it to her. She tapped the black box between us.

"You actually pay—"

"Yes, right, of course," I said as I shoved one piece of plastic into another, the blood swelling in my ears with each passing second.

The next lane over, Travis joined the line, unloading his cart. I looked away so he wouldn't see me watching him, busying myself with signing inside the little box, gathering my receipt, and maneuvering my cart out to the main aisle.

"Have a good day, Mrs. Morgan," he called out as I passed him, my gaze glued to my open purse.

I stopped and offered him a fake smile. "Thank you."

By the time I reached my car, I was hyperventilating. Seconds away from a full-blown panic attack. As I loaded the trunk, I forced myself not to look at the entrance, to go on about my day as though my insides weren't on the verge of exploding.

I slid behind the wheel, my body soaked with sweat. In the rearview, I saw Travis exit the store. My foot itched to punch the accelerator, to get away from him as soon as I could.

But he was watching me. I knew he was. He might even follow me home.

"*Mrs. Morgan, trust me, if I was following you, you'd never know it.*"

He wouldn't even need to follow me. He could easily sit vigil in front of my house all day and night.

Fortunately, the media had not returned. I pulled into my garage, having taken to parking there since my unfortunate late-night encounter with Vanessa's thug, and took a quick glance over my shoulder before closing the door. The street was quiet. I lined my cloth shopping bags along both arms, wanting to make one trip. Once inside, I ran into the kitchen, forgoing my customary neat arrangements, instead throwing the food into the freezer and refrigerator, leaving the non-perishables to fend for themselves on the kitchen counter for the time being.

I snatched up the knife block and hauled it over to the kitchen sink, where I dumped the knives, the clatter of metal on metal causing me to jump back. I ran into the living room, the wood of the knife block damp beneath my hands and yanked the metal screen of the fireplace open, flinging it aside, not caring if it dinged or scratched the wooden floors or cast soot everywhere.

Sweat sluiced down my back as I traded the stumpy logs inside for the knife block. I scrambled for the matches, struggling to get the long, skinny stick to light. Finally, on the fourth try, the flame exploded for a second before dying down. I threw it into the fireplace, watching as flames ate into the knife block. For good measure, I tossed one more lit match into the fireplace, watching the hunk of wood slowly disintegrate before I bolted back into the kitchen. I grabbed a black garbage bag from the roll under the sink and picked up the knives one by one, the blades clinking softly against each other as they dropped to the bottom of the bag.

I wiped my forehead with the back of my hand as I headed for the garage and the vanity toolbox Charles had kept on one of the metal shelves. In thirty plus years of marriage, I don't think I'd ever seen him so much as hammer a nail. Even that power saw was only around for the landscaper's use a few times a year. Still, he felt it appropriate to keep a set of tools close at hand.

I dragged the toolbox down from the shelf, flipping it open to reveal the hammer right on top. I grabbed it, dropped to my knees, and brought the hammer down on top of the knives, the crack of metal on metal thundering across the garage. Grunts escaped my lips as I banged and banged and banged, salty sweat stinging my eyes, skin, my shoulders and neck burning.

The hammer's handle was soaked with sweat and grime while the formerly smooth black wooden knife handles now lay in splinters. There was minimal damage to the blades, but that was okay. As long as the handles and knives weren't together.

I got to my feet and ran back inside, glancing at the fire, still working to obliterate the knife block. I took a poker and moved the wood around. A burst of fire followed and I watched the orange and purple flames dance and crackle around the decomposing block of wood.

I grabbed my gardening gloves along with another trash bag and ran back into the garage. Sifting through the wreckage of the knives, I separated the blades from the shards of wooden handles, dumping them into the other bag. I triple-knotted the bag with the blades, my breath nothing more than wet, jagged wheezing and brought both inside. I carefully scooped the former knife handles out of the bag and into the fire, which crackled and hissed with each new addition.

What about the blades? What do I do with them? Toss them into an anonymous dumpster? Charles had tried that. It hadn't worked out so well for him. Bury them in my backyard? Yes, all I needed was for my neighbors to spy me randomly digging a hole in my backyard. Travis said he was going home to sleep for a few hours. Now would be the perfect time. Of course, that could have been a ruse, an utterance designed to fool me into doing something stupid, something predictable where he could catch me red-handed. I had to be smarter than him. Trash day. Of course. Tomorrow was trash day. Drop them into the bottom of tomorrow's trash so they could disappear into a landfill, never to be seen again.

I ran to the kitchen and jammed my foot against the pedal of the trashcan, dropping the bag inside. I'd wait until I saw the truck winding its way down the street in the morning before I ran outside, apologetic for neglecting to wheel the can out to the curb the night before.

I stumbled back into the living room and slumped against the edge of the fireplace, the flames heating my back. I would go this afternoon and buy a new set of knives, paying cash. Just another nondescript block of knives. Ones that couldn't be traced to me.

I glanced back at the fire and couldn't help but to wearily chuckle to myself at the irony.

Another fire extinguished.

27

I abhorred small talk.

I excelled at it, of course. The sparkling conversationalist, as at ease talking to the Queen of England as the coat-check girl. The gracious and charismatic hostess who could always be counted on to captivate whatever braggart she'd been subjected to that day. Usually, I could do it in my sleep.

Today though, I wasn't up for it. I had things to do. Namely, launching my salvo against Vanessa. I'd run through my plan last night, and it was solid—airtight. I couldn't wait. The sooner I was done with her, the better.

Instead, I was here, so it would have to wait until tomorrow. Celia —over Charlotte's strenuous objections—had pressed me into this Morgan Family Foundation luncheon to represent Chase and Gabe's interests, of course. "We're family, dear," had been her haughty insistence. I was alternately gawked at and clucked over. It had been a few days since my run-in with Travis and there hadn't been a peep out of him. The media appeared to have moved on, all the more reason Celia thought it was good for me to come. "Hold your head up high, dear. We're a united front. We're Morgans. We're family."

Of course, with family, came the obligations.

This loathsome couple at our table, for example—some nouveau riche nightmare recently moved here from Alabama or some such god-forsaken place, to be closer to their daughter and her newborn son—was typical of the obligations one came to despise in the name of family. I, of course, had the duty of sitting next to the wife—Gloria —and playing nice with her. C.K., my cousin-in-law, was glad-handing the husband, some good old boy who'd amassed his wealth by gobbling up low-rent TV stations across the south and turning them into tabloid news juggernauts, eventually developing lucrative cable networks.

The wife's molasses twang snapped against my ears like broken guitar string as she blathered on about her daughter and grandchild, how much she missed their sprawling plantation and her weekly bingo games. She actually had the temerity to ask if I knew where she could find a game. I couldn't decide if she really thought herself the epitome of high-end fashion or was totally clueless about her cartoonish appearance. With her purple press-on nails, black roots pushing through her bleached blond hair, and woeful 80s Escada knockoff that she or some hack designer had further desecrated with all manner of tacky appliqués, it could have gone either way. Don't get me started on the seersucker suit her husband showed up in. How on earth they'd slipped past the Morgan family gate and wangled an invitation to this soiree was beyond me. The only explanation I could summon was that C.K., never one to turn down an opportunity, was priming this gasbag for some sort of hefty endowment.

"I don't know if I'll ever adjust to the big city. I mean, my *gawd*, it's like living in a tin can. How do you do it?"

She was living in a thirty-room mansion in Glencoe yet was crammed into a tin can.

"What's that, dear?" I asked.

"I'll tell you, if it weren't for that precious little grandbaby, I'd be on the next Amtrak back to Mobile tomorrow—I hate to fly, you know. How do you live in this city?"

"I grew up near Philadelphia, so Chicago wasn't much of an adjustment."

"My goodness ... another big ol' city. I guess you would be used to it then, wouldn't you?" She took a huge gulp of her Manhattan. "Now where near Philadelphia are you from?"

"Bala Cynwyd. The Main Line. My family still lives there, but for me, Winnetka is home."

"The Main Line." Her eyes lit up. "Wait a minute. Grace Kelly was from there, isn't that right? Oh, she is just my absolute favorite."

"Yes. As it happens, I'm an extremely distant relation on my mother's side."

"My goodness," she said, her eyes growing wide. "It's like sitting next to a real-life movie star."

"Well, sort of," I said, twisting my lips into a tight bow.

She glanced over her shoulder before leaning down conspiratorially. "To tell you the truth, I've been waiting for the right moment to ask you this, but ... aren't you the woman who just killed her husband? Shot him? And he was having an affair and was arrested for killing his girlfriend?"

I had to hand it to Good Ol' Gloria. She went right for the jugular.

"Why, yes. That is me." I laid a soft hand on her arm. "If you'll excuse me, I must run to the ladies' room to polish my pistol."

Her face burned crimson as I rose from my seat with as much civilized indignation as seemed appropriate for the occasion and escaped to the restroom. I smoothed back a few loose strands of hair, my hand on the door to push it open.

"Hello, Jillian."

I froze, my heartbeat accelerating a little. It appeared we'd be getting this show on the road today after all.

I did a slow turn. Vanessa, clad in gold-mesh Louboutins and a bright red shift dress, ruffles rimming the long sleeves, standing in the hallway of The Drake. Grinning. Hand on one hip. Chest stuck out.

Mentally undressing me, no doubt. I took a deep breath and squared my shoulders.

Curtain up. Act One, Scene One.

"Vanessa," I said. "What a surprise."

"I was at a luncheon for women's heart health over in the Gold Coast Room," she said as she sauntered over to stand directly in front of me. "I happened to see on the marquee the Morgan Family Foundation was also having a luncheon. Thought I'd drop by, hoping to find you here." She smiled. "And here you are."

"Yes," I said as I pushed the door of the ladies' room open. She followed right behind me. We had the facilities to ourselves. "I'm here for Chase and Gabe," I said. "They now share Charles's seat on the Foundation's board of directors."

"You know, Jillian, I'm sure you've heard this before, but you are such a good mother. Really. So attentive to your boys and their needs. I'm sure you'd do anything to protect them."

Ah, yes. Invoke my sons in a thinly veiled threat. She didn't even try to pretend.

"Any mother would do anything to protect their children," I said. "I'm no different."

"I've been waiting for your call."

"As a matter of fact, I planned to call you tomorrow."

She folded her arms across her chest. "That so?"

"I would have done it today, except for this luncheon—"

"I'm starting to think you've been avoiding me."

"Not at all."

"So, what's your answer?"

"Well, I—"

"Before you say anything, I'd like to share something with you." She picked up her purse from the counter and extracted her phone. She swiped and tapped before holding it up.

"Dr. Shayne, this is Detective Dorian Travis of the CPD returning your call. Sorry I missed you, but please call me back at—"

"Shut it off," I whispered.

She smiled and complied. "What do you think? Should I call him back? Tell him what I know? Show him what I have?"

Oh, yes. She deserved everything that was coming to her.

I gulped. "Please. Don't do that."

"I thought I'd made my expectations clear," she said. "I have to say, I'm surprised at you. I thought you were smarter than this."

You have no idea. But you're about to learn.

I glanced over my shoulder and—on purpose—fiddled with the buttons of my suit. Let her think she was getting under my skin, making me nervous.

"Expectations," I whispered. "That's just it. I've never done this before. I'm not sure what to expect."

"Oh, Jillian." Her face softened as she tilted her head. "There's nothing to be afraid of. It'll be like falling off a log."

I looked down sheepishly, warming to my role. "That's what I was trying to explain to you. It's not that I was avoiding you. I've just been trying to figure out how this all works. It's quite new to me."

"I should have been more sensitive." She chuckled. "I guess my excitement got the best of me."

"I didn't want to admit this to you during our lunch, but there was someone I thought about once. In college. It was before I met Charles. It never went anywhere, nothing ever happened." I fingered my bracelet. "I think some part of me has always wondered though..."

She grinned. "Then think of this as coming full circle."

"You caught me off guard and I didn't know how to respond." I reached out and touched her forearm, letting a finger trail ever so slightly across the mist of reddish blond hairs. *That ought to get her going.* "I hope you'll keep that in mind and be patient with me as we ... navigate this."

"Oh, Jillian." She bit her bottom lip, her eyes drowsy slits. "You don't have to worry about a thing. I'll be with you every step of the way."

"Thank you for that," I said, a gush of relieved laughter spilling from my lips. "I can't tell you how much that means."

"So, when should we have our first date?"

"Is that how it works?" I asked shyly. "A date?"

"We'll start with something simple. Dinner. Tonight?"

"I can't tonight. Would Saturday work?"

"Saturday it is. What kind of food do you like?" She smiled. "Other than spinach salads?"

I laughed and she joined in. Oh, the comedy of it all. "Why don't you pick someplace? Someplace fun. Something different."

She tapped her finger against her chin and smiled. "I know just the place. I'll text it to you."

"I'll look forward to it."

"Wonderful. Even though it's only a few days, Saturday seems so far away." She ran her tongue across her bottom lip. "I'm so excited to see where the night takes us."

I picked up my purse from the counter. "I should get going. Celia will wonder if I fell in."

"Can't let Celia think that, can we?"

I chuckled sheepishly as we exited. "No, never that. I guess I'll see you Saturday night."

"Until Saturday."

She turned to sashay down the hall, then peered over her shoulder to throw me a flirtatious little wave. I smiled and waved back.

And ... scene.

28

THE SWISH AND grind of the Reformer drummed against my ears, shutting out the soft grunts and whimpers around me. Teardrops of sweat wobbled and dripped like rain to the glossy wood floor, the handles of the machine slippery in my palms. My thighs burned. My arms strained in their sockets and my toes threatened to cramp from the precision points they'd been in for the last eighty-seven minutes. My breath, heavy and wet, rumbled in my chest as my arms flew above my head before floating back to my sides in a long, graceful wingspan. My legs quivered above the padded bar as I pushed myself up then down. Up. Down. Up. Down.

"All right, everyone, that's time," the instructor called out, her own pale skin flushed red.

I came to a stop, releasing the handles of the machine and letting my eyes drift shut for a moment, listening to the deep echo of my breath, my ears ringing from a grueling ninety minutes of pure, raw labor. Footsteps padded away from me, accompanied by the soft, stunned murmurs of my classmates hobbling to the locker room for long steamy showers.

I took a deep breath and hoisted myself up in one swift motion, ignoring the throbs and stings of my own joints and tendons and muscles. I grabbed the stiff white cotton rectangle management claimed was a towel and mopped my face as I shuffled into the locker room to retrieve my belongings. My nose wrinkled involuntarily at the sight of all these women brazenly parading their nudity around the room before they ambled into the showers. I'd never been one for public showering. Public restrooms were enough of a chore. Flashing my nakedness in front of a cast of thousands had never been part of my wiring.

I splashed some cool water on my face from the sink in the locker room and slung my bag and purse over my shoulder before slipping out to my car. It was early, just past eleven. I would shower in my own bathroom.

Except I didn't quite feel like rushing home. I had no errands to run. No dry cleaning to drop off or pick up. No library books to return. No children to cluck over.

No husband to spar with.

I headed north on Green Bay Road back to Winnetka, deciding to linger over tea and something sweet at the little café downtown. I would read my book, while away the time, appreciative of any little respite I could get before subjecting myself to Vanessa in a few days.

I parked on the street, feeding my credit card to the meter before shuffling toward the café three short blocks away. It was quiet as usual this time of day. Of course, this little quad had grown ever more silent over the years, patrons sucked away by behemoth malls and nearby bustling shopping corridors brimming with trendy boutiques.

I'd never forget the first summer I came to visit Charles at Fairmore, a manse that rivaled my own childhood home. He wanted to show me off to his parents, see if I could pass the Charlotte test, which I did with flying colors. No surprise, I'd charmed everyone, since charm had been pumped into my veins at conception. One afternoon, he'd brought me to Winnetka for ice cream from his favorite shop and a stroll through downtown's quaint cobblestones. As I licked a vanilla cone that blistering summer day, I fell in love with this little hamlet. I told Charles this was where I wanted to raise our family, build our life together. He'd turned his nose up at the idea, lobbying instead for a condo in the city or setting down stakes somewhere else altogether. I couldn't be swayed and I got my way. As if there could have been any other outcome.

The bell over the door tinkled as I entered the tiny café. The whir of machines cranking out rich, pungent coffee filled the small room. There weren't many people. A mother in one corner feeding shards of chocolate chip cookie and something out of a pink and green sippy cup to what I presumed was her curly-headed child captive inside the mammoth stroller parked next to their table. Two elderly women chattered to each other in between sips from gargantuan cups of coffee. A young woman tapped the keys of her laptop, hot pink earplugs snaking out of her ears.

I ordered a green tea and scone. The morning Pilates session would burn up whatever I was about to consume. I settled into a table near the young mother and child and pulled out my book, surprised at the quicksand of the story, as the opening pages hadn't been all that impressive to me when I'd started it the other night.

The bell over the door chimed. I looked up.

My stalker.

Nostrils flaring.

Eyes bulging.

Veins bursting.

Storming straight toward me.

Just like I wanted.

29

It had been a Tuesday morning.

I went out my back door, locking it behind me before stealthily walking through the backyard to the fence. I unlatched it, taking care to lock it as well before passing by the Finches' backyard. Amelia Finch saw me through her kitchen window and offered a tentative wave. I returned the gesture.

It was a cold, sunny day, similar to the day Vanessa's hooligan had chased me. It was the exact same time. In fact, I'd been coming out at the exact same time for the past week.

Watching.

Waiting.

He'd been curiously quiet.

That wasn't likely to last.

Whatever Vanessa was paying him, I'd double it, triple it. That should buy some cooperation. At the very least some peace of mind.

I headed toward the beach, my eyes darting everywhere, searching for his coat, his smirk, his girth. All I saw were the same elderly couples and lone joggers pounding down the beach in search of what, I wasn't sure. I hated jogging.

My breath billowed out in front of me as I continued down the path, my tennis shoes crunching into the twigs and rocks embedded in the sand. I glanced at my watch. Nine thirty.

Still curiously quiet.

Defeated, I turned around to make my trek home, putting my head down for a second.

Which is all it took.

When I looked up, there he was. Standing on my corner.

Watching.

I took a deep breath.

Finally.

I stopped short and looked around. Our little street was quiet as usual this time of morning.

No witnesses.

He made his way toward me, his grin evident, his fists two determined balls at the end of his arms, swinging with purpose.

"Who are you?" I called out as I shifted my feet a little and swiveled my head around as though I was looking for someone to come and save me. Let him think I was scared. I pursed my lips. "What do you want?"

He didn't answer. He was no more than a few feet away. The zipper of his coat was undone, the droop of his stomach flopping out of the black sweater studded with pills and over the waistband of his faded black pants. He reeked of sulfur and burnt coffee. I backed away a little and he laughed.

"Oh, you scared, huh?" he sneered.

"You're the one who followed me home, aren't you? Nearly ran me off the road?"

"I almost had you, too. I was about to break down the door to your house, but changed my mind."

"And New Year's Eve? That was you, too?"

He grinned. "Sure was."

I straightened up. Time to cut the pleasantries.

"How much is Vanessa paying you?"

He frowned. "Who?"

"Vanessa Shayne. She's the one paying you, right? To terrorize me, follow me?"

"I don't know what you talking about. I don't know no Vanessa."

I blanched with surprise and raised my eyebrow, intrigued, a little scared. So, he wasn't tangled up with Vanessa the Vile after all. There was some accounting for taste.

Then who the hell are you?

"You got something that don't belong to you," he said, as though he'd read my mind. "I need you to give it to me."

I narrowed my eyes. "What is it you think I have?"

"I want the box."

The wind had sailed out of me. The box. That stupid puzzle box. Like a goddamned bad penny.

30

I JUMPED UP, the book sliding from my hand and thudding to the floor. The two elderly women murmured to themselves, pointing. The mother clumsily maneuvered her monstrous stroller toward the door, preparing to escape.

"You can't get away from me now," he hissed, his breath ripe with rotten eggs, his skin blanketed in the stench of burnt coffee and sulfur. "I got you. I got you. You got nowhere to go."

It's exactly where I want to be.

"What do you want?" I whispered, waving my hand behind me in search of something to land on, something to break a potential fall as I edged away from him.

He didn't speak, lunging for me instead. I screamed and dodged his grasp. The café manager came running from behind the counter.

"Sir, I'm gonna have to ask you to leave—"

He turned and shoved the manager, sending the hapless young man plummeting to the black and white checked tile below. The quiet little café erupted in a clatter of dishes and screams. Another employee ran from behind the counter to assist her fallen colleague. I looked down at my tea.

His head whipped around toward me.

I flung the liquid in his face and he screamed, clutching at his cheeks. I grabbed my things and bolted past him, running out the door to the nearly empty street. I tripped but managed to keep upright, jerking only momentarily. I stole a glance over my shoulder in time to see him barrel out of the café and head straight for me.

I grappled with my purse, grasping for my keys, cursing as they slithered out of my hand and fell to the ground. I didn't have any time to waste, as I'd timed all of this down to the second. I couldn't afford for this not to happen today. I bent down to retrieve the keys and there he was, hovering over me. There was no time to get tangled up with him.

The bus would be coming soon.

I sobbed and got up, turning to make a run for it. But he was quick, grabbing the collar of my coat and pulling me toward him, his breath hot and putrid in my face.

"Where is it?" he hissed, shaking me. "Brought me all the way up here, told me you had the box and you ain't got shit."

My heart raced and I whimpered against his assault. We were on the sidewalk in front of the bank where Charles took the boys to open their first savings accounts, mere steps from the street. In my original incarnation of this plan, at this exact moment, I should have been sprinting across that street to my car, him close behind. I glanced up at the bank's clock.

Except he had me in his grip.

And the bus was late.

I would need to stall.

"Listen," I said, looking back at him, licking my lips. "This has all been a big misunderstanding. If you'll just give me some more time—"

"You ain't got no more time," he said, his face inching closer to me. "Now, we about to go back to your house and tear it apart until I find it, you hear me?"

The whine and sigh of the bus heading toward us triggered a

flood of relief. I glanced over to my right to see it lumbering down the street and I tamped down the urge to smile.

Finally.

"You hear this, *Neil*," I said. "You should have left well enough alone."

He tightened his grip on my coat, his jaw dropping open to spew more menace. I took one more look toward the bus.

It was time to take my shot.

In quick succession, I jammed the point of my car key into his cheek three times. Blood trickled from the gaping spigot. He screamed and crumpled away from me, yelping, grasping his cheek, his free arm flailing. I backed away before turning to run.

"Bitch! Come back here!"

I ran into the street, a car swerving to avoid me. I was steps from making it to the sidewalk on the other side. I whipped my head around as he staggered to his feet, stumbling forward then back.

He darted into the street, blood mottling his cheek. He was so focused on catching me, he seemingly ignored the screams of warning, though the insistent bleating of the oncoming bus's horn did catch his attention.

However, like the impatient driver who thinks he can outsmart the coming train, he'd sorely miscalculated.

31

I BLINKED. "Box? I don't know what you're talking about. What box?"

"I know he took it when he killed Tamra. I need it back. Her mama wants it back. It's been in her family a long time. They don't even make them anymore. She just wants it back."

"Oh." I fell quiet, the enormity of this situation, this powder keg, sinking into me. "That's how you knew my husband. Through ... her."

"Her name is Tamra. Not 'her,' not 'she.' Tamra. And I loved her. I loved her and I wanted to marry her, spend the rest of my life with her."

I shook my head. "I still don't know—?"

"Me and her was together." He plowed on, lost in his memories of his dear departed tramp. "And it was good. We was in love and everything was all good. Then that motherfucker, that prick, had to go and show up, using her, lying to her. Ruined everything."

My eyes flicked involuntarily up and down at this rancid blob of a man. The slut had certainly traded up with Charles. I couldn't imagine tethering myself to this hulking lump of dough for any length of time, much less life.

"Maybe if you'd done your job, he might not have been playing Tamra." He sneered. "He would have been home with you. He wouldn't have killed her—"

"I'm not responsible for whatever my husband—you can't blame me—"

"Bitch, I do blame you. It's all your fault, all his fault. If Tamra had never met him, had never—if he hadn't taken that box from her, from her mama—"

"I don't know what you're talking about," I said, my voice full of pleading, desperate—and okay, fake—tears. "I don't know about any box of my husband's—"

"It's not his box!" he yelled, grabbing my wrist. "It don't belong to him. He took it, and Tamra's mama wants it back."

I jerked to get away from him, but his grip was strong.

That goddamned box.

"Look, I don't know what you're talking about, but if you don't get away from me right now, I will scream," I hissed. "I will scream at the top of my lungs and I'll bring everyone out of their house and in this neighborhood—"

He laughed. "You threatening me? Huh? Huh?"

"No, I'm not." I took a deep breath to steady myself. "It's just that you're scaring me and I don't know what I'm saying."

"I bet you would do something like that. Scream and cry. Send all them neighbors or whatever running into the streets." He scoffed. "Probably tell people I tried to rape you or something, try to get me lynched or some bullshit. I bet you'd do it, too. I bet that's exactly what you'd try to do."

"I already apologized—"

"You killed your husband because of Tamra, didn't you? Huh? He was fucking her and you didn't like it." He sniffed. "I didn't like it either. He used her up like she was some kind of old tissue or something. She was good, you hear me? Way too good for him. She was a good person. Sweet and nice. He wasn't nothing. He was garbage."

"Please," I whimpered, twisting away from him. "Please let me go."

"He thought he could get away with it. But you fixed that, didn't you? You got back at him, didn't you?"

"What happened with my husband was an accident and that's all I'm going to say about it."

"I don't give a fuck what happened. I hope he's burning in hell. I should give you a medal. Throw you a damn parade."

"Listen, sir, please, I don't know what box you're talking about, I swear. But—"

"But what?"

I needed to buy myself some time, figure out how to keep this bomb from detonating.

I gulped. "Give me a chance to see if I can find it. I haven't gone through my husband's things yet, so maybe it is in the house and I just haven't seen it."

He narrowed his eyes at me, like he was trying to decide if he could trust me. "You mean you haven't seen it?"

"What does it look like? Is it a music box, a wood box, metal?"

He loosened his grip on my wrist and his eyes softened. "Her mama said it's black with like some gold or something on it. A puzzle box. She was looking for it when she cleaned up Tamra's apartment and couldn't find it. Police say they didn't have it. Your husband's the only one who could."

"A puzzle box. A black puzzle box with gold. Okay. Can you give me a little bit of time to look for it? Please."

He looked me up and down, his eyes narrowing. "You got one week."

I pulled my phone out of my jacket pocket. "If you would give me your phone number, I'll call you and let you know if I find it."

"Yeah, all right," he said, spitting out the ten digits as I rapidly punched the numbers into my phone along with his name.

"I'll call you," I said. "I promise."

"You don't call me, I'm gonna be back," he said. "Count on that."

I could only nod as I backed away. He didn't say anything as I headed toward my house, feeling his eyes burn into my back, resisting the urge to turn around. I didn't hear his footsteps pound behind me, didn't feel his breath on my neck.

I dug the house keys out of my pocket as I calmly walked up the driveway, even though inside I was alternately fuming and terrified. Out of the corner of my eye, he moved closer to me, but never broke his smooth stride. I unlocked the front door and closed it carefully behind me, working to keep my breath steady before walking over to the window facing the street. I pursed my lips and took several breaths, moving my head slightly until my eyeball was just this side of the drape. He couldn't see me, but I could see him, continuing to stroll down the street toward his car, whistling to himself now. Mission accomplished. He finally got into a tiny silver box of a car with an emblem stamped across the bumper. A rideshare of some sort.

I edged back from the window, my mind racing. One week to figure out how to fix this. If his past actions were any indication, he wouldn't give up. He was likely to break in here and tear my house down to the foundation in his futile search, or worse, tip off the police, which would unspool everything.

I could not have that. I could not have the police hauling me in every other day to question me about this box. I could not have them deducing that I'd murdered Tamra, a gateway to figuring out I'd gunned Charles down in cold blood.

I could not have them connecting any dots.

So, I had to do something.

32

THE BUS SMASHED INTO HIM, bending him in half before flinging him into the air, its brakes squealing and whining as it skidded to a stop in the middle of the street. My genuine, terrified screams were lost in the symphony of screams exploding around me.

The commotion brought patrons from the surrounding shops outside, caused drivers to screech to a halt for a closer look, stopped passersby in their tracks. The bus driver ran over to Neil, crouching down for a closer look before yanking his cell phone from his pocket and dialing furiously. Several people rushed to administer aid. If the mangled body was any indication, the only thing that could be done for him now was to drape a sheet over the carnage.

I couldn't say anything. All I could do was stand there, shell-shocked, trembling, and numb.

I'd done it. My plan had actually worked.

How many times over the years had I seen pedestrians rush through that intersection to beat that bus, coming dangerously close to being run over? Too many to count. For years, concerned citizens had lobbied for a stop light or stop sign.

All to no avail.

I'd come to the café after my "summit" with Neil, needing to think, to come up with a plan. It just so happened I saw two girls at two separate times that day narrowly avoid poor Neil's fate.

And there it was. The answer to My Big Fat Problem.

All I needed was to work out the timing of when a city bus with no stop lights or stop signs to impede it would come speeding down the street.

Down to the minute.

The second.

All I needed was an app.

I'd parked my car near that intersection for almost a week straight and timed the bus.

And every day, that bus had come barreling down the street at the exact same time.

Just like clockwork.

From there, it was easy. A well-timed call from a new burner phone purchased with cash to tell him I'd found the box and arranging to meet at the café. Asking the young mother next to me if she would watch my things so I could slip into the restroom to call and tell him there was no box.

He'd be angry as he rushed down the street. Oh, so angry. Seething.

Confrontational.

He'd burst into the café, raging, ready to accost me. I'd escape and he'd chase me into the street and *bam*! My Big Fat Problem solved.

It was a huge risk. So much could have gone wrong. He could have said something to tip the crowd off that we knew each other in some tangible way. The bus could have been (and was) running late. He could have been late. There could have been traffic, weather, mechanical failure.

We both could have been a broken, bloody pile of bodies in the middle of the street.

But I had to take my shot.

And thank God I won.

The driver paced, his cell phone glued to his ear as he shouted at whoever was on the other end that *he came out of nowhere* and *I laid on the horn and tried to stop, but it was too late.* A crowd had gathered around My Big Fat Problem, obscuring my view of his crumpled body, though the blood, fresh and red, continued its insidious swirl into the blacktop. I swallowed, looking away. Even though this was what I wanted—what I'd planned for—it was still gruesome.

The shriek of sirens wailed in the distance and a cavalcade of fire trucks, ambulances, and police cruisers came screaming toward us. A small cluster of looky-loos had gathered around me, as though they were protecting one of their tribe. Someone offered me their water bottle, while someone else kept tugging on my sleeve, commanding me to sit down. An arm snaked around my shoulder and I let it linger there. Frantic fingers pointed in my direction and the eyes of the police officers soon followed. A husky older officer adjusted her glasses and sauntered over to me. I took a deep breath.

Curtain up.

"Ma'am, these witnesses say this man was chasing you. Can you tell us what happened?"

I opened my mouth and no sound came out. I tried again, my jaw cranking, my lips flapping, but try as I might, I could not make the words form. This really was a struggle.

"Ma'am, do you need some more water? Can I call someone, maybe?"

I cleared my throat and tried again. "I—he was following me. He's been following me for weeks. I ran—" I screwed up my face, the memory of that horn sounding in my ear.

"I saw him," the woman standing beside me offered. "I was in the bookstore next door and saw the whole thing. He came storming down the street—" She twisted around to point to where My Big Fat Problem had materialized from. Her words receded as I watched a police officer attempt to speak with the frenzied bus driver still on the phone, the bus passengers peeking out from the windows.

"Ma'am, did you know this man?"

"No," I murmured as I watched the paramedics drape a sheet over the body. "I have no idea who he was."

"No clue why he would have been following you?"

"No."

The officer cracked her gum and shifted her feet. "Did he say anything to you?"

"Just that I couldn't get away from him." I looked away, grappling with my composure.

"What did that mean?"

I shook my head. "I don't know."

"He called her a bitch," the woman next to me said, nodding her head. "He said, 'Bitch, come back here.'"

The officer sighed and adjusted her glasses. "All right, ma'am, I'm gonna need you to come down to the station to make a statement."

33

DETECTIVE TRAVIS FLUNG open the door of the interrogation room and stared at me for a few moments before sitting down at the table across from me. I looked up, surprised to see him as I dabbed at my eyes with my snotty, balled up tissue. There was no need to command the tears to flow.

For a change, they were real.

"Mrs. Morgan," he said, putting a box of Kleenex in front of me. No handkerchiefs dripping in Laundress today. A shift in our relationship.

"What are you doing here?"

"They called me in to talk to you. Since we know each other."

"Oh." I sniffed and pulled a fresh Kleenex from the box. "Where's your partner?"

"On assignment." He flipped open his manila folder, clicking his tongue against the roof of his mouth as he perused the contents. "So, if I'm reading these statements correctly, you were chased out of the Dancer Café on Elm Street in downtown Winnetka by the victim, is that right?"

I nodded. "Yes."

"All right, why don't you start at the beginning and tell me what happened?"

My hands shook. Everything vibrated. I was no longer in control. I wiped the back of my hand across my nose and took a deep breath before reciting my story. Travis's face was impassive as he listened.

"And how did you know this man?" he finally asked.

"I don't." I swallowed. "Didn't. But he's been stalking me for weeks."

Travis leaned forward, nonplussed. "He was what?"

"For the past few weeks, he's been everywhere. My husband's memorial service. Outside my home. I'm almost positive he came to the Ladds' on New Year's Eve, banging on the door. That he followed me home another night, nearly running me off the road."

He thumped the end of his pen against the table. "Did you tell anyone about these incidents?"

"I—I didn't know what to do, where to turn, what to say. I was terrified."

"If you were so scared of him, why didn't you report it?"

"And say what?" I scoffed. "'Detective, there's a strange man following me, he hasn't said anything, hasn't approached me in any way, hasn't done anything at all, but do something about it?'"

His face flickered with the realization I was right. "All right, so you say this man had been following you all this time and today for the first time, he actually approached you?"

"Yes."

Travis tapped his pen against the table again. "Witnesses say when he grabbed you, it looked like he was saying something to you. What did he say?"

I closed my eyes. "That he'd gotten me."

"Go on."

I finished my recitation, unable to stop seeing the images of the body flying through the air, smacking against the pavement. The pool of blood around his head, gushing from his mouth onto the street in a dark and sticky stream. Even though it's what I wanted, it still made my stomach clench like a fist.

"And that's it?" Travis asked, sarcasm and incredulity lacing his words. "The bus hit him, just like that?"

"What, do you think I pushed him?"

"Did you?"

"I told you, I hit him with my car key, he let me go and I ran."

Travis sat there calmly, watching me whimper and wipe my nose. He clicked his tongue against his teeth a few times.

"And you really didn't know who this man was?" he asked quietly.

"I already told you I didn't."

"His name was Neil Yancy."

"Who?"

"Tamra Washington's ex-boyfriend."

I gasped. "What?"

Travis bolted up from his chair and hunched over the table, his gaze trapping me. "What are the odds, Mrs. Morgan, that the ex-boyfriend of your husband's mistress was stalking you and then *bam!*—" He slammed his hands against the table and I jumped, nearly falling out of my chair. A fresh wave of genuine tears flooded my eyes. "Hit by a bus."

"Detective, I told you, I didn't know that man. I don't know why he was following me—"

"I don't believe you."

Travis kicked his chair back, the metal feet scraping across the concrete floor like gears grinding. He came to calmly stand over me, looming like the foulest, darkest of clouds.

"Mrs. Morgan, I think you're lying. I think you lie like people breathe. That's how easily and how often you do it. Now, I don't know what you're lying about today, but I know you're not telling me the truth."

"Detective—"

He leaned closer until he was mere millimeters from my face.

The sounds of our breath, tense and thick, filled the room. "All right," he said, his voice low and calm. "I'm giving you a chance, right here, right now to come clean. Tell me everything about this web you've spun around yourself."

I took a deep breath. I'd come too far. There was no turning back. The show had to go on.

"There's nothing to tell, Detective."

Travis straightened up and sucked in his breath, tapping his middle finger against the table. It echoed around the room. My left thigh burned and I wanted to shift in my seat to relieve the pressure.

I didn't dare make one move.

Our impasse continued. His eyes locked onto mine, him attempting to intimidate me, me lapsing into steel and stone and ice.

"Do you still smoke, Mrs. Morgan?"

I blinked. I didn't mean to. He'd caught me unaware.

Damn.

"I'm trying to quit," I said.

"Still smoking a pack or so a day?"

"Something like that."

He clicked his tongue against the roof of his mouth, like a metronome. "Doesn't sound like you're having much luck. Maybe you should try a program."

Good Lord. *This again?*

"I'm not sure what my unfortunate smoking habit has to do with anything," I said.

He paced for a few moments, rubbing his hand across his chin. "What time did you get home the night your husband was killed?"

"We've been over this—"

"What time did you get home that night, Mrs. Morgan?"

I sighed. "Seven forty-five."

"What did you do when you walked in the door?"

"As I've already told you, I unlocked the door, walked in, heard a noise—"

"Right, you heard a noise, thought it was an intruder and *boom!* Bye, bye cheating husband."

I didn't say anything, instead, taking a deep breath to steady myself and keep from slashing him with my tongue.

"You know, my girlfriend smokes," he said. "Like a chimney."

"Maybe she needs to get into a program," I said.

"Oh, I've tried. Believe me, I've tried. It is one of the filthiest, most disgusting habits in the world."

"I can think of worse."

"I'll just bet you can."

"I suppose we can't all possess your superb willpower, Detective."

"There was one cigarette butt sitting in your ashtray," he said. "In the living room."

I rolled the tip of my tongue around the inside of my mouth, understanding, finally, what he was slowly, ever so slowly getting at.

There was a flaw in my story.

A big one.

"How many cigarettes are in a pack, Mrs. Morgan?"

"I have no idea."

He scoffed. "I doubt that."

"I've never taken the time to count."

"Twenty," he said. "Twenty cigarettes in one pack."

"Now I know."

He opened his fat manila folder and plucked a piece of paper from the top, flicking his eyes over the words and letters and drawings.

"We found three ashtrays in your house. One in your bedroom, one in your den, and one in your living room. Three butts in the master bathroom trash, two in the kitchen. Except the ashtray in the living room. One butt. And fourteen cigarettes in the pack in your purse."

I'd smoked a cigarette while Charles and I sat in our darkened living room, moments before I shot him.

Travis wanted me to know he knew. I'd had time to smoke a cigarette. I couldn't have possibly stumbled upon Charles the Intruder.

Play dumb.

"Your point?"

His eyes narrowed to razor thin slits. "I think you came home, had a nice little conversation with your husband while you smoked a cigarette. Right before you shot him."

Boom.

I matched him razor blade for razor blade as I stared him down, never saying a word. I wouldn't be the first to blink this time.

And I wasn't.

"Okay, Mrs. Morgan," he finally said, sighing. "I just want you to remember you had your chance. And you didn't take it. That's fine. But know this. One way or another, that flimsy little web of yours is going to bust apart like wet tissue."

"I have nothing more to say, Detective. If you need anything else, call my lawyer."

He scoffed.

Slowly, I pushed back from the table, my eyes never leaving his. "Good day, Detective." I stepped around him, slinging my purse and bag over my shoulder. I tossed my hair for good measure as I crossed the room and opened the door of the interrogation room. I ignored the dissonance of ringing phones, grumbling voices, and pinging e-mails as I marched out of the station.

I skidded into the garage and rushed into the house, slamming the door behind me. I slumped against it, my heart racing, the blood pounding against my ears. My mouth was cotton and I needed water desperately. Except, I didn't exactly trust myself to move to the kitchen, for it was possible I could collapse into a puddle of sweat, exhaustion, and fear.

The jelly of my knees threatened to drop me to the floor as I took one tentative step toward the kitchen then another until I was grabbing the water pitcher from the refrigerator. I took a glass from the cabinet, gripping it so hard, I feared it would shatter in my hand. When I put the glass down, it shook against the countertop. The water I poured sloshed out of the glass, forming puddles across the granite. I finally managed to get enough water into the glass and inhaled it in two mighty gulps, repeating this countless times until my thirst was finally quenched.

I closed my eyes, seeing his body fly through the air, hearing it slap the pavement, the squeal of the tires, the smell of bus exhaust and burning rubber curling into my nose.

The images continued to play on a loop as I staggered up the stairs toward the bathroom, stripping off my clothes with trembling fingers and pushing them to the bottom of my trashcan. I stood in front of the bathroom mirror, a naked, shivering mess before turning on the shower, twirling the hot water faucet until it could twirl no more. I stepped inside, grabbing my soap and loofah and scrubbing my skin red as the steam engulfed me. My fingers slid against the slippery shower tiles as I coughed. I knew I should get out, that I was minutes, possibly seconds away from inflicting real damage, visions of skin melting from my bones swirling through my head.

I couldn't see anything. Steam dripped from every pore. It crawled down my throat, choking me. I yanked open the shower door and tumbled to the ground, my body wracked with coughs, a tsunami of cool air flooding my skin. I lay there on the floor of my bathroom, not having the energy to reach up and turn off the water.

And all because of a box.

34

LOOKING FORWARD TO TOMORROW NIGHT! XOXO

I rolled my eyes at Vanessa's cheery text message. She knew what had happened, calling me to extend her manufactured concern, but not once offering to let me off the hook from this "date" we were to have. It was just as well. Better to deal with her now than later.

I looked toward the front window for the twentieth time in as many seconds. I picked up the remote, turning the already barely imperceptible volume on the TV to practically mute. I stood up and edged over to the window, trying to convince myself yet again the flickering shadows weren't Detectives Potts and Travis lurking in the bushes outside, ready to slap handcuffs around my wrists. It had been three days since Neil Yancy had met his untimely end. Three long days of ears peeled for sirens, of breath held every time the phone rang, or the rare times the doorbell chimed. Joss assured me there was no crime against being in the wrong place at the wrong time, so there wasn't anything the police could do to me. The media had reappeared briefly on my doorstep, but dissipated quickly due to the emergence of a local political scandal.

Gabe had called. Chase had not.

Sweat prickled across my palms and I itched for a cigarette. I'd run out this afternoon and though it was only eight p.m., I was too afraid to go out for a carton.

It would have to wait.

I pursed my lips and marched around the house for the two hundredth time that night to check that all the windows were locked, drapes drawn, doors locked.

Sealed in tight.

I paced a few more times across the living room, the attempt at television viewing all but abandoned. A glass of wine would have settled me down, but I felt as though I needed to be sharp, on high alert.

The branch scraped across the roof and I gasped. It took a few moments for my breathing to return to normal. Perhaps I'd call the landscaper tomorrow to come out and cut the branch.

My phone chirped from the coffee table. I peered over at it, hoping it wasn't Celia again with another invitation to something. Last week, she'd tried to press me into a gala of some sort next month. Yet something else to put me on high-profile display, the last thing I needed or wanted. I hadn't figured a way out of it just yet, but I would.

I perched on the edge of the couch, watching the phone ring, feeling no compunction to answer. It wasn't Celia, but that reporter again. Isabella something.

Within minutes, the voicemail indicator flashed and I hit play.

"Hi, Jillian, this is Isabella Lombard calling again. As I've mentioned in my previous messages, I'm working on a book about you and your husband. I'd love the opportunity to sit down with you so you can tell me your side of the story. This is your chance to let people know your thoughts and feelings about your husband and what happened. Please give me a call at—"

I hit delete before she could offer me her phone number. The fifth time she'd called. I stuffed myself into a ball in a corner of the couch, the TV still whispering in the background.

When the phone rang again, I jumped, nearly toppling off the couch.

Chase.

I pounced on the phone. "Hello? Hello? Chase?"

"Hi, Mom."

Tears pricked my eyes. "Oh, sweetheart. It's so good to hear your voice."

"Gabe told me what happened. About the guy."

I dabbed at my eyes with a Kleenex. "Yes. It was horrible."

"What happened?"

"He—well, he'd been following me, stalking me and he was unhinged really. He came flying into the café, yelling and screaming and all I could think about was getting away from him. I was running to my car and..."

Chase was quiet for a moment. "Are you okay?" he finally asked.

"I'm okay, just shaken up." I paused. "I'm glad you called."

"How's everything else going?"

"Chase, I want to apologize—"

"It's not necessary."

"Sweetheart, please ... I want you to know how terribly, terribly sorry I am for losing control that day and hitting you and for everything. You have to know how horrible I've felt ever since."

He let out what sounded to be a brooding sigh. "I appreciate you saying that."

I couldn't stop the tears. "Oh, Chase, I love you so much. You and Gabe ... you're all I have left."

"It's okay, Mom."

I blew my nose and straightened up. "So, how are you getting on at school? How's this last semester been?"

"It's all right. I'm clerking for a local firm and it's going well. Things are going pretty good with Jacqueline, so..."

"I'm so happy to hear that," I said. "I really like her. You're good together."

"Yeah." He sighed. "Listen, Mom, I've got to go. I just wanted to check in on you."

I nodded, even though I knew he couldn't see me. "I can't tell you how much it means."

"Yeah. I'll call you soon. Maybe next week."

"I'd like that," I whispered.

We said our goodbyes and ended the call. I sat on the couch sobbing for a good half hour, prostrate with love, grief, relief, sorrow, happiness. It was as though I'd been cracked open and everything I'd been holding in for all these months—years, most likely—gushed out in an unyielding torrent.

My phone beeped with another text message from Vanessa. I'd take care of her tomorrow. I stumbled toward one of the built-in bookshelves and took down a photo of Chase from Thanksgiving and fell asleep on the couch, clutching it to me.

35

I CUT the engine to my car, staring up at the restaurant Vanessa had chosen for what she was calling our first outing. An outing. As though we were getting together for milkshakes, hamburgers, and Frankie Valli on the jukebox. And conveniently located near her house. Vanessa was nothing if not strategic when it came to making her point. Even if she did use a sledgehammer.

It was the first time I'd been out since the Neil Yancy incident. I was feeling calmer, back in control.

More importantly, it was time to continue the show.

I pulled my compact from my purse and ran a swipe of powder against my nose before I exited the car. I smoothed down the front of my black wool coat, hiding my standard skinny black pants and white turtleneck underneath. I took several deep breaths to calm my rattled nerves. I searched the bar for Vanessa, scanning the room for her red hair. True to form, she was late, which was fine. It gave me some time to be alone, prepare for my performance as it were.

I ordered a Sauvignon Blanc, drinking it slowly. The place wasn't a dive, surprisingly, though it wasn't anything I would have chosen, to be sure. Just your basic neighborhood burger-fries-and-beer establishment with flat screen TVs, a dartboard in the back, a bevy of regulars, and assorted tacky paraphernalia lining the brick walls. I flicked my eyes around the bar, taking note of the greasy sixty-something man all but licking the lollipop of the twenty-something girl draped across him, enormous jugs of silicone planted atop her stick of a body, her long, straight black hair retreating into intermittent tangles. Neither of them showed any shame. There was another young girl nervously checking the door every few seconds. Blind date. Or an old date whose heart she planned to break, the fragments of her well-rehearsed speech in danger of disintegrating inside her enormous glass of red wine. Another grizzled gentleman occupied a stool in the corner, hunched over his beer and a newspaper. A regular.

The door swung open and Vanessa slithered in. She smiled when she saw me, waving merrily as she sauntered over.

Curtain up. Act Two, Scene One.

"I hope you haven't been waiting long," she breathed as she slid out of her coat.

"No, not long."

"Oh, good." She looked me up and down as she took the barstool next to me and I had to bite back the acidic barb sitting on my tongue. "You look lovely."

"Thank you." I took a sip of my wine. "I love your outfit."

"Really?" She smoothed down the front of the flouncy pink print blouse that looked to be a Carolina Herrera and skinny black pants similar to mine, an ensemble I actually approved of. "I'm glad you like it."

"Yes, it's very becoming."

Her cheeks flamed crimson and she picked up the water the bartender had just set down in front of her, taking a greedy slurp, all while trying to hide her smile. She cleared her throat and placed the half-empty glass on the bar before looking up at me through fluttery lashes.

"Have you recovered after that awful accident?" she asked.

"I'm doing much better, thank you for asking."

"How horrific." She shuddered. "I can't imagine having something like that happen in front of you. Still, selfishly, I'm glad you were up to meeting me tonight."

I fingered my collar, smiling sheepishly. "I've actually been looking forward to tonight."

A huge smile spread across her face. "Really?"

I returned her smile. "Yes, really."

She plunked her chin in her hand, her green eyes laser focused on me, a gooey look on her face. "You know, there's something else I wanted to say to you. Well, ask you, really."

"Oh?"

"You always smell fantastic and I wanted to ask what, exactly, is the perfume you wear?"

I refrained from rolling my eyes, surprised she had any kind of nose for quality, considering the bug spray she seemed so fond of.

"Shalimar," I said. "It was a high school graduation gift from my Aunt Biddy. She said it was time I moved on from talcum powder and Love's Baby Soft. I guess you could say it's been my signature scent ever since."

Vanessa threw her head back, laughing as the bartender came back and she ordered a Chardonnay. "How funny. I didn't wear perfume until I graduated from medical school. I could never afford things like perfume."

Dear, Lord. Was I up for hearing about the hardscrabble childhood Vanessa had to claw her way out of? There wasn't enough wine in the world.

However, the show had to go on.

Besides. It wouldn't be for much longer.

I cleared my throat. "You know, Vanessa, after all this time, I don't believe I know where you're from."

"Las Vegas. Born and raised."

"Well, that's quite a long way from Chicago."

She chuckled and took a sip of her just arrived wine. "The longest. There's five of us—my daddy died when I was eight. Heart attack. I'm the youngest. Anyway, Mama did the best she could, but you know that's a lot of mouths to feed as a waitress who bartended on the side."

"So that's why you went into cardiology. Because of your father, I mean."

Vanessa shook her head. "Actually, I wanted to go into dermatology. I had dreams of being the high-priced, best-kept secret of Beverly Hills, tending to the facial maladies of the rich and famous. When I did my cardiology rotation, I worked with a lot of women with heart issues and it was amazing. Dermatology was boring after that."

"How interesting."

"Tell me, what drove Charles's interest in cardiology?"

Another inward eye roll. As if she didn't already know.

"He always used to say the logic of the heart intrigued him," I said, signaling to the bartender for another glass of wine.

"I could see that. He, of course, being such a logical person."

"That he was."

"Charles was a superb physician," Vanessa said. "His patients adored him."

"Yes," I said, watching the bartender refresh my wine. "Cardiology was most definitely his passion."

She looked over her shoulder. "Should we get a table? I'm starving."

"You must have read my mind. I'm surprised you couldn't hear my stomach rumble."

"Great minds think alike." Vanessa winked as she picked up her glass of wine and slid off her barstool.

"Indeed," I said, following her to the host stand, where she requested a table for two.

"Should we get a booth?" I asked.

"Can we?" Vanessa turned to the hostess who indicated we should follow her, where she seated us at a booth so obscure, so tucked away, we might as well have been in a cave.

"Oh, this is perfect." She rubbed her hands together. "This gives us lots of privacy."

"Yes. The privacy is nice," I said, perusing the menu. "Everything certainly looks good. What do you recommend?" I asked.

"Well, there aren't any spinach salads." She winked. "Actually, what they're famous for are their burgers. Fantastic."

"I must confess, I'm not much one for hamburgers. Or red meat in general."

"Oh, you have to have a burger. Really. Out of this world good." She chuckled. "Surely you can't be worried about your girlish figure."

"Oh, no, no, it's not that. It's just, sometimes red meat doesn't sit well with me." I tilted my head to the side. "I wouldn't want anything to impact our evening."

"No, we definitely don't want that," she said, running the tip of her finger along the lip of her wineglass. "That definitely would not do."

I turned my attention back to the menu. "I think I'll have the chopped salad."

"Well, I'm going to have the burger." She slapped her menu shut. "With fries."

"Perhaps you'll let me steal some of your fries."

"Oh, Jillian. You don't even have to ask."

I forced myself to smile and hold her gaze. She looked at me, dreamy desire oozing across her face. Her reverie was broken by the waitress who came to take our order.

"I'm just going to run to the ladies' room, wash my hands." She rubbed her fingers together. "I won't be gone long."

"Take your time," I said as she winked at me again.

I nibbled on a roll from the bread basket while I awaited her return. It was still early, so the bulk of the restaurant's population was still in the bar. I spotted the nervous young girl from earlier seated three tables away with her date. She threw her head back and laughed at some bon mot from him. At least I hoped it was something witty, and not something asinine that she was merely playing along with to assuage his ego. I couldn't discern if it was indeed a blind date or a second or third date to determine if there should be a fifth, sixth, or seventh.

A flushed Vanessa ambled back to the table, a wide smile on her face. "Hello again," she said.

"Hello again."

She leaned forward, folding her arms across the table. "I was just thinking about what you said earlier about how we've known each other all this time, but we don't really know each other."

I rubbed my earlobe. "Well, tonight seems like the perfect time to remedy that."

Vanessa took a hearty sip from her wineglass. "Is it really true you're related to Grace Kelly?"

I chuckled. "Yes. Very distantly. On my mother's side."

"Tell me more."

I shrugged. "There's really not much to tell. She was a thirteenth cousin, seventeen times removed or something like that."

"Well, I'm pretty sure I'm not related to anyone famous on either side. Unless you count my Aunt Lolly who was Miss Cactus Flower 1960. She tried to work her way up to Miss Las Vegas, but it wasn't in the cards for her."

"One could say she peaked early?"

Vanessa giggled and took another slurp of wine. "Yes, I would definitely say she flamed out fast. Don't feel too sorry for her, though. She married an oil baron."

"Were pageants something you did?" I asked as I tore a roll from the breadbasket in half and buttered a small piece.

She shook her head. "Too shy. People used to tell me all the time I was so pretty and that I should, because I'd do really well. Honestly, I couldn't imagine parading around in a bathing suit and smiling and waving to a bunch of strangers."

"Take out the bathing suits and you've basically got a cotillion."

"Oh, that's right," she said. "You were a debutante."

"That I was. Tradition and all of that. It was fun. For the time and all, doing those things that seem so important in the moment, but don't mean much later. Honestly, if I'd had daughters, I doubt I would have subjected them to it." I folded my hands in front of me. "Are you close with your siblings?"

"Well, my oldest sister died when I was in college, so not her, obviously."

"I'm sorry to hear that," I said.

"She was a two-dollar junkie. It was a matter of time before something happened to her." She shrugged. "Anyway, my brother is a high school science teacher in Arizona, one of my sisters still lives in Vegas and is a housewife and the sister just ahead of me, Mia, is a big HR VP out in Maine. I'm closest with her."

"How nice."

"I'm also favorite aunt to all of my nieces and nephews. I host Christmas every year and Mia and I go on vacation, just the two of us every summer." She cocked her head to the side. "Maybe you and I can plan some trips together."

Fortunately, before I was forced to answer, the waitress interrupted us with our meals, a large bowl of salad for me and for Vanessa, a basket crammed with curly fries alongside a monstrous burger, a plastic toothpick adorned with a bow of green cellophane poking out of the shiny dome of the bun.

"That does look like quite a burger," I said as I speared a tomato. I watched as she cut her burger in half with her knife.

"I'm so excited."

"How is it?" I asked as she bit into it, a trickle of juice running down her hand.

"So good," she said, wiping her hands and mouth with a napkin. "I don't have burgers that often, but theirs are totally worth it."

I nodded and smiled as I popped a forkful of lettuce, cucumber, and avocado into my mouth, watching as she took another huge bite of the burger followed by a gulp of wine.

"And the salad?" she asked. "Good?"

"Hmm? Oh, yes. Quite good."

She put a huge chunk of her burger in her mouth before pushing the basket toward me. "I think I promised you some fries."

"Yes, you did. Thank you," I said as I pulled a few from the basket, setting them down on the little plate next to my half-eaten roll, keeping one to nibble on.

"Do you like live music?" she asked.

"I'm afraid my live music experiences don't extend much past the symphony, the opera, or Ravinia."

"Do you know in all the years I've lived in Chicago, I've never been to Ravinia?"

I swirled the wine in my glass. "I've heard of people like you. I thought you were an urban legend."

"We should see a few shows this summer so you can show me the ropes."

"That sounds like fun. They always have a lot of great shows."

"Getting back to my question, there's a little piano bar not too far from here and I thought we could drop in for a little while after dinner."

"I must confess when you said live music, I had visions of a mosh pit and head banging."

"I'll save that for next time," she said, laughing as she reached for the last bite of her burger and frowned. She blinked several times and put her hand to her mouth. "Oh."

I popped a cherry tomato in my mouth and chewed it slowly as I watched her. "Are you okay?"

She fanned herself with the greasy, smelly ball of her napkin and coughed a few times. "All of a sudden, I just feel a little overheated."

"Oh no." I motioned to her water glass. "Maybe some water will help."

She nodded, grabbing the glass and holding on for dear life as she sucked in hearty gulps. She plunked the sweaty glass down on the table, pushing the mostly devoured burger away from her, grimacing at it.

"Vanessa, you don't look well at all," I said. "Is there anything I can do?"

She couldn't answer, instead shaking her head and clamping her hand across her mouth. She heaved once before she bolted for the restroom, nearly colliding with a server as she raced toward the porcelain God.

I flagged down our server, who rushed over. "I'm sorry, but my friend has come down with something and I just wanted to run into the restroom to check on her. Can you make sure no one clears the table?"

"Oh, of course. Would you like me to go in and check on her?"

"No, no, that's all right. I won't be gone long. I didn't want you to think we skipped out on the bill."

"Yeah, wow, thanks for that," the server gushed. "People can be the worst sometimes."

"Yes," I said. "The worst."

I excused myself and headed toward the back. When I pushed open the door of the ladies' room, the scratched red soles of Vanessa's high-heeled sandals looked up at me from beneath the stall. She roared into the toilet, her vomit surging out in one long stream.

"Vanessa? Vanessa, are you okay?"

She groaned before more of her dinner dropped out of her.

"Vanessa?" I tried again. "Is there anything I can do?"

Her feet went slack and I guessed she was slumped against the toilet, her face likely planted against the seat.

She moaned. "I think I have to go home."

"You seemed fine when you got here. Maybe the flu has snuck up on you?"

"I don't think it's the flu."

"Oh, no. Do—do you think maybe you have food poisoning?"

She didn't answer, retching once again. I frowned at the sound of all that waste pouring out of her mouth.

"Is there something you have at home that you can take?"

She didn't say anything. I leaned closer to the door.

"Vanessa?"

"Compazine," she panted. "I have some Compazine at home. I can take that."

"Well, you should definitely get home and take some."

"I walked here," she said. "It was a nice night and this isn't far from my house. God, I just hope I don't throw up in the cab."

"I'll take you home. The smell of a cab will probably make you sicker than anything."

"Oh, Jillian, no, it's okay, I—"

"Don't worry about it. If you get sick, well, I have been saying I need a new car."

She laughed weakly. "Thank you," she said, her voice small and meek.

"Don't even think about it."

"God. Now I have to get up."

"Do you need any help?"

"No, I think I've got it." She groaned again and slid her feet across the tiles, dragging herself up to standing.

I rushed to the sink and wet a wad of paper towels with cold water. The door of the stall swung open and she staggered out, her eyes pools of water, her nose bright red, tracks of mascara and eyeliner trailing down her face.

"Here you go." I handed her the compresses, which she used to wipe her face with.

"We should probably go before it starts up again."

"Why don't you wait here while I pay the check and bring the car around? About ten minutes?"

She moaned and nodded. She convulsed again but despite her proximity to a sink and toilet, she didn't make it. I jumped back as vomit splattered out of her mouth and down her chin and the front of her shirt.

"Oh, my God," she sobbed. "What is wrong with me?"

"You poor thing." I wet another clump of paper towels and helped her clean herself up. "Don't worry, Vanessa. I'll take good care of you."

36

I FINISHED HELPING Vanessa then rushed out to the dining room, which had filled up considerably since my flight to the ladies' room. I found our server and paid the bill before I ran the two short blocks to my car. By the time I pulled up, Vanessa had managed to drag herself outside. Even in the conflicting casts of moonlight and streetlamps, she was green.

"I just threw up in the bushes next to the door." She shook her head. "I can't ever show my face around here again."

"Well, you'll be home soon," I said as I helped her into the passenger seat. She rolled down the window and hung out of it. The cold bite of air made me shiver, but I ignored it as I took side streets to avoid traffic on Clark to get to her house faster. I asked her how she was every few seconds and she'd offer frail affirmations that she was hanging in there. Fortunately, she didn't have any episodes in my car. I found a spot right out front and helped her to her front door. She fumbled with her keys, taking a few tries to stick it into the lock. Once inside, she deactivated the alarm and struggled up the short flight of stairs to her living room. I had forgotten she lived in a Cotton Candy Wonderland of pink flowers, pink couch, and pink curtains. I grimaced as I took in the dolls in display cases and cloying pictures of balloons and clowns adorning the pink walls.

"Vanessa, if you tell me where the medication is, I can bring it down for you, if you'd like to sit for a while," I said.

She wiggled out of the pink print top, carefully pulling the hole over her head to avoid coming into contact with the wet, rank stains running down the front. She took a deep breath and dry heaved. It was clear she wasn't done.

"Upstairs. Third floor. In my study. My medical bag," she managed before she bolted for her kitchen.

I headed up to the third floor, poking my head into rooms until I found one with a desk. Her medical bag was tucked under it. I grabbed it and hurried back downstairs.

She was leaning over the kitchen sink in her bra, spewing yet more.

"Vanessa, I found your bag—"

She didn't say anything as she yanked it from me, plowing through its contents until she came across a small clear vial and a syringe. She expertly stuck the needle into the bottle to extract the fluid. Within seconds, she jammed the fine point of the needle into a vein in her arm, slumping as she did so.

"It should start to work in about a half hour," she said, fatigue lacing her words.

"Is there anything else I can do?" I asked.

She shook her head and dropped into a kitchen chair. "I'm not really supposed to, but I may even take a sedative and go to bed. I'm not even sure I can manage a shower."

"Of course. Why don't I rinse out your blouse for you? At least that will be one less thing you'll have to worry about."

"That would be nice." A feeble smile. "Thank you."

"Of course. I'm just glad I can do something."

"I'm so sorry about tonight. I was really looking forward to us having a lovely evening."

I patted her shoulder. "Don't even think about it."

"Rain check?"

"Of course." I smiled. "I'll rinse out your blouse then make you some tea to take with your sedative. How's that?"

She winced and blew out a rancid cloud of breath as she patted her chest. "Sorry. Ugh. I thought one last wave was coming on."

"Quite all right. I'll take care of your blouse and start that tea."

"I've changed my mind. I'm going to try a quick shower after all. I should be out by the time you're done."

"Take your time," I said. "I'll be up in a bit."

She nodded and staggered up the stairs, clutching her medical bag while I collected the putrid pile of blouse from the floor. I pointed my nose away, frowning as I ducked into the kitchen, holding my breath. I heard the shower come on upstairs as I scrubbed the sink of her waste, then washed out the blouse with dish soap. Personally, I would have called the blouse a loss, but a glance at the tag confirmed it was Carolina Herrera, so perhaps she'd decide to hang onto it. I found her mud room and a hanger, and left the blouse to drip over the small wash basin, before locating her tea, mug, and a small tray, putting on a kettle of water to boil.

I carried everything upstairs, blowing into the hot pool of water in the giant pink mug. I poked my head into her room. Fragrant steam rushed out and she was lying on the bed, shrouded in a pink terry cloth bathrobe, her eyes closed. She stirred and sat up as I carried over the tea.

"Feeling better?" I asked.

"I am. Thank you," she said taking the mug of tea I handed her. She rummaged through her medical bag again and pulled out a bottle of pills, tapping out one small oval into her palm.

"Is there anything else I can get you?" I watched as she placed the pills on her tongue before taking a tentative sip of hot tea, then a heartier one.

She shook her head. "You've done so much already. I owe you the biggest rain check."

"Oh, really, it was no trouble. I raised two boys. This was nothing."

She laughed. "Now I don't feel so bad."

"I hope you feel better in the morning."

"I'm sure I will." She chuckled. "I guess no more burgers for a while. Should have had the salad."

"I wouldn't worry too much about it."

"Hmm." She slurped down some more tea and set the mug down on the nightstand. "God, I'm exhausted."

"I'll see myself out," I whispered as she slid beneath the covers. "Oh. What's your alarm code?"

"Seven-five-five-two. Then hit 'Away.' The door will lock behind you," she murmured, her eyes starting to droop.

"I'll call you tomorrow," I said.

She moaned and threw up a limp wave. I flicked off the light and closed the door.

I smiled.

It had worked better than I'd thought it would.

37

REALLY, the whole thing had gone like clockwork.

Charles always kept Compazine on hand. It had come in handy over the years, what with food poisoning and bouts of the flu felling us on occasion. He'd sometimes administer a mild sedative afterward. It wasn't too far a leap to figure Vanessa would probably do the same for herself. Requesting a booth wouldn't be suspicious. That it was so enclosed was a lucky break. No one could see me slip the ipecac syrup into both her water and wineglass after she ran off to the restroom to wash her hands, something she'd done every time I'd been forced to have a meal with her.

Just like clockwork.

Now, it was time to get down to what I came here to do.

I'd tried her office first. Since she'd been so helpful in mentioning that she, Walter, and Charles all had keys to each other's offices, I took a chance and snuck in there in the middle of the night with his keys, determined to find that picture.

Though I hadn't intended to, I'd gone into Charles's office. I couldn't help myself. The air had been cold and stale. I hadn't been prepared for the shock of not seeing the engraved gold letter opener

I'd gotten him as a medical school graduation gift, or the nameplate bearing Charles Morgan, M.D. Also missing were the family portrait taken for our Christmas card two years ago and what he'd always said was his favorite photo of me, taken the year before we'd had Chase, an unguarded moment at a backyard party at Charlotte's, me laughing with careless abandon. Gabe had mentioned that Charlotte had cleaned out the office and given those mementos to him and Chase.

I'd spent over an hour in her office searching through the morass of musty, yellowing magazine articles, papers, papers, and more papers, coming up empty.

Which meant I had to try her house. And if it wasn't here, I didn't know what I'd do. Cross that bridge if I came to it, I suppose.

I pulled a pair of latex gloves out of my purse and snapped them on, glee ripping through me with the slap of rubber against my skin. I headed into her study and sat down at the desk, gently pulling open the top drawer, another mess of papers, rubber bands, paperclips, and dried out pens. I picked up the nest of papers and laid them on the desk, quickly shuffling through them in search of the damning manila envelope full of incriminating photos.

I continued shuffling through the papers, my heart slamming against my chest, my fingers trembling as I tried to navigate the endless stream of faded Post-it notes, old prescriptions, and scribbled notes.

She certainly wasn't as orderly as Charles. I wept for her accountant.

The pile yielded nothing. A bead of sweat ran down my temple and I swiped at it with the back of my hand. I searched through three more stacks, ready to give up, when there it was.

Stuck to the bottom of a file drawer.

A big fat manila envelope she hadn't even bothered to seal shut.

This had to be it. I held my breath as I ran my finger under the flap, a slow smile spreading over my face when I pulled out the picture. There I was. And there I went as I slid the photo back into the envelope. I kissed it before I pressed it to my chest, hardly believing the serendipity of this moment.

"God, you're so stupid, Vanessa," I muttered before carefully placing the stack of papers back into the desk drawer. I flipped off the desk lamp and grabbed the envelope.

I poked my head out of the door and tiptoed down the hall to her room, slowly turning the knob to look inside.

Dead asleep.

I crept downstairs and retrieved my purse from the couch, plucking out my keys. I punched in the alarm code, waited for the beep.

She wouldn't even miss it. She would turn that room upside down, so certain she had put it in there, swearing up and down it was *right here.* She'd tear this house apart in her futile search. Maybe she'd think she'd thrown it away by accident. Would berate herself for not being more careful.

She'd never even remember this little hitch in her time space continuum.

And even if she did put two and two together and realized what I'd done, so what?

There wouldn't be anything she could do about it.

I slid behind the wheel of my car and pulled away from the curb, humming to myself, barely able to keep the lid on my glee.

Finally, I gave up.

And burst out laughing.

38

I SMILED at the whir of the paper shredder as I fed it the envelope and picture. I'd been so tired when I got home, I hadn't bothered to take it out of my purse. I'd slept like a baby for the first time in weeks and bright and early this morning, I'd put the bow on this loose end before heading out to my Pilates class.

I took a sip of tea and went in search of my phone, pulling up Vanessa's number.

"Hope you're feeling better. Perhaps we can reschedule soon?" I muttered as I tapped out the text message.

Her response dinged within seconds.

FEELING SOOOOOO MUCH BETTER. LOL, HOW CRAZY WAS THAT? #NO MORE BURGERS #WAITWHAT? #HOPENOT AND YES, WE DEFINITELY HAVE TO RESCHEDULE. I'LL LOOK AT MY CALENDAR AND COME UP WITH A FEW DAYS. THANKS AGAIN FOR TAKING SUCH GOOD CARE OF ME. I REALLY APPRECIATE IT!!!

I laughed out loud. "Oh, I took care of you all right." I scoffed to myself at how gullible she was. She'd even bought that cock and bull story about me being attracted to another girl in college. I knew that bit of salaciousness would get her right where I wanted her.

Child's play.

My phone rang and I frowned, irritated that she was already calling me.

Except it was my father.

I put my hand over my heart, my eyes flooding with tears as I answered. "Hi, Daddy."

"Oh, Jillian, Jillian, Jillian." My father's voice broke as he said my name.

"How are you?"

"Why've you been avoiding me, Jilly Girl?"

I wiped the back of my hand across my face, smearing wetness along my cheeks. It was barely nine a.m. in Philadelphia and I could already hear the wobble of drink in his voice. "I haven't."

"I've been waiting to hear from you. Why have you been avoiding me?"

"I'm not, Daddy, I swear."

"You can tell me. Did I do something wrong?"

"There's been so much going on," I said. "I ... I have a few things to take care of."

"You know, I always liked Old Charlie. I did. Do you know, when you very first brought him home, I said, well now there's a fine young man for my Jilly Girl."

"I know, Daddy."

"I took him to McLaughlin's so I could really see what this fine young man was made of."

"Charles told me."

"And he matched me drink for drink." I heard my father take a noisy slurp from his glass. Or the bottle. I couldn't be sure which. "Stayed upright the whole time. I said, now that's a strong young man. He's strong enough for my Jilly Girl."

"Charles—he always loved you, Daddy."

He sighed. "A fine young man, Old Charlie was. Just fine."

"I'm so sorry. For everything."

"Why don't you come home? I'd love having you here every day. We could sit out on the South Lawn and talk. Talk all day long. We always have the best conversations out there on the South Lawn."

"I remember."

"I think your mother would like it."

I had to snap my lips shut to refrain from commenting. Daddy was nice to try to make it sound as though my mother would welcome my presence. She could have cared less what I did. Despite her sometimes overly aggressive nature, I preferred Celia's company to my own mother's.

"Oh, Daddy—" My phone beeped with a text message. I pulled the phone away from my ear to see Vanessa at it again. "Maybe I'll come out in May for a few months. I have some business that needs tending to first."

"I want you to know how much your father loves you," he said, his voice cracking as he dissolved into sobs. "I love you so much, Jilly Girl."

I plucked a Kleenex out of the box in the kitchen, dabbing at my eyes and blowing my nose. "I love you, too Daddy. And I will come home. I promise."

"I really need to see you."

"I have to go. I'll call you soon. Very soon."

We said our tearful goodbyes and I laid down on the couch, a sobbing, broken mess. My father was a sick old man. If I went to jail, it would kill him.

My phone beeped with a new text message. Vanessa again, letting me know when she wanted to reschedule.

I threw the phone across the room.

39

STRATEGICALLY PLACED white candles emitting the scent of lavender burned all around Suzette and me. The flames cast faint, flickering shadows across the soft white leather couches, silk sage green wallpaper, and willow branches jutting out of tall, clear vases lining the glass shelves affixed to the wall.

"I needed this in the worst way."

"Me too," I said. "I don't think I realized how much until this moment."

Suzette turned to look at me as her manicurist lowered her foot into the bubbling, artificially blue water below. "It's good to see you getting back to normal. Relatively speaking."

I closed my eyes, dropping my head against the massage chair. "I'm trying to. Relatively speaking."

She reached over and grabbed my hand. "Thank you again for the invitation."

"I should be the one thanking you for taking me up on it. A weekend away from prying eyes and..." I cleared my throat, Charles's name about to slip from my lips. Since Suzette and I had come up on

Friday afternoon for a weekend at one of Kohler's five-star spas, his grating presence had been silenced and I'd been able to enjoy the day of massages, facials, and assorted treatments in peace.

"What was that?"

"Nothing." I smiled. "I'm sad to be leaving tomorrow. I wish we could stay a few more days."

"Would if I could. Court first thing Monday morning."

"This is it, yes?"

"God, I hope so," she muttered. "I don't know how much more of this I can take."

Much like myself, Suzette had also suffered the humiliation of her husband's tacky affair. He then had the temerity to attempt to leave her penniless after thirty-five years. Like myself, she'd been the epitome of the perfect wife: raised flawless children, maintained a magnificent home, and scrupulously preserved her beauty. Grays did not betray her chic feathered blond bob. Her size four waist did not bulge. The smooth, baby's butt of her skin did not sag, flap, or pucker with cellulite. Neither husband could claim we'd "let ourselves go," as justifications for their indiscretions.

Through the years, merely as an observer, there were times I thought Suzette had been entirely too accommodating to Martin's ego, far too subservient to his whims. He certainly seemed to develop amnesia regarding her excessive catering to his needs. Or had never noticed. Or never cared. The merry-go-round of court dates had been almost too much to keep up with as he and his attorney continued to find increasingly abominable ways to avoid paying Suzette any kind of settlement. She'd finally wised up and engaged a new attorney, a shark from what I could surmise, and now seemed on the cusp of getting her due.

"We'll have to celebrate when it's all over," I said. "Commemorate your true freedom from Martin."

She winced as the manicurist lifted one foot from the water, immediately taking a pumice stone to her heel. "It can't come soon enough. I can barely think about anything else. Dating has certainly taken a backseat."

"You're not still *Internet* dating, are you?" I shuddered as the words slid from my lips. "Even saying it is unseemly."

Suzette laughed. "Oh, I've slowed down a little, dealing with all of this, but I've met a lot of nice men and had a lot of nice dates. It's not as horrible as you think."

"I suppose. Still, I can't imagine ever crossing that threshold."

"Don't be so sure." She stiffened a little as the manicurist gave up on the pumice stone and applied a razor to her heel instead. "Women our age ... well, we have to get a little creative."

"Would you ever marry again?"

"I don't know. Maybe. It depends." She scoffed. "Frankly, I never should have gotten married in the first place."

"Understandable that you would feel that way," I said. "Considering."

"No, I mean, I knew marrying him at all was a mistake. Still, I did what I thought I was supposed to do. What my mother demanded I do."

I chuckled. "It is what our mothers taught us, isn't it? Get an MRS degree?"

"I thought I'd be an old maid." She fingered the belt of her plush white spa robe. "Can you imagine? Twenty years old and I thought my only option in life was to say yes to this handsome, charming asshole. Crazy to think now. Sad to think now."

"I wanted to marry Charles," I said more to myself than to her. "I really thought we'd live happily ever after."

"I don't think there is such a thing." She moaned a little as the manicurist placed hot towels on her legs. "I don't want to talk about Martin anymore. What about you? What's next for you?"

I watched the steam rise from the hot towels the manicurist wrapped around my legs. My phone beeped from the pocket of my robe. Vanessa responding to my text message from earlier confirming our next date. I took a deep inhale, and smiled, burrowing deeper into the chair. "I still have a few more threads to snip."

"What does that mean?"

I fingered my phone, my glee surging. "Just some things I need to do to get my house in order."

40

I PUT on a pair of white satin pajamas then carefully wrapped the wet strands of my hair in a fluffy white Egyptian cotton towel. I'd had a wonderful Pilates session late that afternoon with my favorite instructor and after a long and steamy shower, I felt refreshed. Reborn.

It promised to be a wonderful night. The best I'd had in some time.

My trip to Wisconsin with Suzette had ignited a frenzy of productivity when I'd returned home. I tackled some long-neglected projects around the house, from reorganizing the kitchen in anticipation of a remodel to clearing the garage of abandoned trash and the odd treasure. Suzette had a good week as well, as she was granted her long-awaited divorce settlement, a stunningly beautiful eight figures. Well-deserved severance for decades of misery.

I floated downstairs toward the kitchen, smiling as I passed the living room. The new taupe paint color had turned out better than I'd thought it would. The new wood floors gleamed like shiny pennies. Chase and I had talked this morning and in fact several times since our initial conversation following the Neil Yancy incident. I had hope our relationship was on its way back to being a good one. Even Gabe was coming around to his charming, impish self. And not a peep out of Detective Travis. Not that I really thought there would be. He could try, but it didn't mean he'd win.

My life was falling back into the nice, neat squares I craved.

I poured myself a cold glass of Chardonnay, giddy as the buttery gold slid down my throat. I shuffled over to the Bose, flipping through the songs until I found what I was looking for. I smiled as the gentle opening strains of "Moon River" filled the room.

I hummed to myself as I went in search of my phone, flopping down on the new couch, delivered yesterday, as I scrolled through my contacts for Vanessa's phone number. My finger hovered over the keypad and my eyes slid shut. I cleared my throat a few times and frowned, trying to affect the right mood, the right tone. I murmured a few of the phrases I'd tried out in the shower, mentally scratching out and rewriting what I wanted to say. I shrugged my shoulders up and down a few times and took some deep breaths.

It was time.

I opened my eyes and smiled as I hit the dial icon for her number.

She answered on the first ring. "I just got out of the shower. I can't wait to see you." She laughed. "And no hamburgers!"

I laughed, too. "No, definitely not." I lowered my voice. "What are you wearing tonight?"

"I'm not sure. I've narrowed it down between three outfits."

"Whatever you wear will look lovely."

"You're sweet. I can't wait to see what you're wearing."

"Will you do me a favor?" I asked.

"Well, that depends," she purred. "Is it something I'll enjoy?"

"Oh, I think so." I smiled. "We both will."

"Then I'm all ears."

I perched one foot on the edge of the coffee table, and crossed my legs. "Did you receive my gift earlier today?"

"I did. I have to say I'm intrigued by what it is. It was hard not to open it, but you'll be glad to know I waited, just like you asked me to."

"I think you're really going to love it."

"So." She laughed. "Do I get to open it now?"

"Please do."

I tapped my phone while I waited for the inevitable oohing and aahing to commence.

"Oh, Jillian." She gasped. "You shouldn't have."

"It was nothing. Really."

"I'm going to wear some tonight. I mean, if that's okay."

"Actually, that's what I wanted to ask you," I said. "If you would put some on. Right now. While we're talking."

She laughed. Embarrassed. Titillated. "What?"

"Does that sound strange? I just ... I want to hear you, hear your first words once you spray it on yourself."

"That's a new one for me," she said. "I had no idea you were so creative, Jillian."

"Are you sitting down?"

"Yes." She giggled. "This feels very strange. But I like it."

"Okay," I said. "I'm ready."

A little moan escaped her lips and I smiled.

"Do you like it?" I asked.

"Oh, Jillian. It's delicious. It smells absolutely delicious. You never know how a perfume will smell until you spray it on yourself."

"You're so right," I whispered.

And then I heard it. The quickening of breath.

"Oh, God," she said.

I fingered the handle of Charles's hulking black medical bag resting next to me on the couch. "Vanessa? What's wrong?"

"I..." She was gasping now. Clutching and clawing for life. "It feels like I'm having a heart attack."

I examined my nails. The no-chip manicure I'd gotten during spa weekend was holding up quite nicely. It might become my newest indulgence. "Oh my God, Vanessa—are you serious?"

"Jillian, you have—"

I reached into the bag, extracting a syringe. "What? What is it, Vanessa? What is it you need me to do?"

"C-C-Call. 911."

"You need me to call 911? Is that what you said?"

"Yes, please, I ... can't breathe. I can't breathe."

I pushed the plunger on the syringe, watching a thin arc of liquid squirt out of the needle and into the air. Like a water and light show. Watch the poison dance, dance, dance.

"I'm going to switch over, okay? I'm going to put you on hold and call 911. Vanessa? Can you hear me? Vanessa?"

"Okay," she said, her voice feeble. Fading. Dying.

"Hang on, Vanessa. Just hang on."

"Okay," she whispered.

The phone went dead.

She went dead.

I waited a few moments.

Silence.

Snip, snip on that nasty thread.

I placed the syringe on the coffee table and extracted the vial of cyanide from the bag and examined it, remembering the day the bag fell off the closet shelf onto the floor next to me. It was kismet the bag was even in the closet. It was usually in Charles's study or the trunk of his car. It must have gotten moved during the police stampede through the house and they put it in the closet by mistake.

As I stared at it, I had a flash of Charles telling me he always carried cyanide around, as it could slow down blood pressure, an often critical action for someone in cardiac distress.

Of course, the hulking old medical journal I found on one of the bookshelves in his study told me it was lethal. Quietly so. Quickly so.

This would solve everything. I just needed a way to do it.

Spritzing myself with Shalimar one morning provided even more inspiration. She was always blathering on about how good she thought I smelled. To the point of mania, it seemed.

It was perfect.

Thirty dollars in cash later, I had a small bottle of Shalimar spray from their low-end line, purchased in disguise from a beauty supply store in a dank, non-descript shopping center in a dank, non-descript suburb two hours away. It wasn't the genuine parfum, what I paid hundreds of dollars for, but she'd never know the difference, so happy for this little crumb I was throwing her.

From there, it had been so simple.

The long injection of cyanide into the bottle's opening. All while wearing surgical gloves. Of course.

No tampering.

No mess.

Just a smooth and slow injection.

For a quick and painful death.

One spritz.

And she'd never know what hit her.

Colorless. Odorless. Lethal in the wrong hands.

Or the right hands, depending upon your point of view.

I'd leave Charles's bag in the closet in his study. I had a doctor's appointment Monday afternoon. I'd drop the vial and syringe into the medical waste bin in the exam room when the nurse stepped out to let me change clothes.

And no one would ever know.

I'd act surprised, of course, when the news was delivered to me. I'd send a tasteful flower arrangement. Attend any memorial services. Offer Walter my condolences on losing both of his practice partners in the space of a few months. Such a tragedy.

But so necessary.

I picked up my glass of wine and held it up in the air. "To Charles. Thank you for helping me solve a very thorny problem."

He would have been appalled by this turn of events, of course. He took his duty as a physician very seriously. First do no harm and all that.

Well, what was done was done. Goodbye, Vanessa. You will not be missed.

The Bose continued to pump out Henry Mancini. I picked up my phone and tapped the food ordering app I liked to use, choosing chicken noodle soup with dry toast, a baked chicken breast, tea with extra lemon, and some honey packets. This would be lunch tomorrow. Fitzgerald's chicken noodle soup was actually quite tasty. Not as good as mine, of course, but good. I'd cut up the chicken breast into a Caesar salad. I hadn't seen "Breakfast at Tiffany's," one of my favorite movies, in at least a year. This was a good night to watch it while I ate my dinner. I headed into the kitchen and took a hearty slice of the leek and goat cheese tart I'd made earlier and put it on a plate with some simple greens. The strawberry panna cotta for dessert was velvety and luscious. The perfect indulgence for a job well done.

Curtain down.

And scene.

41

"Detectives. It's late." I frowned as I opened my front door in response the doorbell. "What do you want?"

Potts and Travis. Right on schedule.

"Mrs. Morgan." Travis gestured toward my living room. Compared to our last meeting, he seemed oddly deflated. "May we come in?"

I blew my nose into the Kleenex I was holding. "Why?"

"We'd like to talk about this inside," Potts said.

"I'd prefer it if you just told me what this is about."

They exchanged an agitated look. "Mrs. Morgan, we stopped by to inform you that Dr. Vanessa Shayne is dead," Travis said.

"Oh, my God." I gasped, my hands flying to my mouth. "I just talked to her last night."

"That's why we're here. Her phone showed you as the last person she talked to."

Fear flashed through me as I did a quick mental scan of the text messages between Vanessa and me, searching for anything unseemly or suspicious. Nothing came to mind. Coordinating innocent lunch and dinner dates. Queries as to my state of mind. Following up on her oh-so-unfortunate bout with food poisoning. All easily explained, all completely benign.

"What happened?" I asked.

"An autopsy is under way, but it looks like a heart attack," Potts said.

"A heart attack. My God." I gripped the doorknob. "I know she lives alone. Who found her?"

"A neighbor returning from a two-week vacation went over to retrieve her mail and found her this afternoon," Travis said.

"What did you and Dr. Shayne talk about last night?" Potts asked.

I blew my nose again before letting my hand drift over my mouth for a second as I shook my head in shock, I tell you, utter and complete shock.

"We'd planned to have dinner last night. However, I didn't feel well, so I called her to reschedule."

"You and Dr. Shayne. You were close?" Travis asked.

"She's been a good friend ever since ... Charles. We'd had dinner a few times. Lunch. She was easy to talk to."

Yes, when one wasn't dodging her ceaseless innuendo and subtle threats, Vanessa was an absolute delight.

"And when you talked to her last night, how did she sound?" Potts asked.

"Fine." I shrugged. "We didn't talk long. We said we'd touch base next week to reschedule."

"What'd you do last night?" Potts asked.

"I ordered some chicken noodle soup and tea, then went to bed."

"Anybody who can corroborate that?" Potts asked.

"The delivery driver I would imagine."

Paid with a credit card. Good tip in cash. Nothing obscene, but enough that would definitely make me memorable.

"We're gonna need the phone number of where you ordered from."

"It was through FoodQuick."

"Can I take a look at your phone?" Travis asked, holding his hand out toward me.

"Why?"

He cocked his head to one side and smiled. "What happened to you being cooperative, Mrs. Morgan?"

I scoffed and told them to wait while I extracted my phone from my purse, scrolling, swiping, and tapping before I handed it over to Travis. His face seemed to fall as the app confirmed that indeed, after I'd hung up with Vanessa, I had ordered a light dinner suitable for an ailing individual. He twisted his mouth around, clicking his tongue against the roof of his mouth, silently fuming.

I'd sent no note with the Shalimar. I'd been careful not to handle it with my bare hands. As usual, they had nothing.

"Were you and Dr. Shayne friendly before your husband's death?" Travis asked as he handed my phone back to me.

"We were social acquaintances, mostly. Charles and I had been to her home a few times, she'd been here a few times. Various functions and the like over the years. But that was the extent of our relationship."

"And the past few months," Potts said, jotting this down in his little notebook, "just a few dinners, some lunches. And she always seemed fine to you?"

"Yes."

"Is there anything else you can tell us about last night?"

"I've already told you, I had a little soup then went to bed."

"Anyone who can corroborate that?" Potts repeated.

I folded my arms across my chest. "No."

Travis scoffed and shook his head. "Mrs. Morgan ... there's a saying. Once is an incident, twice is a coincidence and three times is a pattern. What do you have to say to that?"

"What do you want me to say?"

"How about why three people connected to you in some way have died over the past three months?" he asked. "Why don't you explain that?"

I reared up, looked him dead in the eye. "Detective," I said, my own voice hushed with an intensity matching his. "You can come at me all you want, but I promise you, it will all be for nothing."

"You should know that I love a challenge."

"Bully for you, Detective. And *you* should know that we're done here. I won't be stepping foot inside your interrogation room anymore. No more questions. No more dropping by my house. No more bumping into me at the grocery store. We're done."

For once, Potts was mute as Travis pulled back a little, a smile tugging at the corner of one lip.

"For now."

I slammed the door in their faces.

42

"*When will it end, Jillian?*"

"It's over." I stubbed my cigarette into the ashtray, overflowing after my visit from the Goon Squad the night before. I blew out a cloud of smoke as I carried the ashtray into the kitchen and dumped the contents into the trash. I'd called Joss to fill her in on this latest turn of events. I think it was safe to assume she was moments away from hanging up on me. I couldn't say I blamed her. After all, the stench around me was blooming hot and fast.

"*They're getting closer to figuring it out.*"

"They're not getting closer to anything. They've got nothing. Absolutely nothing."

"*You sure about that?*"

I jammed the heels of my hands over my ears and paced the living room, my breath rattling in my chest. But this was it. There wouldn't be anything or anyone else. I had eliminated every last one of my problems, snipped all my threads.

The doorbell rang. I flinched, frozen as I stared at the door, as though I expected it to explode, burst into flames.

Or a brigade of police to come barreling through it.

It pealed again, and I tiptoed over to peer through the peephole. A young man in a police uniform stood on the other side. Fear rippled through my heart until I realized if I were being arrested, it wouldn't be by this lone young man.

"Yes?" I said as I opened the door. He held a few large brown grocery bags, the tops of which were folded over and stapled. A suitcase stood next to him.

Charles's suitcase.

"Jillian Morgan? Officer Corona, Winnetka Police Department." He held the bags toward me. "We're returning the rest of your property to you from our investigation. I just need you to sign for it."

"Oh." I looked at the bags, afraid. "Did these things belong to my husband?"

"I don't know. All they told me was that they were done with everything and to return it to you."

"Where do I sign?"

He opened the bags and directed me to look inside. I only glanced at the contents, but the assortment of ties, shirts, and pants looked as though they'd belonged to Charles. He unzipped the suitcase, empty now, asking if this indeed did belong to me. I nodded and signed the sheets of paper he stuck in front of me.

"Have a good day, ma'am," he said, saluting me with a lazy flip of his pen. I hauled everything upstairs, turned the bags out onto the bed, and pawed through the clothes. He'd been packing that night, moving out. I stuffed the clothes back into the bags. I'd see if the boys wanted anything and whatever they passed on, I'd give to charity. Or burn.

I turned the last bag over.

A plastic bag tumbled out.

A plastic bag camouflaging a box.

A black puzzle box.

I liberated the box from the plastic bag, my fingers trembling as I traced the intricate loops and swirls of black filigree over gold peeking underneath. I sank down to the bed, turning the box over in my hands. Over and over and over.

My index finger brushed against one of the seams. The box exploded in my hand, the elaborate carved pieces hanging onto a tiny wooden spindle in the center. I dropped it on the bed, half afraid of what might come crawling out from beneath the crevices. My heart pounded in my ears and I rubbed an uneasy hand across my chest.

"You've been more trouble than you were ever worth," I whispered.

I mashed the pieces in a frenzied attempt to put the box back together again. Finally, the pieces closed in on themselves to become a box once more.

I picked it up and walked downstairs, careful now not to handle it, to keep my fingers still, lest it detonate on me again. I threw it in the fireplace, the weight on my shoulders lifting as I did. I lit a match, hurling that into the fireplace, too. The fire caught instantly, blazing and curling in a spectacular *poof!* before dying down and getting on with the business of destroying the wretched thing.

Good riddance.

43

FOUR MONTHS LATER

LIFE HAD FINALLY RETURNED to normal.

Vanessa the Vile was laid to rest in her hometown of Las Vegas. There was a local memorial service which I forced myself to attend. How would it have looked if I hadn't? I went and gushed my crocodile tears and feigned utter shock and disbelief at this *dedicated physician being struck down in her prime*, or whatever tripe her medical school mentor had uttered during her eulogy.

I was happy to spend three weeks out east for Chase's graduation from Harvard Law. Charlotte and I turned ourselves into contortionists to avoid each other, and I think everyone breathed a sigh of relief that we didn't recreate some screeching catfight from *Dynasty*. I extended my stay by taking refuge in my childhood home in Bala Cynwyd. I'd lucked into choosing a time when my mother was gone for some horse show, so it was Daddy and me for two weeks. Every day, he burst into tears about how happy he was to have his Jilly Girl home. I was reluctant to leave and seriously considered bringing him here to live with me. In fact, the more I thought about it, the more I thought I should. It would probably be a relief for him and my mother.

Aside from that, all had been quiet at my little sanctuary in Winnetka, which was a respite I couldn't describe. I'd thrown myself into projects around the house, Pilates, reading my books, and gardening.

No disgruntled stalkers demanding puzzle boxes. No trailer park trash redheads attempting to blackmail me into sordid, backstreet liaisons. No detectives harassing me.

Normal as normal could be.

Sometimes, I'd forgotten what I'd done. It was odd in a way, how I was able to compartmentalize murdering four people in cold blood. Almost as though my crimes had never been committed. Mind you, I had no regrets about any of them. Well, Charles, sometimes. That's only natural. But the rest? Hardly. They were but a blip on my radar, and most days they didn't even rate that.

I looked up from my recipe box on the kitchen table at the sound of keys jangling in the door. I ran into the living room in time to see Chase and Gabe come bounding in, loaded down with suitcases and smiles.

"Oh!" I ran for them, my arms outstretched. "I've been so excited all day waiting for you."

I drew them into fierce hugs, both individually and together, simultaneously smothering them in kisses. I held Chase's cheek in one hand. At his graduation last month, he'd hedged about coming home for a few weeks. He and Gabe had clearly wanted to surprise me. I was still getting used to the new sinewy angles of Gabe's already lean frame I'd observed a few weeks before. His defense was training for a marathon.

"You came."

"I came," Chase said.

"Sweetheart—"

"We can talk later."

"It's so wonderful to have you both here. I thought we could have dinner at home tonight, just the three of us. Celia and Clayton want to have us to the house Tuesday night, then of course, just a quiet little dinner for my birthday next Saturday."

"Sounds good." Chase said. "Jacqueline gets in Tuesday afternoon, so that's perfect."

"When does she start her new job?"

"After the fourth." He looked down at his shoes, the tips of his ears burning cherry red. "We're going to Michiana for a few days with Aunt Charlotte."

"Of course." I nodded. "I'm glad you'll have a chance to get up there before you have to start your new job. I know it's not the usual Labor Day festivities with all the family, but you'll have a lovely time nonetheless."

Awkward silence draped over us. I cleared my throat. "Well, why don't you both get upstairs and freshen up, unpack, and I'll start dinner. I thought we'd have something simple, something light. Some grilled salmon, a salad, some asparagus."

"You know what would be fun?" Chase asked.

"Yeah, we were talking about it on the way in from the airport," Gabe said.

"Okay," I said, my head pivoting between the two. "What?"

"Pizza night," Chase said, his eyes twinkling.

"Oh." I giggled as I looked at both of them. Tears sprung to my eyes. "I can't remember the last time we did pizza night. It's been years. Years and years."

"Can't get good deep dish out east," Chase said. "Besides. Gabe could use a break from carbo loading."

"Pizza's got carbs." Gabe grinned. "So does beer."

"Ah." I playfully pinched his arm. "No beer for you yet, young man. At least in front of me."

Chase ribbed his brother. "I'll get you some near beer."

"Gross," Gabe said. "No, thanks."

"Well, okay, pizza night it is," I said.

Gabe leaned over and kissed me on the cheek and Chase hugged me.

"Thanks, Mom," Gabe said. "Feels good to be home."

"It feels good to have you both here." I smiled. "It's going to be a perfect few weeks."

44

I TOOK a deep breath as I looked up at the staircase, waiting for Chase to come down. He'd agreed to go on a walk with me to the beach this morning, just the two of us.

Dinner last night with my boys had been magical. It had reminded me of all those times when they were little and Charles was working. It was often just the three of us, making our own little traditions, separate from their father. On Friday nights, I'd order a pizza and rent a DVD and we'd huddle in front of our TV, enthralled by some children's movie or suitable PG tale. They always wanted chocolate ice cream for dessert and I'd allow them to douse it with whipped cream, chocolate sauce, and nuts. Of course, as they got older, they drifted away from me and in some sense, from each other, as they navigated their way toward Friday nights out with new friends and old, Saturday roller skating parties, and lazy Sunday afternoons filled with comic books, trading cards, bike rides, and video games. Eventually, girls came to the fore, which of course pulled them away from you even further. Still, you always seek out those little opportunities to remind them of those times when you were the most important thing in their life.

It felt like old times as I ordered a large pepperoni, sausage, and mushroom pizza and filled white porcelain bowls with heaving scoops of chocolate ice cream, smiling as I watched the boys fight over the chocolate sauce and whipped cream. I didn't even remember what movie we'd watched on Netflix (Gabe's choice). What didn't leave me, even after I'd drifted off to sleep that night, was the laughter, the ease, the camaraderie.

I finally had my boys back.

I heard Chase's bedroom door open, along with his footsteps in the hallway. I finished the last of my tea and waved as he thudded down the stairs in his tennis shoes, baggy black running shorts, and royal blue workout t-shirt.

"Good morning, sweetheart," I said. "I made you some coffee. How'd you sleep?"

"Great," he said. "You?"

"Better than I've slept in a long time."

"Last night was fun." He leaned against the counter. "I'm glad we did that."

"Me too." I rinsed out my mug before putting it in the dishwasher. "I can get you a to-go cup for your coffee if you'd like."

"Yeah, thanks, that would be great," he said.

I filled up the stainless steel cup and screwed on the top before handing it to him. Like Charles, Chase preferred his coffee black.

"Ready?"

He nodded and we headed out the front door. Though it was early, the sun was hot and piercing, giving a preview of the day. We made small talk about his upcoming job as an associate with a law firm in Boston and Jacqueline's new position as a meeting planner for an international relations firm.

In so many ways, listening to Chase, it reminded me of when Charles and I had started out—his residency at Northwestern, me excited to search for a job in the arts. That first left turn happened when we'd returned from our honeymoon to find Celia and Clayton had bought the house as a wedding gift, cancelling the lease on the studio we'd rented. Charles had gone apoplectic. I'd been disappointed. Oddly, I'd been looking forward to uncovering how to cook gourmet meals on a hot plate, laughing over leaky faucets, and lamenting noisy neighbors through paper-thin walls.

What if Charles had stood up to his parents and refused to allow them to push us under their thumb? What if I'd stuck to my dream of working in an art gallery or managing a fashionable boutique, rather than allowing myself to fall in line with Celia's expectations of a young society wife? How different would our lives have been? Would we have descended into the toxicity and bitterness that ultimately tore us apart?

We'd never know.

Sometimes, fate is fate. There's no running from it. We could have done everything differently, everything we'd wanted to do and still wound up in the same quicksand.

"Mom?"

I blinked and looked at Chase. "Yes?"

He laughed. "You look like you spaced out there for a minute."

"Oh. I was just thinking about when your father and I first got married, starting our lives together. We thought we had the world on a string." I wiped away a tear. "You know, in a lot of ways, to me, he'll always be that handsome young man reading *Gray's Anatomy* on Harvard Yard."

Chase sighed and looked out at the water. "You really did love Dad, didn't you?"

"I did," I whispered. "I really did. Still do."

"I want you to know that I know you didn't do it on purpose. I know it was an accident."

I kicked at a loose pebble with the toe of my tennis shoe, a twinge of guilt rippling through me. "It means a lot for me to hear you say that, Chase."

"When I think about it, yeah, sure you guys had your troubles. I mean Gabe and I could see it sometimes—"

"I—"

He held up his hand. "But I could also see how much you guys loved each other, too. All of those times you'd surprise Dad with breakfast in bed or the little gifts he would give you. The way you looked at him. The way he looked at you." Chase turned to me. "I'm putting it all behind me. You're my mother. The only one I've got and I'm with you one hundred percent."

I grabbed Chase, pulling him to me. "I can't tell you what it means to hear you say that."

"I love you, Mom. Really and truly. I love you."

I sobbed against his shoulder. Finally, he handed me a Kleenex from the pack in his pocket and we both laughed. Charles had always carried a pack of Kleenex, as he'd abhorred handkerchiefs. Charles's voice hadn't roiled around in my head for some time. I suppose that meant he was really gone for good.

I was finally free of him.

I hooked my arm through the crook of Chase's elbow as we turned toward home.

45

"AND THAT'S when I told him, 'I'd do it, but I might fall in!'"

The flames from the tall Roman candles standing in a proud line down the middle of the long rectangular dinner table flickered across all our faces as we all laughed, indulging Clayton's witticisms about some run-in he'd had on the golf course with an overeager new caddy. I looked over at Jacqueline, freshly arrived that afternoon, her blue eyes sparkling with unfettered adoration as she gazed at Chase, then bent down to listen to whatever Celia whispered in her ear. She so reminded me of myself at her age. Blond, blue-eyed, brimming with charm, poise, and sophistication far beyond her years. The world at her feet, the man she loved by her side. Chase took a swig of his beer, then, clearly besotted, grabbed Jacqueline's hand and kissed it. She smiled back, biting her bottom lip.

It was almost like old times.

Almost.

A chill blew through me as my gaze drifted yet again to the far end of the table where Charles's chair sat dark and empty. Every Sunday, we'd come here for dinner and Charles had always sat at the far end of the table, me to his right, Chase to his left, Gabe next to him. We'd all paused a little as we involuntarily sought out our regular places before shuffling the deck and choosing new seating assignments for ourselves. Of course, Clayton and Celia retained their usual spots—the patriarch at the head, the matriarch to his right. Charlotte, usually across from me, was conspicuous in her absence.

My gaze clicked over to Gabe, listlessly picking at the wobbly mint jelly atop his barely eaten lamp chop. I frowned. He'd been subdued all day, barely saying two words since yesterday morning.

"Gabe, you've been practically mute," Celia said. "Is it your intention that we get our updates on you through osmosis?"

He straightened up in his chair, gripping his fork. "Sorry, Grandma."

"Perhaps you're coming down with something," she said. "Jillian will take you to the doctor in the morning, get you a full examination, make sure everything's in working order."

"I'm not sick, Grandma."

"You do look a little flushed, so perhaps you are coming down with something," Clayton said. "I always say it's best to work through a cold. Buck up, son."

"Well, if he's contagious, Clayton—"

"Oh, pish posh," he said, sending a careless wave of his hand in Celia's direction. "The boy is no more contagious than I am."

"I'm not sick," Gabe repeated. "Really."

"Will you be working at the country club again this summer?" Celia asked Gabe, pointedly ignoring Clayton.

Gabe nodded. "Yeah."

Clayton gave him a look, not unlike the ones Charles used to give him when he wanted Gabe to polish his grammar. Gabe caught it and pursed his lips.

"I meant yes, I will be working at the country club again this summer."

"Well, that's fine," Celia said. "Just fine. Always good for a young man to have responsibility. Learn the value of a dollar and a hard day's work."

"I'll—I mean, I want to stay in New York next summer to see if I can get an internship at a newspaper or magazine or something."

"Well, son, we can manage that." Clayton rubbed his mouth with his white linen napkin. "We know the heads of every TV station and newspaper here in Chicago. All it will take is a phone call."

"I'm good, Grandpa, thank you," Gabe said. "I appreciate the offer, but I've already decided to stay in New York next summer."

"Hmm." Clayton harrumphed. "Well, that's a year away. A lot can change."

I smiled at Gabe, proud of him for standing his ground with Clayton. He was his father's son.

"And what about you, Chase?" Celia asked. "When do you start your new position?"

"Not until late July. Jacqueline's starting her new job a little before that."

"I assume we'll be hearing wedding bells sooner rather than later," Celia said. "You aren't getting any younger."

"Jeez, you sound like Grandma Marion." Chase grinned and he and Jacqueline exchanged a glance.

"Go on," Jacqueline said. "It's okay."

"Are you sure? I thought we were going to wait?"

"Chase, sweetheart ... is there something you'd like to tell us?" I asked.

He and Jacqueline giggled a little before he took a deep breath.

"Well," he said. "Last week, I asked Jacqueline to marry me and she said yes."

A whoop went up from Celia and tears pricked my eyes as we descended on the lovebirds with well-wishes. Gabe hugged his brother as Jacqueline dug her engagement ring out of her purse. Unconsciously, I rubbed at my own engagement and wedding rings, still snug on my finger after all this time, remembering when Charles took me to Marliave and dropped the ring in the bottom of my champagne glass. I'd filched the glass from the restaurant, wrapping it in the red linen napkin and stuffing it in my purse when I was sure no one was looking. I still had that glass and napkin.

"Well, this is good news, good news," Clayton said as he palmed Chase's shoulder, beaming. "Indeed. This calls for champagne." He called out to his butler to put their best bottle on ice.

I glanced over at Charles's chair, surprised to see him leaning back in it, scowling.

"You deprived me of all of this. I hope you're happy."

The butler came in twenty minutes later bearing the champagne and we all oohed and aahed at the foamy arc of bubbles shooting into the air. I shivered as I accepted my glass, looking at Charles once more.

"Mom? You okay?" Chase asked.

"I'm fine." I smiled. "How could I not be? This is wonderful news. I'm so happy for you, for Jacqueline."

"Okay. Good." He hugged me. "It *is* pretty wonderful."

I took a sip of my champagne, peering over the glass at Charles. "Yes. Everything is wonderful."

46

My car whined and sighed as I rolled to a stop in front of Charlotte's house. I looked up at the muted red brick of the three-story mansion. Friday afternoon. I knew during the summer months she often worked from home on Fridays.

I inhaled and closed my eyes, drowning momentarily in the silence of the quiet, tree-lined street, children having been banished to day camps and summer jobs. I desperately wanted a cigarette but had given them up shortly after the Vanessa Incident as I called it. Trying to live a clean life and all that.

I got out of the car, my footsteps seeming to grow louder as I drew closer to the house. I raised a shaky finger to push the doorbell. The muffled chimes seemed to ring in my ears long after the doorbell itself had ceased.

And now, silence.

I rang again, pushing harder, pushing with determination.

From inside, a voice floated out to hold on a second. The door swung open. The blond strands of Charlotte's hair swooped back from her face before settling down around her shoulders. Her jeans and simple white t-shirt hugged her athletic frame. Her face fell as she realized it was me, the corners of her mouth confirming her displeasure by drooping downward.

"Hello, Charlotte," I said. "How are you?"

She folded her arms across her chest. "What are you doing here?"

"May I come in?"

"Why?"

I sighed. "Charlotte ... don't you think it's time we moved on? Cleared the air? We're family—sisters—and I can't bear us going on like this."

"Am I supposed to fall to your feet now?"

"For the sake of the boys, for Clayton and Celia, I think it's time we called a truce."

"Oh, I see. You want me to forget you shot my brother."

I looked down at my feet, pursing my lips. "I don't expect you to forget any more than I can ever forget. But I was hoping that we could find a way to move forward."

She was quiet, her eyes looking everywhere but in my direction. Finally, she sighed and focused her gaze on me.

"I guess I haven't talked to you since that incident with that man," she said. "I read about it in the paper. Mother and Daddy went on and on about it."

"It was horrifying."

"I take it you've recovered."

"I have, yes."

"Did the police ever figure out what he wanted with you, why he attacked you like that?"

I shrugged. "No idea."

The silence settled over us. Birds chirped behind me and from inside the house, Charlotte's cell phone pinged incessantly. She looked behind her, scratching her ear, twitching, as though she couldn't wait to bolt for that little piece of life-and-death plastic.

"I'm having a quiet birthday dinner at the house tomorrow night. Nothing fancy, just a few friends." I paused, eyeing her carefully. "Family. I would be honored if you and Rex came. And

Chelsea. That is if she can stand an evening with a bunch of decrepits."

I think in spite of herself, Charlotte chuckled. She shook her head.

"I doubt she'd grace us with her presence, but, uh, let me check with Rex, see if we have anything on the calendar for tomorrow."

"Okay," I said. "I'll look forward to hearing from you. And hopefully seeing you."

She gripped the door as her phone detonated again. "I'll text or call you."

"Goodbye, Charlotte." I turned toward the steps.

She merely smiled, the same dismissive, we'll-see-but-don't-count-on-it smile I'd flashed a million times in my life.

The door clicked shut behind me.

47

I SELECTED the diamond earrings I planned to wear that night and stuck them into my earlobes before spritzing myself with Shalimar. Finally, for the first time in a long while, I was looking forward to something. A quiet birthday dinner at home. Tina and Walter (who'd rebounded beautifully with two new practice partners). Francine and Raymond (who'd finally come around), Suzette and her current beau, my in-laws, Chase, Jacqueline, and Gabe. I said he could invite Brynn, but they were off again it would seem, so he would be solo tonight. I wasn't holding out much hope that Charlotte would appear. I'd checked my phone for calls and texts all day, but it had remained void of any contact from her.

I pulled out my diamond teardrop pendant. Charles's wedding gift to me. A lifetime ago. I could wear it and feel not even a hint of guilt.

I gave myself one last look, smoothing down my simple black sheath, before heading downstairs, smiling as I looked around the living room. Elaine had done a masterful job in transforming the room with new paint, flooring, and furniture.

You'd never know a cold-blooded murder had happened here.

The smells of dinner being prepared by the private chef I'd hired wafted up to greet me. Beef Wellington, scalloped potatoes, garlic green beans, field green salad. My favorite white chocolate cake with a "Happy Birthday" topper. Guests would be arriving soon.

I went into the kitchen, checking on progress, finding myself pleased. A server handed me a cold glass of Sauvignon Blanc. Delicious.

I set the Bose to play the *Breakfast at Tiffany's* soundtrack. I hummed along as I did another round robin of the house. Flowers. Candles. Everything in its place.

The doorbell rang. I took a quick sip of wine as I went to answer it.

"Happy Birthday, darling," Suzette said as she lowered a monstrous flower arrangement.

"Thank you," I said as we air kissed each other's cheeks. "What can I get you?"

"I'll have whatever you're having." She handed me the flowers. "They were so beautiful, I couldn't resist."

"Where's your new beau?" I signaled to the server to bring her what I was having. "I thought you were bringing him tonight."

"He had a last minute fire with work to put out, but he'll be here shortly."

"I'm looking forward to meeting him. Let's see if he lives up to the advanced praise."

She laughed. "The Jillian Morgan Stamp of Approval would be graciously accepted."

"Oh, you're such a dear. Listen, before everyone arrives, I just wanted to say thank you for being here tonight. And for the past few months. It means so much."

"I know it's been a horrendous year and I'm so happy you can finally put it all behind you," she said.

"I'm starting to feel like myself, like I can finally move on with my life."

"Aren't Chase and Gabe going to be here?" she asked as the

server handed her a wineglass. "I could have sworn you said they would be."

"Chase and Jacqueline said they had an errand to run, so they'll be here shortly and Gabe—" I frowned as I looked upstairs. "Still getting dressed, I suppose. I'll go up and wrangle him in a minute if he doesn't come down."

The doorbell pealed again, and Francine and Raymond bustled in, followed in short order by Walter and Tina and my in-laws. Soon, we were all swept away by passed hors d'oeuvres and wine, as Chase and Jacqueline finally made their appearance.

The chime of the doorbell elicited a gasp from me. It had to be Charlotte and Rex, as everyone else was already here. I smoothed down the front of my dress as I went to open the door, hoping my nerves weren't showing.

"Hello, Jillian." Charlotte stepped forward to hug me. I pressed her extra tightly, the peach shampoo of her hair tickling my nose. "Happy Birthday."

I pulled back to look at her. "Thank you." Dare I say it, but I might have felt a tear threaten to roll from my eye. Rex offered me a chaste kiss on the cheek before handing me a glittery gift bag bursting with huge tufts of hot pink tissue paper.

Charlotte and I linked arms, like old times. "I'm very glad you're here," I whispered. "I can't tell you how much this means."

"You're right. We have to find a way to heal and move forward."

I nodded, placing the gift bag on the table in the foyer, and offered to get them drinks. I scanned the room, frowning that Gabe hadn't come down yet. He'd been gone most of the day, having left early this morning, returning early in the afternoon, barely tossing a hello over his shoulder before bounding up to his room and slamming the door. I looked up toward his room, vacillating between letting him be and going upstairs to check on him. He sometimes got like this when he was coming down with something. If this continued, I'd call his doctor on Monday to make an appointment.

The crush of the crowd momentarily swallowed me as I circulated through the revelry of well-wishes. Warm happiness oozed through me. My cheeks burned with laughter. I glowed.

Finally, Gabe appeared at the top of the stairs, dressed in jeans and a t-shirt. I frowned, perturbed he hadn't put on a nice pair of slacks and button-down shirt. As he got closer, I saw that his face was pale, his eyes rimmed in red, as though he'd been crying. I greeted him at the bottom of the steps.

"Sweetheart, how come you're not dressed?"

"We need to talk, Mom."

"Are you sick? Are you running a fever?" I planted my palm against his forehead. "You do feel a touch warm."

He gently removed my hand. "Can we go in Dad's study? It's important."

"Oh—" I looked around at the assembled. Everyone seemed to be enjoying themselves. "All right, but just for a minute. It's rude to leave our guests."

He didn't say anything, just shuffled off in the direction of Charles's study.

I could practically feel Charles's spirit zooming out to greet us before whooshing back in. The room felt cold. Stiff. I hadn't been in here since before Vanessa died. Perhaps I could nudge the boys to go through it over the next few weeks and determine if there were things they wanted to keep. Then I could redecorate. Perhaps it would now be my study. I'd been thinking about resuming my artistic pursuits— painting, photography and the like. A studio of my own.

Gabe sat down in his father's chair and it jolted me to see him behind that desk. Yes, Chase favored Charles and Gabe resembled me, but at this moment, he looked exactly like his father.

I closed the door behind me and sat on the edge of one of the massive leather chairs. "All right. What did you want to talk about?"

He clasped his hands on the desk in front of him, looking down. He didn't say anything.

"Gabe?"

"I'm sorry, Mom."

"What are you sorry for, sweetheart? Not being dressed in time? Don't worry about that. You can go upstairs now and put on something nice. No one will even notice."

"That's not what I mean."

I touched my temple, exasperation bubbling in my veins. "Okay, then, what are you sorry for?"

"Your party. For tonight."

"I'm afraid I don't understand, Gabe."

"There's not going to be a party tonight because the police are coming here to arrest you."

My throat clamped shut. Everything went black. "Excuse me?"

"They're coming here to arrest you for murder."

48

I BLINKED, certain I hadn't heard right. My mouth fell open as I clutched for words.

"What did you just say?"

"Mom." Gabe lowered his voice. He swallowed a few times, as though he was working up his courage. "I know."

"What do you mean, you know? Know what?"

"I know you killed that woman. I know you killed Dad on purpose," he whispered, his voice thick with tears.

I seized my throat, desperate to rip it open, to let in some oxygen, which was suddenly in short supply.

"Sweetheart, we've been over this. What happened with your father was an accident. And as far as—" I had to catch myself from calling her a slut. "And as far as what happened to your father's ... friend ... the police determined that was his doing."

"Stop it."

"I don't know what else you want me to say."

"I want you to stop lying."

I sighed. "Yes, I was upset with your father about a great many things, but in no way was what happened intentional."

Without a word, Gabe reached into his pocket and extracted his phone, swiping across the screen a few times before placing it on the desk. Within seconds, it crackled to life.

"*Charles. And what brings you by?*"

"*I'm out on bail. Until my trial. If it gets that far.*"

"*You sound supremely confident.*"

"*You have no idea.*"

My heart went into freefall. The last real conversation Charles and I'd had. In the living room just beyond the door of this study. He must have ... dear God, when he heard me drive up, when he was sitting in the dark, waiting to confront me because he'd found that damn puzzle box, that must have been when he turned on his phone's recorder. Shoved it back in his pants pocket.

And then I'd handed the phone over to Gabe.

None the wiser.

"*I suppose I shouldn't be surprised you figured it out. You always were smart. One of the many ways you tricked me into falling in love with you. So smart, so brilliant. So ... headed places. And where he's headed, I want to be right there next to him.*"

"*Jillian.*"

"*I wonder, I wonder, I wonder, I wonder. What did I do?*"

"*You killed her, didn't you?*"

"*Did I?*"

"*You didn't have to kill her.*"

"*Didn't I, Charles?*"

"*Gabe, please—*"

Charles laughed. "*Are you—is this a joke?*"

"*I guess to you it is since you're the only one laughing.*"

"*What the hell are you doing with a gun?*"

"*I had planned to get rid of this tomorrow morning. Seemingly fortuitous that I didn't.*"

"*So, what, you're going to shoot me now?*"

"*I'm a woman alone in this big house, her deranged husband just*"

out of jail. No one told me you'd been released. I came home, was star-
tled to find you here ... Who could blame me?"

"Turn it off. Please." I barely recognized the wisp of my voice.

"You'd really shoot me, Jillian? Just like that?"

"I sure would. Because I call the shots."

The room exploded with gunfire. I grabbed at the phone, needing
to shut it off, not wanting to hear Charles's agonized grunts, his pleas
for his life. I pawed at the device, frantically tapping the screen until I
could make it stop. I dropped the phone on the desk and stared at it as
I gripped the sides of the desk. Words clogged in my throat. Sweat
rolled down my back. Jagged breaths battled to travel from my lips to
my lungs.

"This is a copy," Gabe said quietly. "The police have the
original."

"Oh, God. I'm so sorry." The tears detonated without warning,
burst from my body in a sudden gush of water and shame. I sobbed
brokenly under the quiet heartbreak of his gaze.

My precious, beautiful Gabe knew I was a monster.

"How could you do this?" he whispered. "To me, to Chase?
Dad?"

"Sweetheart, if I could go back, if I could change this—"

"You'd do the exact same thing," he said bitterly. "Because you
hated Dad. Because you wanted to punish him, in any way you could
think of. Even if that meant killing him in cold blood."

I blanched at his bluntness, his brutality. "Don't say that, Gabe."

He scoffed. "Stop lying. Please. Just ... stop."

I jumped out of my seat and ran around the desk to him, sinking
to the floor, grabbing his arms. "Please, Gabe, please forgive me,
please. I'm throwing myself at your mercy. I don't think I can get
through this unless I know that you forgive me."

"Stop it." He couldn't even look at me as he worked to untangle
himself from my grasp.

Except there was no hiding the disgust and disappointment on
his face.

I reached for him, trying to cradle his cheeks in my palms. He gripped my elbows, wrestling my hands away. "The police will be here soon."

I sobbed again as I stared at him, hoping for a last-minute reprieve, a sudden change of heart where he would take my hand, smile and say, "Don't worry, Mom. Things are cool."

Instead, he backed away from me and picked up his phone from the desk, shoving it in his pocket. He continued to look everywhere but at me.

The doorbell pealed.

49

"I GUESS THAT'S THEM." I wiped the tears from my face, my fingers black with mascara and eyeliner. "I guess it's all over now."

Gabe leaned against one of the built-in bookshelves, his hands in his pockets, his gaze pinned to the floor. I dug the heels of my hands into my eyes and inhaled deeply, a pitiful attempt at calming myself. Oddly poetic that murdering Charles and his tramp is what brought about my downfall. Vile Vanessa and Neil the Barbarian couldn't take me down in life or death.

The door loomed large in front of me. Once I stepped through it, my life would be over. It had been over long before, though. Years.

It was now or never.

I did what any good debutante would do. I squared my shoulders and threw my head back as I marched over to the door, slowly turning the knob.

There wasn't a sound. Detectives Potts and Travis stood just inside the living room. The assembled faces wore confusion.

"Mrs. Morgan—"

I held up my hand to indicate Detective Travis should wait. I searched for Chase, finding him, his eyes clouded with bewilderment.

He broke away from Jacqueline and came over to me. I reached for his hand.

"Mom, what the hell is going on?"

I cupped his cheek before I kissed it. "Your brother will tell you everything."

"At least let me go down to the station with you."

I looked over my shoulder at Gabe, who had followed me out of the study, his stoicism gone, replaced by raw tears streaming down his face.

"No," I said, my eyes still on Gabe. "You need to stay here. You need to help your brother."

"Mrs. Morgan, we're here—" Travis tried again.

"Yes, Detective Travis, I'm well aware of why you're here." I looked around the room at my guests. A bitter laugh burst from my lips. "Well, I guess you've all surmised there won't be a celebration this evening. At least not with me in attendance."

"Jillian—"

"It's all right, Suzette. These fine detectives are here to arrest me for the cold-blooded murder of my husband, Dr. Charles Morgan and his slut, Tamra Washington."

A gasp went up around the room as they all stared at me.

"How could you do this?" Celia asked, her voice shaking with tears. "How could you lie—tell bald-faced lies to us, after everything—"

"Oh, come off it, Celia. The way you harangued Charles, the way you picked, picked, picked at everything he ever did. Do you know, in thirty-two years, I never heard you say a kind word about your son? Nothing. Ever. Not one, single, solitary thing." I looked at Clayton. "And you were no better, though I suppose you knew that. Of course, you treat Charlotte like a second-class citizen, too, which I suppose you also knew, because you know everything. Everything about the way the world works."

"That's enough, Jillian," Celia said.

"Yes, I have had quite enough." I swiveled my head until Charlotte and I were face-to-face. Tears gushed from her eyes.

"Well, Charlotte, you were right all along. Congratulations. Yes, I murdered your brother in cold blood. I murdered him because he cheated on me with a tawdry, backwater slut. I murdered him because he was a wretched husband who held his career in higher esteem than his wife and sons, because he missed practically every birthday, every occasion, every everything, for years. I murdered him because he made my life utterly miserable. I murdered him because he couldn't be bothered to offer me a kind word once in a while or a thank you for all the nights I sat in this house alone while every other priority on his list took precedence. I murdered him because I just couldn't stand to be married to him one more day." I wiped the back of my hand across the slick of my nose and laughed. "Happy, Charlotte? Happy to have your answers?"

"You miserable bitch."

"How original. Really, I expected better."

This slap, like the first one all those months ago, was a surprise, though it shouldn't have been. I laughed again and rubbed my cheek. "I hope you enjoyed that. It'll have to last you the rest of your life."

I turned my head toward the detectives and thrust my wrists in their direction. "I suppose this is the position you'd like me in."

The two men glanced at each other before Potts sighed and retrieved a pair of handcuffs from his jacket pocket, pulling my hands behind me. I winced at the deafening click of the cuffs as they clamped around my wrists.

"Jillian Morgan, you have the right to remain silent..."

I didn't hear the rest. Suzette shook with tears, reaching out to grab me as Potts paraded me past her grasp. Her friend hadn't yet arrived. Well. One less witness to my downfall. Walter groped for words and Tina looked away, embarrassed. Shaken. Francine, like Suzette, wept, while Raymond shook his head, his face smeared with smirking disbelief. A shocked and stoic Clayton cradled a weeping Celia. Charlotte stood stone-faced. Rex was pale.

And Chase and Gabe. Brothers standing side by side. Trying to be strong for the other. Trying to absorb the shock of their mother being arrested for murdering their father.

"You had to know you wouldn't get away with it, Jillian."

I scoffed to myself as Detective Potts guided me into the nondescript sedan parked across the street. Charles. He was fond of telling me I always had to have the last word, that he could never win with me.

As we pulled away from the curb, the revelation pained me.

For the first time ever, Charles had won.

END

AUTHOR'S NOTE

One of the perks of writing fiction is you get to take a little creative license. In TELL ME A LIE, I took some liberty with the use of ipecac syrup. Once commonly used to force vomiting to treat orally ingested poisons, production of ipecac syrup officially ceased in 2010 after numerous studies concluded it did more harm than good.

In Jillian Morgan's world, ipecac syrup is an easily attainable substance ready to take care of ... whoever needs to be taken care of.

ACKNOWLEDGMENTS

When I first had the idea for LIVE TO TELL, there was never a plan for a sequel. However, Jillian tapped me on the shoulder, demanding I give her equal time to tell her side. I had so much fun telling her story. I hope you enjoyed reading it.

Thank you as always to First Reader Kathryn for your bottomless well of funnies and, well, being First Reader. Many, many thanks to Lanee and Joy for beta reading and catching things I missed. To my editorial team of Samantha Stroh Bailey and Wendy Janes ... you are both awesome and I love working with you. You make my words so much better. As always, all the mistakes are mine and mine alone. Thank you to Nick Castle of Nick Castle Design for the gorgeous new covers for the series!

Mr. D. Thank you for making me laugh. Thank you for having my back. Thank you for listening. The only other words I have are these: first letter P, second letter—

And to my readers. Thank you for reading, tweeting, e-mailing, posting messages on Facebook. Your support means so much—more than I can express. Thank you.

WANT TO KNOW HOW IT ALL BEGAN?

BUY THE PREQUEL TO
"TELL ME A LIE" TODAY!

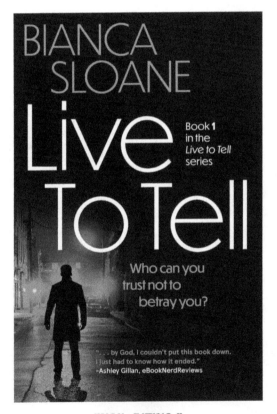

"NAIL-BITING."
-GOODREADS REVIEWER

WWW.BIANCASLOANE.COM

HAVE YOU READ THEM ALL?

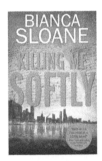   

ABOUT THE AUTHOR

Bianca Sloane is the author of the suspense novels *Killing Me Softly* (previously published as *Live and Let Die*), chosen as "Thriller of the Month" (May 2013) by e-thriller.com and a "2013 Top Read" by OOSA Online Book Club, *Sweet Little Lies*, *Every Breath You Take*, and *Missing You*: A Companion Novella to *Every Breath You Take*). When she's not writing, she's watching Bravo TV or Investigation Discovery, reading, or cooking. Sloane resides in Chicago.
To connect with Bianca:

www.biancasloane.com
Bianca@BiancaSloane.com